Poppy Harmon
and the
Backstabbing Bachelor

Books by Lee Hollis

Hayley Powell Mysteries
DEATH OF A KITCHEN DIVA
DEATH OF A COUNTRY FRIED REDNECK
DEATH OF A COUPON CLIPPER
DEATH OF A CHOCOHOLIC
DEATH OF A CHRISTMAS CATERER
DEATH OF A CUPCAKE QUEEN
DEATH OF A BACON HEIRESS
DEATH OF A PUMPKIN CARVER
DEATH OF A LOBSTER LOVER
DEATH OF A COOKBOOK AUTHOR
DEATH OF A WEDDING CAKE BAKER
DEATH OF A BLUEBERRY TART
DEATH OF A WICKED WITCH
DEATH OF AN ITALIAN CHEF

Collections
EGGNOG MURDER
(with Leslie Meier and Barbara Ross)
YULE LOG MURDER
(with Leslie Meier and Barbara Ross)
HAUNTED HOUSE MURDER
(with Leslie Meier and Barbara Ross)
CHRISTMAS CARD MURDER
(with Leslie Meier and Peggy Ehrhart)
HALLOWEEN PARTY MURDER
(with Leslie Meier and Barbara Ross)

Poppy Harmon Mysteries
POPPY HARMON INVESTIGATES
POPPY HARMON AND THE HUNG JURY
POPPY HARMON AND THE PILLOW TALK KILLER
POPPY HARMON AND THE BACKSTABBING
BACHELOR

Maya & Sandra Mysteries
MURDER AT THE PTA
MURDER AT THE BAKE SALE

Published by Kensington Publishing Corp.

Poppy Harmon
and the
Backstabbing Bachelor

LEE
HOLLIS

Kensington Publishing Corp.
ww.kensingtonbooks.com

KENSINGTON BOOKS are published by

Kensington Publishing Corp.
119 West 40th Street
New York, NY 10018

All Kensington titles, imprints and distributed lines are available at special quantity discounts for bulk purchases for sales promotion, premiums, fund-raising, educational or institutional use. Special book excerpts or customized printings can also be created to fit specific needs. For details, write or phone the office of the Kensington Special Sales Manager: Kensington Publishing Corp., 119 West 40th Street, New York, NY, 10018. Attn. Special Sales Department. Phone: 1-800-221-2647.

The K and Teapot logo is a trademark of Kensington Publishing Corp.

Library of Congress Control Number: 2021951539

ISBN: 978-1-4967-3040-4

First Kensington Hardcover Edition: May 2022

ISBN: 978-1-4967-3042-8 (ebook)

10 9 8 7 6 5 4 3 2 1

Printed in the United States of America

Twinkle, twinkle, little star,
How I wonder what you are.
Up above the world so high,
Like a diamond in the sky.
Twinkle, twinkle, little star,
How I wonder what you are.

Chapter 1

Poppy Harmon was having a devil of a time operating her electric wheelchair. When she pushed the joystick forward, the wheels seemed to veer right, not straight ahead, and she banged into a wall in the hallway after maneuvering out of the bedroom, trying to steer herself toward the living room.

Poppy sighed.

She was never going to get the hang of this.

She tried cranking the knob to the left, but only managed to drive the wheelchair away from one wall and crash it into the opposite one. The noise alerted someone in the kitchen, and within seconds a young woman in her twenties with long, straight black hair, emerald green eyes, and a bright smile that mostly disguised a somewhat hardened face suddenly appeared in front of her.

"Oh, you're up. How was your nap?"

"Fine," Poppy spit out, frowning, continuing to push the knob forward but getting nowhere. "I hate this new wheelchair. My old one was a lot easier to operate."

"Here, allow me," the young woman said, slipping behind Poppy and manually pushing the wheelchair by the handles out to the living room and parking it in front of the large flat-screen TV hanging on the wall. "I have some tomato soup heating up on the stove for your lunch. Would you like Ritz crackers or saltines to go with it? I have both."

"Saltines, please," Poppy answered gruffly.

"Coming right up," the woman said before snatching up the remote and turning on the TV. "Now you just relax and watch your British Bake Off show, and lunch will be ready in just a few minutes."

She bounded back to the kitchen.

Once she was gone, Poppy adjusted the itchy, stringy gray wig she was wearing, straightened her burgundy housecoat, and checked out her face in a wall mirror across from her. The retired Tony Award–winning Broadway make-up artist the Desert Flowers Detective Agency had hired to transform Poppy into a ninety-two-year-old woman had done an incredibly convincing job using liquid latex, eyeliner, and face paint. Poppy looked at least thirty years older than her actual age.

And more importantly, Tanya Cook, the self-described "professional home care nurse" who'd answered her ad to help out with shopping, errands, meals, and to administer medications, was totally buying the disguise.

Poppy heard a thump.

It had come from down the hall, the small guest bedroom that she had set up as her office.

Poppy tried to pick up the remote off the coffee table to lower the television volume but couldn't quite reach it. She stretched her fingers as far as they would go, but the remote was still about an inch away from her grasp. Frustrated, Poppy swiveled her head around to make sure Tanya had not wandered back into the living room, and then, with lightning speed, she jumped out of the wheelchair, grabbed the remote, and quickly sat back down. She muted the TV and waited.

Sure enough, she heard another thump.

Poppy pulled back on the joystick, the wheelchair rolled in reverse, and then she buzzed back down the hall. The door to the guest room was closed. She leaned forward, turned the handle, and pushed the door open, surprised to find two more young women, both around Tanya's age, and just as pretty. One was blond and the other auburn haired. The blonde was seated at a desk meticulously going through drawers while the other one held a half-filled plastic garbage bag that she appeared to be stuffing with valuables.

"Who are you? What are you doing here?" Poppy cried.

The two girls froze in place, not quite sure what to do.

Tanya appeared in a flash. She stepped in front of Poppy's wheelchair and knelt down so they were at eye level, a reassuring smile on her face. "There's no cause for concern. These are my friends, Bella and Kylie. I invited them over to help tidy up the house. Don't you want your lovely home to be nice and clean for when your grandkids come to visit?"

"I suppose so," Poppy said. "How much is this going to cost me? I used to do my own housework. . . ."

"Oh no, Edna, this is included in the service. You don't have to pay anything extra. I am just here to make things easier for you."

Poppy nodded. She had momentarily forgotten her cover name was Edna Greenblatt, so she was grateful that Tanya had just reminded her. She smiled warmly at the two nervous-looking women in the office. "Thank you, girls. I may have some gingersnap cookies in the kitchen. Would you like one?"

They exchanged quick glances, and then the one with the garbage bag, Bella, shook her head and muttered, "No, we're fine."

Tanya firmly gripped the handles of the wheelchair and rolled Poppy out of the room and back down the hall. "Come on, Edna, time to eat your soup."

"I spotted some dust bunnies underneath the desk. Do you think they can sweep those up, too?" Poppy asked.

"Of course, the whole house will be spotless when they're done, I promise," Tanya said, parking Poppy back in front of the TV in the living room. "Now stay put while I finish preparing your lunch tray."

Poppy detected a slight annoyance in Tanya's tone. She was obviously getting tired of being nice to this high-maintenance old crow.

Because the fact of the matter was Tanya was no professional home care nurse. Tanya Cook and her two cohorts, Bella and Kylie, were professional criminals, allegedly running a massive financial fraud and theft scheme by infiltrating the homes of susceptible senior citizens and gaining access to their bank passwords, cash, checks, credit cards, valuables, and personal documents. Basically bleeding their victims dry right in their own homes! Tanya would scout out a vulnerable target, someone in need of in-home care; apply for the job with forged credentials; then show up at the door with a friendly smile and a promise to take good care of them. She would play nursemaid for about a week, gaining the trust of her charge before bringing in her two accomplices to rob the unsuspecting senior blind, even insidiously redirecting social security direct deposits to a dummy bank account.

Their last mark, however, a feisty widow by the name of Cecile LaCrosse, an eighty-nine-year-old battle-ax who unfortunately fell victim to the scam, was not about to let them get away with it. And so she brought in Poppy and her crew at the Desert Flowers Detective Agency to set up a sting and bring this evil coven of Gen Z witches down.

Poppy, along with her two partners, Iris Becker and Violet Hogan, took a very personal interest in this particular case because they felt a strong kinship with the victims. Although still in their sixties, they knew it was only a matter of time before they themselves might be confused, defenseless elderly victims preyed upon by opportunistic, heartless swindlers.

And so Poppy had insisted that she pose as an elderly widow, drawing on her years of acting experience from when she was a starlet in the 1980s, in order to bust up this enterprising, depraved crime ring.

And so far she had played it to perfection.

Tanya was confident enough after only three days of playing nursemaid to bring in her two sidekicks to finish the job by pillaging poor Edna Greenblatt's home until she was left with nothing but her electric wheelchair, which had a mind of its own.

Tanya appeared with a wooden tray and set it down in front of Poppy. "I garnished the soup with a few garlic croutons. My own grandmother used to love the extra kick."

"It looks lovely," Poppy said, picking up the spoon with a shaky hand and scooping some up, making sure to dribble a little on her housecoat just to be convincing.

"Can I get you anything else?" Tanya asked.

"Oh, no, dear, you've done quite enough," Poppy said with a thin, knowing smile.

And she meant it.

Tanya and her friends had certainly done enough.

And they were about to discover just how "done" they actually were.

Chapter 2

Violet's loud, piercing, high-pitched voice of concern blasted through Poppy's ear. "Poppy, Poppy, what's happening in there? Are you okay?"

Poppy dropped her spoon on the tray and raised her hand to adjust the small earbud resting in the crevice of her right ear, and urgently whispered into the tiny microphone that had been pinned on the inside of her housecoat, "Violet, turn down the volume on your mic, you're going to burst my eardrum!"

"Oh, sorry," Violet said, lowering her voice. "Iris, how do you adjust the volume on this thing?"

"Here, let me do it," Iris snapped.

There was a pause.

"Hello? Hello? Is this better?" Violet bellowed, even more deafening than before.

Poppy sighed. "No, she just made you even louder."

"Hold on," Violet said.

Poppy could hear her two friends and partners bickering in the background away from the microphone that they were using to communicate with Poppy.

"Is that better?" Violet asked, almost whispering.

"Yes, much," Poppy said.

"Who are you talking to?"

The stern voice came from directly behind her. Poppy used her joystick to turn her electric wheelchair around.

Tanya stood staring at her, a plate of gingersnap cookies in her hand.

"What?" Poppy asked innocently.

"I heard you whispering to somebody," Tanya said suspiciously, eyes darting around to see if anyone else was in the room before returning her mistrustful gaze back to her charge. "Who was it?"

Her tone was unsettlingly sinister.

"Abe," Poppy said softly.

"Who's Abe?"

"My late husband. He comes to talk to me every now and then," Poppy said with a sad, drawn face. "I miss him so much. He would have loved this tomato soup." Poppy picked up her spoon to take another sip, making sure to get a garlic crouton. As she slurped and crunched, Tanya seemed to size her up, ultimately opting to believe her story, then held out the plate of gingersnaps toward her.

"Cookie?"

Poppy slowly reached out with her trembling hand and took a cookie, then shoved it into her mouth and talked with her mouth full. "Yummy."

"I'm going to see if Bella and Kylie would like one," Tanya said, turning around to head down the hall, but stopping at the window. "Have you noticed that van parked across the street?"

"What van?" Poppy asked innocently.

"Desert Florists," Tanya said, staring out the window.

Poppy swallowed hard.

The van had been rented by the Desert Flowers Detective Agency. They had slapped a fake florist shop decal on the side so as not to arouse suspicion. Inside were Violet and Iris, keeping a careful watch over the house. However, they had underestimated how smart and observant Tanya Cook could be.

"If they're just here to deliver flowers to a house in the neighborhood, it's taking them a really long time," Tanya said warily, checking her wristwatch. "It's been there since I arrived this morning."

"Oh, that van is parked there all the time," Poppy quickly explained. "It belongs to one of the neighbors. That's his business. He's always leaving it there and getting a ticket because he forgets to move it on street-cleaning day."

Tanya peered at the van a few more seconds before deciding to buy Poppy's on-the-spot made-up explanation. She then continued on down the hall with her tray of cookies.

"Is everyone in place?" Poppy whispered.

There was silence.

"Violet?" Poppy asked.

Still nothing.

She had lost communication.

Either her earpiece battery had suddenly died, or there was a problem with the transmitter in the van.

"*Violet?*"

"I'm here, Poppy, I accidentally hit the mute button! Sorry! Yes, we're ready, it's go time!"

"I knew I should have been in charge of the communication equipment!" Iris snorted.

Poppy braced herself just as Tanya returned from the guest bedroom/office with her empty plate. Something outside caught her eye and she raced back to the front window in time to see a uniformed police officer ducking down and circling around the house. Tanya gasped, her mouth dropping open in surprise. She quickly found her voice and started yelling, "Cops!"

Bella and Kylie came crashing out of the guest room, Kylie holding a stuffed garbage bag in her arms.

"Are you serious?" Bella asked nervously.

"Yes!" Tanya cried. "I just saw one sneaking around the side of the house! Run!"

Bella sprinted toward the kitchen, Kylie following close behind but weighed down with the bag. She finally let go of it and it dropped to the floor with a thud as she raced to catch up with Bella.

Poppy heard a man yell, "Police! Put your hands up!"

Tanya's eyes popped open in surprise and she made a mad dash for the front door. Poppy, anticipating the move, jammed the joystick of her wheelchair all the way forward, full speed, and whizzed over in front of the door, blocking her escape.

"What are you doing? Out of my way, old woman!" Tanya screeched, furious, struggling to get around her.

Poppy sprang up to her feet and forcefully pushed Tanya back.

The miraculous sudden strength and agility of the ninety-two-year-old stymied Tanya briefly, but she was still not to be deterred. She charged forward, trying to physically shove Poppy out of the way. Poppy held her ground, knowing she was no match for the young, physically fit woman, but determined to keep her from getting away. Poppy and Tanya grappled, Tanya trying to scratch Poppy's face with her nails in the hope she might release her grip, but as Tanya withdrew her nails, she was stunned to find latex hanging off them, not blood.

"What the—?"

Two uniformed cops suddenly bolted into the living room from the back door off the kitchen, their guns drawn.

"It's over, Tanya!" one of the cops yelled.

She shuddered at the mention of her name because she knew at this moment this had all been a sting.

A con job. A trap.

And she had willfully, stupidly, walked right into it.

Tanya slowly raised her hands in the air while glaring defiantly at Poppy, who busily wiped the old-age makeup off her face with the napkin from her lunch tray.

One of the cops, a boyish, inexperienced one, struggled

to unhook a pair of handcuffs from his belt loop. Finally, he glanced apprehensively over at his more seasoned partner. "Sarge?"

The older cop sighed, and assisted him in releasing the handcuffs from the officer's belt so he could snap them on Tanya's wrists.

Once her face was free of powder and latex and added wrinkles, Poppy removed her gray wig.

Tanya gaped at her, undoubtedly kicking herself for so easily buying into her now obvious disguise.

The older cop studied Poppy, then stepped forward with a big smile. "Hey, I know you . . ."

The younger cop snapped to attention and stared at Poppy, still clueless. "You do?"

"*Jack Colt, PI!*" Sarge crowed, slapping his forehead. "You're Daphne, Jack's secretary!"

The younger cop still appeared totally confused. "Who?"

"The TV show, it was on in the nineteen eighties!" Sarge exclaimed.

"I wasn't born until nineteen ninety-seven," the younger cop said.

Both Poppy and Sarge chose to ignore him.

Sarge was almost giddy. "Detective Jordan said he had recruited an actress to help with this operation. I just never imagined it would be *you*! This is so cool!"

Of course, Poppy knew that it was she who had contacted Detective Jordan, bringing him into the case, not the other way around, but why clarify such things and potentially bruise Jordan's fragile ego?

"I am a private investigator these days," Poppy felt the need to explain.

"Wait, a *real* one? Are you joking?" Sarge asked, still beaming from ear to ear.

Poppy nodded shyly.

Sarge fumbled for his phone. "Hey, do you mind if I get

a selfie with you? My poker buddies are never going to believe this!"

Poppy did not feel this moment was appropriate for that kind of thing, but she also did not want to disappoint a fan.

Sarge basically bodychecked a handcuffed Tanya out of the way to get to Poppy.

"Maybe I should read this woman her rights first, Sarge," the younger cop quietly suggested.

"That can wait, kid, hold on a sec," Sarge barked before holding his phone up and beaming while snapping a photo. He checked it and frowned. "It's a little blurry. Do you mind if I take another one?"

"No, not at all," Poppy said, keeping one eye on Tanya, who glowered at her menacingly.

Sarge tried again, this time satisfied. "Thank you, Daphne, you made my day!"

"Of course," Poppy said, grabbing the handles of the wheelchair and pushing it out of the way so the officers could escort Tanya Cook outside to their waiting squad car.

The young officer gripped Tanya by the arm to lead her out, but she refused to budge, her eyes angrily fixed on Poppy. "So you're telling me the cops recruited some washed-up, old has-been Hollywood *star* to take us down?"

Sarge nodded. "Yeah, and unfortunately for you, it worked like a charm, didn't it?"

Tanya sneered and looked dismissively at Poppy. "Why bother with the old lady makeup? You're already old enough to be my grandmother."

Poppy bristled on the inside, but was not about to show any emotion on the surface to give this she-devil the satisfaction. Instead, she calmly replied, "Yes, Tanya, you may have many more years ahead of you in life than I do, but a lot of them will no doubt be spent behind bars . . . so there's that."

Poppy opened the front door, allowing the two officers to leave with Tanya, who looked as if she wanted to smack Poppy right across the face but couldn't because her hands were handcuffed behind her back, so instead, she just raised her head high contemptuously and began to softly whistle the children's nursery rhyme "Twinkle, Twinkle, Little Star."

Poppy scoffed at Tanya's labored attempts to ridicule her Hollywood past. But given what was about to come, that unfortunately would turn out to be a very grave and dangerous mistake.

Chapter 3

"Tell me, what's the Rock really like?" Violet asked breathlessly as she and Iris crowded around the desktop computer at the Desert Flowers Detective Agency's garage office.

"He's a sweetheart," Matt said, beaming, his handsome face filling the screen. "Next time we do a Zoom call I'll try to wrangle him to swing by and say hello!"

Violet's eyes widened. "Oh my, that would be, I mean a big movie star like that, oh my!"

"Calm down, Violet, he's just a regular person like you and me," Iris sighed.

"I would hardly say he is anything like you and me, with those muscles and abs and that to-die-for gorgeous smile," Violet protested.

Iris rolled her eyes and turned back to the computer screen to address Matt. "Where are you now?"

"Hanging out in my trailer. I have some time to kill before my next scene," Matt said.

"And it's going well?" Poppy wanted to know, trying her best to squeeze in between Violet and Iris so she could participate in the video call as well.

"Better than I ever imagined. I mean, who would have thought three months ago that I'd be in Prague shooting a movie with Dwayne 'The Rock' Johnson! I mean, seriously, it's totally unreal!"

He was certainly right about that.

None of them could ever have predicted the turn of events that had unfolded after their last case. Both Matt and Poppy had accepted key roles in a Netflix reboot of the classic 1960s romantic comedy *Palm Springs Weekend* while working to ferret out a stalker hounding the film's female star. Once the case was wrapped up, Poppy and Matt honestly believed that that was the end of it. It was time to return to real life and finding their next case.

But then the movie was released and became an instant hit, and Matt in particular impressed the critics with his stellar performance and was singled out as a breakout star. The next thing they knew, Hollywood was suddenly sitting up and taking notice. A big-time talent agency offered to represent him, and then it was only a matter of weeks before he landed his first co-starring role in an A list studio picture, playing the young sidekick to Dwayne Johnson in his latest big-budget action blockbuster. It was all very unexpected and heady, and none of them could get their heads around Matt's sudden and meteoric rise as a bona fide Hollywood star.

Least of all Matt himself.

"I keep expecting to wake up in my bed back in Palm Springs and realize it was all just a wild dream," Matt said.

"It is not a dream, it is well deserved, and the three of us could not be more proud of you," Poppy gushed, grinning from ear to ear.

"Wyatt too!" Violet interjected.

"Where is Wyatt?" Matt asked.

"I know he seems very mature for his age, but he is still only thirteen years old, and has to go to school."

Matt chuckled. "I hear I have reason to be proud of the three of you, too, busting up that crime ring."

"The client is very pleased," Iris reported. "And the police expect she will get back a good portion of the money those girls stole, minus our fee, of course."

"I have to admit, it was quite satisfying taking down those three arrogant and entitled young girls who thought they were smart enough to get away with it, only to be outwitted by three old broads who could be their grandmothers," Poppy said.

"I would *not* say we are old enough to be their grandmothers, glamorous older aunts maybe, but hardly *grandmothers*," Iris snorted.

"Stop kidding yourself, Iris, and just do the math," Poppy said, laughing.

"Sorry I missed out on all the fun," Matt said. "But I'll be home soon."

There was a long pause.

The mood in the room turned slightly more somber.

Matt leaned forward, studying the ladies. "Did I say something wrong?"

"No, of course not," Poppy said, shaking her head. "We just miss you!"

But Matt was a smart guy.

He knew he had triggered something, and it quickly became obvious to him what it was. "Hey, listen, you three mean the world to me, and I know this whole acting thing is new, and who knows where it's going to go, but I want you all to know I will never abandon you, or the agency. We're a team, and nothing, not even a big Hollywood movie, will ever jeopardize that!"

The women nodded, although it was evident from their pained expressions they remained somewhat unconvinced, which Matt instantly picked up on.

"I'm not blowing smoke, I mean it," Matt insisted.

"Of course, Matt, we all know that," Poppy said quietly.

They heard a knocking sound behind Matt and someone talking but the words were indecipherable.

Matt whipped his head around toward the door of his trailer. "Be right there!" Then he turned back to face the screen. "They need me on set. I've got to go. I should be wrapped in the next couple of weeks barring any delays! Love you all! See you soon!"

"Bye, Matt!" Violet shouted, waving.

And then the Zoom call cut out.

"He is never coming back," Iris said matter-of-factly.

"Iris, don't say that!" Violet gasped. "You heard him! He is not going to just ditch us. He is a big part of our success, right, Poppy?"

Poppy put a hand on Violet's shoulder. "I believe Matt is being sincere when he says he has no plans to quit playing Matt Flowers for us, but neither he, nor we, can predict what might happen. Matt is very talented, and this is a big movie with an even bigger star, and it could lead to many more opportunities, and sooner or later, it might just be physically impossible for him to continue in his role here. I just think we need to be prepared for that possibility."

Violet's eyes began pooling with tears.

"Oh, Violet, please, control yourself," Iris snapped, although Poppy could see that Iris herself was getting emotional and her eyes were moistening.

"Look, it's not something we have to worry about right now. And by the way, the three of us just solved a case while Matt was in Prague, so we are quite effective on our own," Poppy argued confidently. "He was always supposed to be just the face of the agency anyway, for people too close-minded to hire women of a certain age. Cecile LaCrosse didn't blink an eye when we told her it would be just the three of us working on her case."

"Because she's even older than we are," Iris said.

"Well, lucky for us, Palm Springs is full of old people with problems who will be open to hiring us to solve them," Poppy said. "Now, I'm going to go home and take a long bubble bath and relax these tired bones. I'll see you both tomorrow."

"But I bought champagne to celebrate us cracking the case!" Iris exclaimed, pointing to a bottle sitting on the counter in the kitchen area.

"You two have fun, I'm exhausted. Let's have a martini lunch together tomorrow. Bye!"

Before they could protest, Poppy flew out the door to her brand-new white Cadillac, parked on the street. She had debated with herself about buying the pricey luxury car—a sixty-something-year-old woman in Palm Springs driving a Cadillac was almost a cliché—but in the end she just could not resist, especially with her boyfriend, Sam, in her ear, encouraging her, insisting she deserved to spoil herself a little. And all the technological gadgets and the superb smooth ride only bolstered her confidence that she had made the right decision.

When Poppy pulled onto her street and swung into the driveway of her midcentury home, she noticed a woman around her age sitting in a Lincoln Town Car across the street. She was trying to start the engine, which would initially start, rev a few times, then sputter and die out. The woman tried again, but got the same result.

Poppy slipped out of her Cadillac and walked down the driveway and across the street to where the woman was struggling to get her car started. "Having some trouble?"

The woman jumped back in the driver's seat. Her window was down and she threw a hand to her chest at the sight of Poppy. "Oh, dear, I didn't see you standing there!"

"I'm sorry, I didn't mean to startle you. I'm Poppy Harmon. I live right across the street."

"Yes, I've seen you out and about. We've waved at each other a few times, but we have never formally met. Adelaide Campbell. I'm your new neighbor. I just moved here two weeks ago."

She spoke with a distinct accent.

"Are you from Australia?" Poppy asked.

"Yes, Melbourne. But I lived in Florida the past twenty years, until my husband died six months ago."

"I'm sorry."

"Thank you. He had suffered a long time. Cancer. It was almost a blessing when he finally passed." She paused before continuing. "I needed a fresh start and always wanted to visit Palm Springs, so I came out a few months ago, took one look around, and said to myself, 'Adelaide, I think you've found your new home.'"

"Well then, welcome. I'm sure you're going to love desert living," Poppy said.

Adelaide tried the engine of her Lincoln one more time before giving up and getting out of the vehicle. "There is not much you can do around here without a car. Do you know a good mechanic?"

"I'm sure I can help with that."

"Also, is there a market around here that delivers? I was on my way to do some grocery shopping. I only have one carton of Greek yogurt and some wilted lettuce left in my fridge."

"Tell you what, my cupboards are pretty bare as well, so why don't you come with me in my car and we can both go to the store and restock together?"

"Oh, I don't want to be an imposition," Adelaide said.

"You won't be. I would appreciate the company."

Adelaide broke into a wide smile. "That's very neighborly of you, let me just grab my purse."

Adelaide reached into the driver's side and grabbed her bag off the passenger's seat, and then locked her car and walked with Poppy back across the street to her Cadillac.

The nearest grocery store was only five minutes away, and Poppy knew if they didn't dawdle, she could be home in that bubble bath relaxing in less than an hour.

They both grabbed carts and parted ways, agreeing to meet at the checkout counter in thirty minutes. Adelaide veered off toward the frozen foods and Poppy made a bee-line for the produce section. She was perusing the organic vegetables when suddenly another cart banged into hers, causing her to nearly drop the plastic carton of organic cherry tomatoes she was inspecting.

"Excuse me," a man said in a raspy voice.

Poppy spun around to see a young man, probably some-where in his midtwenties, with shaggy hair, a scruffy beard, and wearing a ball cap and dark sunglasses.

"That's quite all right," Poppy said with a tight smile.

The man didn't move his cart or make any attempt to leave. "Is there any difference?"

"I beg your pardon?"

"Between organic and regular vegetables."

"I believe it has to do with carbon," Poppy said, trying to be polite.

"I think it's a scam, just an excuse to jack up the price."

"Perhaps," Poppy said, not eager to engage with him.

She tried to push her cart forward, but the young man didn't budge and his cart still blocked hers. She gave him a stern look, but he made no effort to move it.

"Would you please let me get by?" Poppy asked.

"You look familiar. Have we met?"

She studied him. It was hard to tell what he looked like with the bushy beard, hat, and sunglasses. "I don't think so."

"I swear I've seen you somewhere before."

"Look, I'm here with a friend, and I need to get my shopping done, so if you would please just move your cart—?"

He smiled, not a friendly smile, more of a knowing, su-percilious sneer. He still didn't budge.

"If you do not allow me to pass by, I am going to call the manager," Poppy warned.

Finally, the young man lackadaisically rolled his cart back, allowing Poppy to push past him. She had only made it a few feet when she heard the man whistling.

Her blood ran cold.

She knew the tune.

It was a familiar nursery rhyme.

"Twinkle, Twinkle, Little Star."

She was so disturbed she dropped the carton of tomatoes, and they rolled all over the floor.

A stock boy came running to help with the cleanup.

"I'm sorry," Poppy said to the stock boy before spinning around to see the bearded young man still sneering, still whistling the same song as Tanya Cook.

Poppy abandoned her cart.

She was no longer interested in grocery shopping.

She just wanted to find Adelaide and get the hell out of the store.

Chapter 4

"You've got a few issues going on with your unit," Tyler, the air-conditioning repairman, said to Poppy as they stood outside in her backyard, inspecting her system, which was on the fritz. Poppy had awakened early that morning in a puddle of sweat. At first she thought she might be coming down with the flu, but then she quickly realized it was stifling hot in her entire house. She had tried turning the temperature down on the thermostat located in the hall just outside her bedroom, but when she lowered it to sixty-five degrees, the air-conditioning unit still did not kick on. The temperature was already past eighty degrees in the house and it was only seven in the morning. It was going to be a scorcher of a day in the desert, and she still desperately wanted to get a hike in before it reached a sweltering 114, as the local weatherman was forecasting.

Poppy had slipped on her loose-fitting khaki Bermuda shorts, a pink scoop V-shaped T-shirt, matching pink visor and sneakers, and her cherished Dolce & Gabbana sunglasses she was always worried about losing, hoping to get out on the trail after finding someone to come and fix the problem with her air conditioner. She had fired up the computer and asked for recommendations from a neighborhood chat site where residents offered suggestions for house repairs, local restaurants, lost pets, things like that. Within ten minutes of declaring her emergency, she had received several messages praising an appliance repairman named Tyler. After shooting him an e-mail with her phone number, he had texted her back right away and said he could be there within the hour. True to his word, he was at her front door in less than forty minutes.

Tyler was handsome, in his midthirties, dark haired and swarthy, probably Latin, very professional and courteous, but he showed a rebellious streak by painting his fingernails jet black. Poppy thought they made him look hip. She liked him right away, even as he began to spout off all the problems that were wrong with her central air conditioner.

"Right off the top I can see you've got coolant leaks, dirty condenser coils, and a clogged drain line. I can fix those no problem and get it running again, but the unit is old and barely holding up. Your blower motor is on its last legs and pretty soon you're going to have compressor issues," Tyler said solemnly, scribbling on his clipboard with a ballpoint pen.

"When I was in escrow on the house, the inspector told me the air conditioner had not been properly maintained by the previous owners and was on the verge of breaking down, but I just wasn't ready to invest in a whole new unit since it appeared to be working at the time," Poppy explained.

Tyler smiled sympathetically. "They always seem to sputter out on the hottest day of the year. Like I said, I could get it operating again—it will cost you about two hundred and seventy-five dollars—or I can put you in touch with a company I do business with, and they can set you up with a whole new system."

"How much will that put me back?"

"Six, maybe seven thousand dollars for a reliable, top-of-the-line model."

"I was afraid you were going to say something like that," Poppy sighed. She knew she could afford it, but it might take days to schedule a big job involving the installation and ductwork necessary to get it up and running properly. "Tell you what, Tyler, why don't you get this turkey humming again, which will give me a little more time to do some research on buying a new one."

"You got it," Tyler said, kneeling down and opening his toolbox to get to work.

"How long do you think it will take?"

"Couple hours at the most," he said with a smile.

"Would you mind if I popped out for a little hike just to get my heart rate up? I promise to be back in an hour, so I don't keep you waiting."

Tyler shrugged. "Knock yourself out."

"Thank you," Poppy said. She could tell he was trustworthy enough to leave at her house alone while he worked, especially given the outstanding testimonials he had received on the neighborhood help site.

After running inside to fetch him a bottled water from the fridge, Poppy dashed to her car and drove to the Murray Leak Loop, a popular hiking trail located at the intersection of Highway 111 and Gene Autry Trail, east of the Vons supermarket. Poppy parked her car, took a swig from her own bottled water she had brought along with her, and began her ascent up the steep dusty trail toward the peak. The heavily traveled path was unusually deserted today. Poppy surmised the hot weather predicted for today might have scared off even a few of the diehard hikers. A half hour later she was high enough to look down from the mountain and take in the majestic beauty of the Coachella Valley. She was sweating profusely now and poured some of her water down her face to stay cool before pounding onward and upward. She passed a young couple on their way down, who smiled and nodded but didn't stop to talk. After another twenty minutes or so, she decided to lean against a rock and take a break. She finished her water and stuffed the empty plastic bottle into her fanny pack. She leaned back, closed her eyes, and took some time to catch her breath.

She checked the weather app on her phone.

It was eighty-nine degrees.

Time to head back down, she thought.

Normally she would keep going all the way to the picnic tables at the very top, then continue on, sweep around the backside of the peak before looping in to the original trail and back down to the bottom, but today was just too hot. Plus, she was worried that would take too long, and Tyler might be finished and waiting for her to return so he could get paid, and he probably had other appointments. She rested for another minute or two and was about to turn around and retrace her steps back down the mountain to her car when she heard something.

Whistling.

Someone nearby was whistling.

She bolted upright from the rock and scanned the area. Just big granite rocks and prickly cacti for as far as the eye could see. She stood quietly, frozen in place, straining to hear the sound again.

It could be pretty windy up in the San Jacinto Mountains, but today it was still and clear.

A lizard skittered past her.

Other than that, she saw no signs of anyone.

She began trudging back down the trail when she heard it again.

It was definitely someone whistling.

Twinkle, twinkle, little star . . . How I wonder what you are . . .

Poppy's heart nearly leapt in her throat.

She spun around, expecting to find someone behind her. But there was nothing there.

No one seemed to be around for miles.

Up above the world so high . . . Like a diamond in the sky . . .

Her eyes searched the entire surrounding area.

There were large rocks all around. Behind any of them someone could be hiding.

Did the man who blocked her cart at the grocery store follow her all the way out here?

Had he been watching her?

Stalking her?

For what purpose?

And who was he?

The whistling stopped.

Poppy hurried back down the trail, unnerved, feeling suddenly vulnerable and unsafe. She picked up her pace, fearing he might jump out and chase after her. She twisted her ankle on a stone she hadn't seen in the middle of the trail, but fortunately she stopped herself in time and didn't sprain or break it. She kept turning back to see if anyone was behind her, but still there was nothing.

When she rounded a corner and spotted her car at the foot of the trail, she broke out into a run until she was safely back inside her vehicle with the doors locked and driving home.

Poppy shuddered, confused by what was happening.

Either this was someone's idea of a sick joke or someone was out to terrorize her.

Or worse.

Chapter 5

"Why did you wait until the dessert course to bring this up?" Sam Emerson asked, reaching across the table to take Poppy's hand at their favorite dining spot, John Henry's Cafe.

Poppy was picking at her Sunny Lemon Cake, and glanced up at Sam, who then turned to their dining companions, Violet and her date, Phil McKellan, a former Green Beret who worked for a security company whom they'd met on a previous case. They all exchanged concerned looks.

Poppy sighed and set her dessert fork down on the table. "Because I was hoping to avoid this."

"What?" Violet asked.

"This. You three worrying about me. It could be nothing."

Phil leaned forward, shaking his head. "It's definitely *not* nothing, Poppy. The grocery store, the hiking trail, someone is obviously trying to scare or intimidate you. This is classic stalker behavior. I know this stuff, it's my business."

"What can you tell us about this bearded man you ran into at the supermarket?" Sam asked.

"Not much. He had a hat on, sunglasses, the beard covered up most of his face, it was hard to see exactly what he looked like. I honestly don't think I would even recognize him if I ever saw him again," Poppy said. "I have already reported all of this to Detective Jordan. He's on top of it, so there is really no need to be so concerned."

"Well, it's obvious that this man who's following you around whistling a kids' nursery rhyme has to be connected somehow to Tanya Cook, who you are about to testify against," Phil said before taking a sip of his espresso after polishing off the remainder of his Classic Crème Brûlée. "It's got to be some kind of warning."

Violet shuddered. "Oh, I am not going to be able to sleep a wink tonight I'm so upset over this."

"Well, I don't have to drive back to Big Bear tonight. I can crash at Poppy's so she's not home alone," Sam said, squeezing Poppy's hand.

"Sam, you don't have to do that. . . ." Poppy said, smiling.

"I was planning on inviting myself to stay over anyway," he said with a playful wink.

"How is Jordan planning to handle this?" Phil wanted to know, downing the rest of his espresso.

"He said he was going to send one of his men over to the county jail and interview Tanya Cook to see what, if anything, she knows," Poppy said. "It's too much of a co-incidence that she whitstled 'Twinkle, Twinkle, Little Star' to me when she was arrested, before all this began."

"Poppy, I could have one of my guys shadow you, be a kind of security detail, until the cops get a bead on what's going on here," Phil offered.

The company Phil worked for, Cobra Security Force International, was a world-renowned company protecting a wide variety of high-profile clients such as Hollywood celebrities, powerful CEOs, and tech giants, even royalty.

"Don't be silly, Phil," Poppy laughed. "Somehow I don't

think retired actress and fledgling PI Poppy Harmon is an important enough figure for Cobra International. And I certainly don't have the means to pay for your services."

"You would get my personal friends and family discount," Phil promised.

"Ten percent off a million-dollar retainer fee?" Poppy joked.

"Nope, free of charge," Phil said.

"Thank you, but no," Poppy said firmly. "I trust Detective Jordan to get to the bottom of this quickly."

The waiter zipped by with the bill, dropping it down on the table. "You have a good night, folks." Then he continued on his way with a tray of appetizers for a large party across the patio. Both Sam and Phil reached for the check, but Poppy managed to snatch it up first, slapping her credit card down on top of it.

"You've had to endure listening to my problems all evening, so it's only fair I pick up the tab."

"Poppy, no . . . ," Phil protested.

"I have already decided, and I do not want to hear another word about it," Poppy said.

Sam sat back in his chair, grinning. "Trust me on this, Phil, there's no point in trying to change her mind once she's made a decision. I've tried and failed many, many times."

Phil smiled and threw his hands up in surrender.

Poppy stood up. "Now, if you will excuse me, I'm going to go to the ladies' room."

Violet grabbed her napkin off her lap and dropped it down on the table, making a move to get up. "Maybe I should come with you."

Poppy eyed her suspiciously. "Do you honestly need to use the ladies' room, Violet, or are you afraid I'm going to be kidnapped by gun-toting militiamen and spirited away on my way there?"

Violet hesitated, not sure how to answer.

"I thought so. Stay here and keep the men company. I will be back in a jiffy," Poppy promised before locking eyes with a distraught Violet. "Honestly, I will be just fine."

Poppy spun around and headed inside from the patio to the ladies' room. When she reached to open the door, she found it locked. The woman inside heard her jiggling the knob.

"Be right out!"

Poppy stepped back and waited patiently for about two minutes until the door was flung open and a woman around Poppy's age, heavily made up, burst out and then instantly stopped in her tracks.

"Poppy? Poppy Harmon?"

Poppy quickly studied the woman's face. It only took a second to recognize her. "Serena?"

The woman's face brightened and she reached out and grabbed Poppy with both hands. "Oh my goodness, how long has it been?"

"Over thirty years, I think," Poppy calculated.

Serena Saunders.

A blast from the past.

A very distant past.

Poppy had met Serena back in the eighties just as Poppy was coming off three seasons on *Jack Colt, PI*. She had built up some cache as an actress from being a series regular on a highly rated series, so her agent was able to immediately secure her more than a few high-profile TV movie and miniseries roles on the then three major broadcast networks: ABC, CBS, and NBC. Poppy played a wide array of colorful roles including an up-and-coming lawyer blackmailed into representing the mob based on a Sidney Sheldon novel; a woman who endures the horrors of Nazi-occupied France to become a world-famous fashion designer; and her personal favorite, a U.S. diplomat in the Middle East kidnapped by a Bedouin tribe and sold into the harem of the sultan. All cheesy to be sure, but certainly a lot of fun to do.

The only project she had accepted during that fruitful era that turned into an unmitigated disaster was a TV re-make of the 1967 film based on the blockbuster Jacqueline Susann novel *Valley of the Dolls*. The original movie, star-ring Patty Duke, Barbara Parkins, and Sharon Tate, had been roasted by the critics, but had subsequently with time turned into a camp classic. Why the network executives believed there was any kind of demand for a new version with a considerably lower budget was beyond Poppy, but her agent convinced her it would be a good career move. Plus the money would pay off her mortgage. She took the role of virginal Radcliffe graduate Anne Welles, who ac-cepts a job as a secretary at a talent agency and is exposed to the soul-crushing, seamy underbelly of Hollywood. She was most excited about playing opposite Bruce Boxleitner, who had been cast as her boss's business partner and ro-mantic interest, Lyon Burke. When the actress playing the troubled but talented starlet Neely O'Hara had to drop out because she forgot to tell the network she was five months pregnant, the producers scrambled to replace her with a new actress who had made a splash in a recent sci-fi movie starring Tom Selleck.

Serena Saunders.

That's when the trouble began.

Serena was a mess from the start.

Snorting coke.

Wild mood swings.

Not showing up on time.

And Serena took a particular dislike to her "Miss Per-fect" co-star, Poppy herself. Poppy tried to comport her-self with the utmost professionalism, but it was difficult with the mercurial Serena constantly trying to drag her down to her level. Serena would spread rumors in front of her co-stars, even Bruce Boxleitner, that Poppy was having a torrid affair with the director, and sabotage her confidence by breathlessly recounting fake conversations she had supposedly overheard where the producers discussed replacing Poppy because she couldn't act. At one point, Serena went so far as to strategically snip Poppy's costume with a pair of scissors so she had a wardrobe malfunction while shooting a crucial, emotionally charged scene. Their poisonous relationship wasn't on the scale of the Bette Davis/Joan Crawford feud, but word got around town that these two starlets were at each other's throats, even though Poppy tried very hard to dispel that notion and keep the peace on set. She did not want this experience marring her reputation. Once the movie wrapped, Poppy had vowed never to work with Serena Saunders again, and she didn't. However, Serena took great pleasure in taking swipes at Poppy in the press, further fueling the rumors of their divine feud. Poppy was just happy to be rid of her, hoping they would never have to be in the same room ever again.

And fortunately they never were.

Until tonight.

"Do you live here in Palm Springs?" Serena asked with a fake smile plastered on her face.

"Yes, I do. . . ."

"How wonderful. I know of so many old actresses who have come here to retire when they can no longer get work."

"Actually I'm not retired, I have my own business—"

"Oh, lovely, one of those adorable novelty shops on Palm Canyon all the tourists flock to? I would love to see their shocked faces when they discover Poppy Harmon sitting behind the register!"

"No, I—"

"By the way, I live here, too. Well, I have a second home here. I'm still acting. One of the lucky ones, I guess. Busier than ever, in fact. I just shot a movie with Chris Pratt in Georgia, I play his mother, his *very young* mother!"

Poppy could have boasted about her own recent role in the Netflix remake of *Palm Springs Weekend*, but had no desire to engage in a game of one-upmanship with this withering former rival.

"Listen, I have to go. My boyfriend is bringing the car around. He's a dear, but he doesn't like to be kept waiting. I thought younger men were supposed to be more patient. Yes, he's quite a few years my junior—what can I say, I love them young and virile these days, so sue me! But we must get together for lunch and catch up soon!"

Serena plucked a card from her diamond-encrusted handbag and pressed it into Poppy's palm. "Call me. Promise?"

"Promise," Poppy lied.

She hated lying.

But she also did not want to endure another minute engaging with this horrid woman whom she had mercifully forgotten about over the years.

"Ciao!" Serena cooed, hustling off.

Good riddance, Poppy thought to herself, as she scooted into the ladies' room.

By the time she was heading back to the table to join Sam, Violet, and Phil, she received a text from Detective Jordan.

Tanya Cook denied knowing anything about anyone stalking you. However, my detective who questioned her suspects she was lying.

Poppy grimaced.

But unlike Jordan's detective, Poppy did not just "suspect" that Tanya Cook was lying.

She was 100 percent certain of it.

Chapter 6

Poppy felt a pair of strong arms slip around her waist and someone nuzzling her neck from behind as she stood at her stove in the kitchen, scrambling eggs in a frying pan with a spatula.

"Good morning, Sam," Poppy said, then turned around to see him standing close to her, sleepy-eyed and smiling.

He kissed her softly on the lips. "I'm going to miss you."

"I will miss you, too, but you're only going to be gone for a week, so we have all that absence-makes-the-heart-grow-fonder romantic-longing stuff to look forward to when you get back," Poppy said, tapping his chest with her spatula.

Sam was leaving for New York City in a couple of days to work as a consultant on her former *Jack Colt, PI* co-star Rod Harper's one-hour police procedural television series, now in its second season. Although pretty much retired from show business after an illustrious career as a scriptwriter for cop shows and as a technical adviser given his past career in law enforcement, Sam was still called upon on occasion to come in for short periods of time and lend his expertise. The money was almost always too much to pass up. And so, when Rod had called him out of the blue, begging him to wing his way east to help get the details right on a number of upcoming episodes, Poppy had encouraged him to accept the high-paying gig. Sam had been lying low since suffering a heart attack some months ago, but he was feeling like his old self again, and was eager to get back out in the world. This trip seemed like the perfect opportunity.

Sam held Poppy tight against his chest as he went in for a third kiss.

"If you don't let me go, I'm going to burn your breakfast," Poppy said, trying to wriggle free.

"I'll take the risk," he said, burying his face in her neck. "Why do you always smell so good in the morning?"

Poppy reached over to turn off the burner on the stove because Sam was in an amorous mood and he was not about to be deterred.

He grabbed her hand, leading her out of the kitchen toward the bedroom, when there was a knock at the door.

Sam tugged on her hand, pulling her toward him, whispering, "Don't answer it."

"I wonder who that could be. I'm not expecting anyone," Poppy said, curious.

"Good, then no one knows we're here," Sam said, raising her hand and gently caressing it.

"It might be a package I forgot I ordered."

"Then you have a 'Sophie's Choice.' Me or the UPS man."

There was another knock. This one louder.

A woman called out from the other side of the door. "Poppy, are you home? It's Adelaide!"

Sam gave Poppy a puzzled look.

"My new neighbor," Poppy whispered. "She's a widow who recently moved here. I think she's a little lonely."

Sam knew Poppy's kind heart was going to win out, so he reluctantly let go of her hand, defeated.

Poppy smiled, squeezed his arm, and then scurried over to open the door. "Good morning, Adelaide."

"I hope I'm not getting you at a bad time," Adelaide said, glancing over Poppy's shoulder and spotting Sam.

"No, we were just about to have some breakfast," Poppy said, stepping to the side to introduce him. "This is Sam."

"The boyfriend," Sam said with a little wave.

"This is Adelaide. She lives across the street," Poppy said.

"Oh my, he's so rugged and handsome. It's like he just stepped out of the pages of a Louis L'Amour novel!" Adelaide gushed.

"Yes, he's quite the cowboy. I always say he was born about a hundred years too late. Would you like to come in and join us for some eggs and coffee?" Poppy asked.

"I would hate to impose, I just came by to give you the security code for my house," Adelaide said.

"Please, we'd love to have you," Poppy insisted. "Right, Sam?"

Sam nodded in agreement, resigned that his plan to get Poppy back to the bedroom was going to have to be put on hold, at least for the time being. "Yes, come on in, Adelaide."

Adelaide bounced inside, hugging Poppy, then pressed a slip of paper into the palm of her hand. "You keep that in case of an emergency, or if I happen to be out of town and something goes wrong in the house, a busted pipe or something. This way you have access—if you don't mind, of course."

"No, and I will make sure to give you mine as well," Poppy said. "We can look after each other."

"It just gives me some peace of mind knowing I have someone in the neighborhood I can count on for things like that," Adelaide said to Sam as she followed them to the kitchen and plopped down at the table.

Poppy poured coffee from the pot into three mugs. "Cream and sugar?"

"Not with my glucose levels! I take mine black, thank you very much, dear," Adelaide guffawed.

"Extra sugar for me," Sam said, turning to Adelaide. "Everybody says I could stand to be a little sweeter."

Adelaide giggled. "Oh, he's a charmer, too, Poppy!"

Poppy delivered the mugs to Sam and Adelaide, then returned to the stove, where she dished out three plates of eggs and buttered the toast. There were sausage links sizzling in another frying pan that were just about done. Poppy picked up a dish towel to wipe the sweat that had formed on her brow. "Sam, could you go turn the air up? It's getting awfully hot in here."

Sam jumped up and headed to the thermostat down the hall. Suddenly all the electricity in the house went out.

"Oh no . . . ." Poppy sighed, frustrated.

"What's wrong?" Adelaide asked, concerned.

"I'm having major air-conditioner issues," Poppy said, turning back and picking up a spatula to add the sausage links to the breakfast plates.

Sam returned to the kitchen. "I'm going outside to check the breakers."

Poppy carried two plates over to the table, setting one down in front of Adelaide, who prattled on about how delicious everything looked, and putting the other one down where Sam had been seated. She went to retrieve her own plate before sitting down with Adelaide.

"How long have you and Sam been dating?" Adelaide asked, wide eyed.

"Not long. We've known each other for decades. We both worked on the same television show back in the nineteen eighties when I was an actress and he was a consultant, but we only recently reconnected. It's been nice. I try not to have too many expectations at this stage in my life, but I care for him very deeply. He's a good man, the kind you don't come across very often."

"That's lovely," Adelaide said wistfully.

Poppy suddenly felt guilty for prattling on about her relationship with Sam, especially given how Adelaide had only just lost her husband, but Adelaide did not seem to mind.

The house appeared to come alive again as the electricity was suddenly restored. Moments later, Sam ambled through the back door.

"Just a blown fuse, nothing serious," Sam said, crossing back out to the hallway to try the air conditioner again.

Still nothing.

No cool air was running through the vents.

Poppy turned to Adelaide. "I have been avoiding buying a whole new unit, but it looks like I may have no choice."

Sam returned to the kitchen. "Hey, while I was outside, I saw some guy loitering across the street, just staring at me as I was standing at the fuse box working on the circuit breakers."

Poppy took a deep breath. "What did he look like?"

Sam grimaced. "I didn't get a good look at him. I called out and asked if he lived in the neighborhood, and then he just took off." Sam took a deep breath, then said knowingly, "He was wearing a red cap and sunglasses."

Poppy felt her hands slightly trembling. "Did he have a beard?"

Sam nodded.

"It might not be the same man," Poppy said softly.

Adelaide glanced back and forth between Poppy and Sam. "Who are we talking about?"

"I'm scheduled to testify at a court trial tomorrow morning. The defendant is a young woman by the name of Tanya Cook who has been charged with a number of serious crimes, and if she's convicted, it could lead to a lengthy prison term. I have reason to believe that someone connected to Ms. Cook, maybe a friend or boyfriend, is trying to intimidate me into not showing up."

Adelaide gasped. *"What?"*

"That does it. I'm cancelling my trip," Sam announced, slamming the palm of his hand down on the table and startling Adelaide.

"Sam, don't be silly," Poppy protested.

"If anything happened to you while I was gone, I would never forgive myself."

"Sam, you are going to New York. Look, I will be done testifying before you even leave Palm Springs. It makes absolutely no sense for you not to go."

Sam was clearly still wavering.

"I'll be just across the street to keep a close eye on things while you're gone, Sam. I will make sure Poppy stays safe and no strangers are lurking about," Adelaide offered.

"See? I will be fine, Sam," Poppy said firmly.

Sam finally seemed to be appeased and sat back down at the table.

Adelaide took a sip of her coffee. "You should talk to my old neighbors back in Melbourne. I always knew everything that went on within a five-block radius. I am the perfect nosy neighbor. Gladys Kravitz at your service!"

"Who?" Sam asked, confused.

Poppy chuckled and turned to Adelaide. "Sam may work in television, but he sure doesn't watch a lot of it. You wouldn't believe the references that go over his head."

Sam sat up straight in his chair. "Wait. Gladys Kravitz. *I Dream of Jeannie*, right?"

Poppy rolled her eyes. "Eat your eggs, Sam."

Chapter 7

"How old are you, Ms. Harmon?"

Poppy bristled.

She found it downright rude for anybody to ask a lady that question.

But she was sitting in a witness box under oath so she did not have much of a choice except to answer it.

"I am sixty-three years old," Poppy said.

The defense attorney, a wily, slick, off-putting man stuffed in a cheap gray suit, nodded, his chubby hands clasped together at the table. "Sixty-three years old . . ."

"Yes, that's correct," Poppy replied through gritted teeth, not appreciating him feeling the need to repeat it and allowing it to linger in the air.

"Do you find it appropriate for a *woman* of your . . . *maturity*, shall we say, to play dress-up, put on a gray wig and old lady costume, in order to entrap three home care professionals whom you *claim* were running some kind of wild money fraud scheme?"

"No, but I find the characterization of your question inappropriate. It's both sexist and ageist."

There were a few titters in the courtroom.

The judge, whose long face reminded Poppy of a basset hound, chose to ignore the mild outburst.

"I was just doing my job," Poppy quickly added.

The defense attorney rose from his chair and crossed around the table toward Poppy. "Ah, yes, your job. You say you're a private investigator."

"I don't just say it. I have the license to prove it."

The attorney glanced down at his notes. "The Desert Flowers Detective Agency, with your two best gal pals, also in their sixties, Iris and Violet. Too cute for words."

"I don't see how our age is relevant," Poppy said.

The attorney folded his arms. "You don't have to, because you are here to just answer my questions, not to provide color commentary."

Poppy stared at him with a steely eyed gaze that would make a misbehaved moppet cry, but she remained mum.

"So your friend, Cecile LaCrosse, came to you hysterical, crying about a gang of young women ripping her off and you and . . ." He checked his notes again. "You and Iris and Violet took it upon yourselves to set up this elaborate sting, just the three of you, in order to entrap these mysterious rogue nurses?"

Poppy flicked her eyes over to Tanya Cook, who was seated next to Bella and Kylie. All of them were dressed in very modest clothing, very little makeup, Kylie even wearing a pink bow in her hair. All three had made a convincing effort to come across as sweet, innocent, almost virginal young girls, incapable of stealing anything from anyone. Poppy prayed the jury was not stupid enough to buy their act.

"First of all, Cecile LaCrosse is not a friend. She is a client. She came to us for help when those three women conned their way into her house and stole her cash and drained her savings from her checking account," Poppy said, glaring at Tanya, before turning back to the defense attorney. "Second, we did not take it upon ourselves to set up the sting. We worked in conjunction with the Palm Springs Police Department."

"And you are absolutely certain that the three women you targeted are here in this courtroom," the attorney said, his beady eyes fixed on Poppy.

"Yes, they're right over there," Poppy said, pointing in the direction of Tanya, Bella, and Kylie, all of whom remained stone faced.

"Do you wear glasses, Ms. Harmon?"

"Yes, I do."

"I assume you were wearing them when you went undercover as a ninety-two-year old?"

Poppy paused, trying to remember.

"I mean you were pretending to be a little old lady, and from my experience, little old ladies wear granny glasses, am I right?"

"I don't believe I wore glasses as part of my disguise," Poppy said tightly.

"But you do have a prescription to wear glasses?"

"Yes," Poppy said, her stomach suddenly in knots.

"You were wearing heavy old-age makeup, which could have easily gotten into your eyes, which might have obstructed your vision, you didn't bother wearing your glasses, which you have stated you need to see clearly, but you still swear under oath that these are the three women, two of whom you admit only getting a glimpse of that day, *these* are the same three women you lured into your home hoping they would try to rob you?"

"It's them. Our client Ms. LaCrosse also previously identified them as well," Poppy explained.

"Yes, Ms. LaCrosse, who is currently being treated for cataracts. Given her eyesight and yours, I'm surprised you two ladies were able to even identify the gender of the defendants."

"Objection!" the prosecutor called out from his table. He was a wiry, intense, focused young man fresh out of law school. "Who's providing color commentary now?"

"Sustained," the judge agreed.

"Nothing further, Your Honor," the attorney said dismissively, waving away Poppy as if she had just broken down on the stand and admitted she had committed perjury by lying about everything.

The prosecutor popped up to his feet. "Redirect, Your Honor."

The judge nodded and the prosecutor scurried around the table and marched right up to the witness box. "Ms. Harmon, do you have to wear glasses all the time?"

"No."

"Are you required to wear them when you operate a vehicle?"

"No."

"Why not?"

"Because I only need them for reading."

"And why is that?"

"Because I had laser surgery on my eyes back in 2002. Other than reading, I have had perfect twenty-twenty vision for the past twenty years."

"So am I correct in saying if you were looking at a picture of the defendants in a book, you may need your glasses, but right in front of you, in person, or even from a distance, you can see them quite clearly?"

"That is correct," Poppy said, suppressing a smile.

"Nothing further, Your Honor."

The prosecutor was practically beaming as he returned to his table.

The defense attorney began to huffily scribble something in his notebook.

"Thank you, Ms. Harmon, you're free to go," the judge said.

Poppy was about to stand up and leave the witness box when she suddenly noticed a bearded man in dark glasses and wearing a red baseball cap slumped down in the back row of the courtroom, staring straight at her.

Poppy sat frozen for a moment, unable to move.

Was that him?

It was hard to tell.

It looked like him.

But there were a lot of young men with scraggly beards fond of wearing sunglasses, even inside, and red caps.

"Ms. Harmon? Is everything all right?" the judge asked with a look of concern.

Poppy snapped out of it and stood up. "Yes, Your Honor, thank you." She hustled out of the witness box, down the aisle, and out of the courtroom. She felt her testimony could not have gone better, but she had been rattled by the bearded man sitting in the back row. As she clicked down the hall toward the stairs that led her out of the Larsen Justice Center in Indio, she glanced back to see the man in the red cap follow her out. He seemed to pick up his pace in order to catch up to her.

Poppy suddenly made a beeline for the ladies' room and hurried inside, where she waited a full ten minutes, fearing the bearded man was hovering outside, lingering, watching for when she finally came out.

She debated calling the police.

But what if she was wrong?

What if she was totally mistaken and it wasn't him?

Two female lawyers breezed in, chatting about a case.

Poppy washed her hands at the sink, hanging around until they emerged from their stalls, still chattering away. The ladies took a few moments to scrub and primp, then Poppy fell in behind them as they walked out, hoping there would be safety in numbers.

She nervously glanced around, but there was no sign of the bearded man again. She followed closely on the heels of the two lawyers until she was outside in the parking lot, where she jumped into her car and sped off toward Palm Springs.

She kept one eye on the rearview mirror just in case he was trying to follow her, but thankfully there was no further sign of him.

She could only hope that now that her testimony in the trial was officially finished, this whole nightmare might finally be over.

She could not have been more wrong.

It was far from over.

In fact, it was just beginning.

Chapter 8

Poppy was exhausted.

The stress from the past few weeks had taken its toll. Part of her wanted to drive straight to the airport and get on the first plane that would take her to a quiet island somewhere in the Pacific to recuperate, or just get in her car and drive until she found an out-of-the-way resort and spa in Arizona to recharge. But instead, she opted to slip into her floral-patterned Asian wrap Kimono robe, prepare a steaming cup of hot chocolate with marshmallows, and relax on her patio watching the sun go down.

Sam had e-mailed her earlier that morning, still pressuring her to accompany him to New York tomorrow, just to get away and do some shopping, and when he wasn't working they could catch a Broadway show or take a cab down to Little Italy for some pasta and wine. She had declined. She was going to have a new air conditioner installed the following morning and did not want to put off a number of chores she needed to get done now that the Desert Flowers Detective Agency was between cases.

No, her plan was to rest and recuperate right at home, and put this entire unpleasant ordeal out of her mind. She hoped that now that her testimony was behind her and the judge had turned the case over to the jury, which was currently deliberating, there would be no point in the bearded man continuing to stalk her.

After the sun disappeared down behind the San Jacinto Mountains and her street was bathed in darkness, Poppy stood up from her chaise longue and walked back inside to the kitchen, where she washed out her empty mug. She was about to turn on the television and catch up with what was going on in the rest of the world when her phone rang.

Poppy sighed, annoyed. It was her landline. No one ever called on this line except for telemarketers and election pollsters. All her friends and family usually tried calling her on her cell phone.

She didn't want to answer it.

She let the phone ring until it finally stopped. She set the clean mug down on a dish towel and walked into the living room. The TV remote was not in its usual spot on the coffee table so she set about hunting for it.

The phone rang again.

She tried to ignore it until she finally located the remote on a side table next to the couch.

She turned on CNN.

The phone stopped again.

Poppy settled down to watch Anderson Cooper.

She was a little hungry but too tired to make the effort to prepare something. Maybe she would put together a cheese and cracker plate and watch a diverting movie after the news, a romantic comedy, something silly that she didn't have to think too hard about.

The phone rang yet again.

This was getting ridiculous.

Poppy hauled herself up from the chair and marched into the kitchen, grabbed the receiver off the wall, and answered huffily, "Hello?"

Nothing.

Just dead air.

Poppy tried again. "Hello?"

Then she heard the whistling.

Twinkle, twinkle, little star.

"Who is this?" Poppy demanded to know.

The whistling continued.

"What do you want?" Poppy cried.

Finally, she slammed down the phone.

She glanced at her hands. They were trembling.

Why wouldn't this mystery person just leave her alone?

The phone started ringing again.

Poppy stared at it, terrified, then scooped it up and screamed, "If you don't stop doing this, I'm going to call the police!"

"Poppy?"

Sam.

It was Sam.

A wave of relief washed over Poppy's entire body.

"Oh, Sam . . ."

"What's going on? Are you all right?"

"Yes . . . I . . ." She wanted to tell him, but she knew he would only get worried, and there was really nothing at this point he could do. "I'm fine."

"Are you sure?"

"Yes. Why are you calling on this line?"

"I tried your cell, but it went straight to voicemail. I got worried, so I decided to try this number."

Poppy searched the living room for her phone before realizing she had left it on the night table in her bedroom. "I must have turned the ringer off earlier. I just wanted to block out the rest of the world and be alone with my thoughts."

"How did today go?"

"It was difficult, but I got through it. I'm just relieved the whole thing is over. What happens now is completely out of my hands."

"Well, let's hope whoever's been harassing you will finally stop," Sam said.

I should tell him, Poppy thought to herself.

She was about to speak when Sam interjected, "I was calling to see if you might reconsider coming to New York with me."

Poppy smiled.

He was never going to let up until he was physically on that plane at the Palm Springs Airport.

"It sounds lovely, Sam, really, but you're going to be busy working on the show, and I just don't have the energy to run around Manhattan sightseeing and shopping all by myself."

"My hotel in midtown is supposed to be amazing. World-class spa. You could just hole up with room service and pamper yourself with a massage and facial."

It did indeed sound tempting.

"I love you for thinking of me, Sam, but maybe next time."

"Okay, I understand. I will see you tomorrow evening. I'm planning to get to your place around six. My flight leaves at nine."

"I will be here. Good night, Sam."

"Night, doll."

He hung up.

Poppy put the phone back in its cradle.

When she went to turn off the lights in the kitchen she caught a quick glimpse of someone standing underneath the streetlight across the street.

Poppy's heart nearly jumped into her throat.

Was it him?

Was he back, staring at the house again, just like the other morning?

She flipped the light switch off, plunging the kitchen into darkness, then slowly moved closer to the window, peering out. She saw the man had a little Pekingese dog on a leash, and was now bending over to pick something up with a plastic bag from a neighbor's front lawn. When the man stood upright and the light caught his face, Poppy recognized him as the man who lived a few houses down. Satisfied, she headed back to the living room and was about to sit down again when the doorbell rang.

Poppy stood frozen, not sure what to do.

She debated whether or not she should just not answer it and pretend she wasn't home.

The doorbell rang again.

She knew if she didn't do something, whoever was out there might ring the bell all night.

Poppy closed her robe tighter with one hand and slowly, cautiously made her way to the door. "Who is it?"

"It's Violet and Iris," Violet chirped.

Poppy quickly unlocked the door and swung it open.

Sure enough, Violet and Iris stood on her front stoop, both carrying overnight bags.

Poppy smiled, happy to see them. "What are you two doing here?"

"We are going to have a slumber party," Iris said, pushing her way inside. Violet dutifully followed.

"Slumber party? What are we, sixteen?" Poppy said with a grin, closing the door behind them.

"Violet and I were discussing it earlier, and we decided we could never live with ourselves if some marauding madman broke into your house and slashed your throat while you were sleeping in your own bed!" Iris cried.

"Iris, dear, I really do not see the benefit of being so descriptive in your possible nightmare scenarios," Violet admonished, before turning to Poppy. "We just figured there is safety in numbers."

"I'm starving. What do you have in your refrigerator?" Iris asked, crossing to the kitchen.

"I'm sure we can scrounge up something edible," Poppy said.

Iris suddenly came scurrying back in from the kitchen. "It is stifling hot in here! I'm melting! What do you have the temperature set at, Death Valley in August?"

"I'm afraid the air conditioner is still on the fritz, but don't worry, I have plenty of electric fans, and the company will be here tomorrow morning at seven to install a new one," Poppy said.

"*Seven AM*? They'd better not be pounding things and making all kinds of noise and wake me up! I need my beauty sleep," Iris scoffed, gesturing toward her remarkably well-preserved face. "This just does not happen by chance!"

Poppy and Violet chuckled.

"Don't worry, I brought extra earplugs and sleep masks. You won't be disturbed," Violet said.

Poppy touched Violet's arm. "I'm happy you're here."

Violet patted Poppy's hand reassuringly. "We wouldn't have it any other way."

Chapter 9

"Are you sure it's him?" Violet gasped.

"No, I'm not sure," Poppy sighed. "I said it *could* be him."

Poppy, Iris, and Violet sat at a round glass table on Poppy's patio, drinking coffee and eating Violet's homemade scones the following morning while staring at the three men from Atlas Air Conditioning who were busy installing Poppy's brand-new unit. They had already unhooked and removed the rusty old one and hauled it to their truck. The three women were focused on the youngest of the three, who was around five feet ten, had a lanky build, and sported a scruffy beard and blue ball cap.

"I thought you said the stalker wore a red cap," Violet noted, chewing her scone.

"It is possible for him to have more than one hat, Violet!" Iris snapped before turning to Poppy. "I think it's him. I caught him sneaking around inside the house a little while ago."

"He wasn't sneaking, Iris, he was just looking for the crawl space so he could check the ductwork," Poppy explained. Her eyes zeroed in on the young man, who took off his cap and wiped his sweaty brow with his tanned, muscled arm as the harsh midmorning desert sun beat down on him and his two coworkers.

"Well, there is only one way to find out for certain," Iris said, slamming her coffee mug down on the table and standing up.

"What are you going to do?" Violet whispered.

"Ask him," Iris snorted before marching over to the young man and wagging a finger in front of his confused face. His two older buddies, a rotund, balding man in his midforties and a tall, skinny Latino man around the same age, stopped what they were doing to curiously eavesdrop on the conversation.

The young man listened to Iris go on for a bit before reaching in the back pocket of his shorts and pulling out his wallet. He flipped it open and handed Iris his driver's license, which she intently scrutinized before gruffly handing it back to him.

The rotund man, who had been kneeling next to the new unit they were installing, hauled himself up to his feet and crossed over to join them. Iris nodded as he spoke, then, satisfied, marched back over to Poppy and Violet.

"It's not him," Iris announced.

"What did he say?" Violet asked.

"His name is Rusty Coolidge, he lives in Desert Hot Springs with his girlfriend and their three-year-old daughter. Larry, his boss over there, told me he has been with the company for five years and has never been in any kind of trouble."

Poppy watched as Rusty smiled and nodded in their direction, then circled around the side of the house and out the gate to the street to where their truck was parked to get some tools or something they needed. "I hope we didn't offend him."

"What's to be offended by? I was perfectly polite. It is not in my nature to be demanding or aggressive!" Iris exclaimed.

POPPY HARMON AND THE BACKSTABBING BACHELOR   53

Both Poppy and Violet took sips of their coffee to avoid making any kind of response to that last comment.

Rusty ambled back around from the front, carrying a hammer, and made a beeline for the three women. As he approached, he slowly raised the hammer, and the three women instinctively leaned back in their chairs, suddenly a bit nervous.

"What are you going to do with that hammer?" Violet cried.

Rusty glanced at it, realizing he was still holding it, and chuckled. "Oh, Larry needed it, sorry, hold on." He jogged over, handed it to his boss, and then bounded back to the women.

"I don't mean to interrupt, ladies—"

"It's all right, Rusty, we believe you are who you say you are and not some deranged psychopath who is going to butcher our friend Poppy here," Iris said matter-of-factly.

"I really wish you would have stopped after 'we believe you are who you say you are,' for Poppy's sake," Violet moaned.

"I just wanted to let you know there's a man at your front door," Rusty said. "I saw him ringing the bell when I went to get my hammer from the truck, but you probably can't hear it out here on the patio, so I told him I'd let you know he was here."

Poppy tensed. "What did he look like?"

"Black guy, midforties maybe, very serious looking," Rusty said.

Poppy exhaled, relieved. "Detective Jordan." She jumped to her feet. "He said he would come by when he had some news." She hurried inside the house and to the front door, swinging it open to reveal Jordan, who was texting on his phone, eyes downcast. When he was done, he raised his gaze to Poppy and smiled, which was rare. Poppy took that as a good sign.

"Well?" Poppy asked apprehensively.

"Guilty on all counts."

"All of them?"

"Tanya, Bella, and Kylie, all of them."

Poppy threw a hand to her heart. "Oh, thank God, I was beginning to get a little worried the way it was taking so long."

"The prosecutor believes your testimony really made the difference," Detective Jordan said.

"I am just relieved this whole ordeal is finally over," Poppy remarked. "Would you like to come in for some coffee?"

"Thanks, but I have to get to the office. I just felt I should warn you . . ."

Poppy suddenly tensed again. "About what?"

"After the judge read the verdict, Tanya Cook went ballistic, screaming obscenities at the jury, making all kinds of threats against the cops, the prosecutor, the judge . . . even you. . . ."

"She mentioned me by *name*?"

Detective Jordan nodded. "She said she had friends who would help her get revenge, make you and the entire legal system pay for ruining her life."

"The bearded man," Poppy said to herself with a shudder.

"Look, she was probably just mouthing off, trying to get a rise out of everybody because she was upset over the fact that she's now suddenly facing a stiff prison sentence."

"Or she could be dead serious."

"Poppy, I can have a patrol car come by regularly, keep an eye on your place, until all of this dies down. I will also write up a report so we have a record, but until we have more information, like a photo or license plate of this guy, there's only so much I can do."

"I understand, Detective," Poppy said quietly.

"In my experience, threats made in the heat of the moment rarely turn out to be real. They're almost always bluffing, but I want you to be very careful, and I want you to promise me you will call me, day or night, if you think your safety is in any way compromised. Do you hear me?"

"Yes, thank you, I promise," Poppy said with a thin smile.

She prayed Detective Jordan was right.

But deep down she had a sinking feeling he wasn't.

Chapter 10

"I still don't feel right about this," Sam said, grimacing, after parking his SUV in Poppy's garage and retrieving a scuffed black suitcase he had stored in the back.

"Sam, for the last time, stop worrying," Poppy said. "Iris and Violet are closely looking after me, and Matt will be home from Europe in a few days, and you know how overprotective he is."

Sam lugged his suitcase down the drive to Poppy's car, which was parked in front of the house with the trunk popped open. He slid the luggage inside, and Poppy pressed a button on her remote to lower the lid shut.

Sam stopped, flashed her a look of concern, worry lines forming on his forehead, then kissed her gently on the lips. "Just promise me you will be extra, extra careful. . . ."

"Why, Sam Emerson, you really do care!" Poppy joked.

"Of course I do, we make sense together. . . . I wouldn't know what I'd do if you suddenly weren't around," Sam muttered.

"You old softie," Poppy said, smirking. She then headed around the side of the car to slip into the driver's seat. "Come on, I don't want you to miss your flight."

Sam jumped in the passenger's seat, and Poppy drove

the ten minutes to the Palm Springs Airport, pulling up to the curb next to the main terminal entrance.

"No tearful good-byes, please," Poppy said, turning to Sam.

He gave her one last worried look and then opened his mouth to speak, but Poppy cut him off. "I will be *fine*!"

"Okay," Sam said hesitantly before stealing one last kiss and getting out of the car. Poppy pressed a button to open the trunk, where Sam retrieved his suitcase. He waved and finally shuffled inside the terminal. Poppy watched him get in line to check in for his flight before sighing and driving away, on her way home.

She drove out of the airport, heading west on Tahquitz Canyon Way, then turned left on Ramon and continued on. She stopped at a red light and instinctively glanced up at her rearview mirror. A black Cadillac Escalade was idling directly behind her. The windows seemed to be darkened, so she couldn't get a clear view of the driver. The light turned green and Poppy pressed her foot on the gas pedal, speeding up. The Escalade plowed forward, keeping pace with her.

Was the driver tailing her?

A knot slowly began forming in the pit of Poppy's stomach.

Don't panic, she reminded herself.

It could just be a coincidence.

Poppy decided to be certain she wasn't being followed, so suddenly she made a sharp turn onto DaVall, which led her down to Dinah Shore Drive, where she made a quick left toward Rancho Mirage, heading in the opposite direction of her house.

Sure enough, the black Escalade copied her every move.

Someone was definitely tailing her.

Poppy tried to remain calm, but found herself gripping the steering wheel so tightly her knuckles were white.

She stopped at another red light, stealing furtive glances in the rearview mirror, nervously staring at the black-tinted windshield. When the traffic light turned green, Poppy veered to the left out of her lane and raced forward ahead of two cars, then, with her tires squealing, whipped back into the right lane, leaving the Escalade behind as her speedometer crept up to over fifty miles an hour. The Escalade then did the same, overtaking the two slower-moving vehicles, determined not to lose Poppy.

Poppy made another right turn, onto Bob Hope Drive just before the Agua Caliente Resort Casino Spa, and found herself with an open road ahead of her, with no traffic. She slammed her foot down on the gas and sped as fast as she could. Her best chance to lose him was to get far enough ahead, out of his sight, so she could turn off onto a residential street and finally ditch him.

The Escalade was far enough back when Poppy saw her opportunity. She made a hairpin turn onto a side street into a small, quiet desert neighborhood, her car screeching. She once again flicked her eyes up to the rearview mirror to see if the driver of the Escalade had spotted her last-minute turn. But when she gazed back at the road in front of her, she suddenly realized she had veered too far to the right while not looking where she was going. Her car jumped the curb, smashing into a mailbox. The pole holding it up cracked and the whole metal box came crashing down on the hood of her car.

Poppy leaned back in her seat, closing her eyes.

Defensive driving was clearly not her strong suit.

She calmly reached for her purse in the backseat to find her wallet. Inside was a business card for the Desert Flowers Detective Agency. She scribbled on the back that she was the one responsible for damaging the mailbox, and requested the home owner contact her so she could reimburse him or her for the necessary repairs.

Poppy opened the car door, got out, and put her note inside the mailbox. Then she carried the box to the front lawn and set it down. She was about to head up the walk to the front door and ring the bell, in case anyone was presently at home, when she heard tires squealing and the black Escalade pull up behind her car.

Poppy took a deep breath.

She felt defenseless out in the open like this, not sure what was about to happen.

The driver's side door swung open, and much to Poppy's surprise, Phil McKellan jumped out.

Violet's boyfriend.

"Phil, what on earth—?" Poppy cried.

He had a sheepish look on his face. "Violet's not going to be happy about this."

"Why? What did Violet say?"

"She's been worried sick about you, driving around on your own, possibly putting your life in danger, she thought . . ."

"She thought since you were a trained security expert, you could keep an eye on me without me knowing."

"Something like that."

"Phil, that's not necessary."

"I just want to keep Violet happy. In case you hadn't noticed, I like her a lot," Phil said with a sheepish grin.

"That's very sweet," Poppy said.

"For all my years of experience, I sure did botch the job big time, didn't I? The whole point of surveillance is not to be noticed," Phil said, shaking his head, embarrassed.

"Well, I appreciate the effort, Phil. And if it makes you feel better, you can still follow me around, just try to keep a lower profile."

"I promise."

Poppy walked over and frowned at the front hood of her car and the now noticeable dent in the middle of it.

Phil started to head back to his Escalade, but then stopped. "Poppy, one favor . . ."

"I won't say a word to Violet about you blowing your cover," Poppy said, giving him a knowing wink.

"Thanks, I want her to keep thinking I'm really good at my job," Phil said, relieved.

"I'm sure you are good, Phil."

Phil broke into a wide smile. "Just for that, I'll give you a full two-minute head start before I start tailing you again."

Chapter 11

"G'day, Poppy!" Adelaide chirped, standing on Poppy's doorstep.

"Adelaide, how are you this morning?" Poppy said politely, casually checking the time on her phone, which she gripped in her hand.

It was 10:45 AM.

She was running late.

She had to be at the Desert Flowers Detective Agency office by eleven to meet with a prospective new client.

Poppy had finally gotten a good night's sleep after the tension and drama that had unfolded over the past few weeks. But she had overslept, and she was now in a rush to get out of the house and into her car and on her way to her meeting.

"I've had better days," Adelaide sighed.

Oh no.

Poppy did not have time for a long, protracted story, but she certainly did not want to come off as rude to her new neighbor.

"My mechanic called this morning and my car is going to be in the shop for another couple of days. They need to order a new part—I can't for the life of me tell you what it is—but now I'm stuck without transportation and I really need to get some errands done today that I have been putting off."

"Well, I would love to help you out, Adelaide, but I'm in a bit of a hurry. I'm meeting a client at the office in fifteen minutes—"

"Oh, I understand, I won't bother you anymore. I suppose most of my errands can wait, except my prescriptions—I really do need those. How far of a walk is it to the nearest Walgreens?"

Poppy thought about it. "Maybe two, two and a half miles."

"Well, I guess I can try to hoof it there," Adelaide moaned.

"It's going to be over a hundred degrees today, Adelaide. You definitely should *not* walk. What about calling an Uber?"

"A what?"

"Uber, the app, you can request a ride."

"Oh, I just get confused trying to figure out those app things. Maybe I can just call a cab. I just hope it's not too expensive—I'm living on a fixed income."

Poppy felt guilty, but she needed to get moving. She suddenly noticed how nice Adelaide looked, with her hair done, wearing a lovely shade of lipstick, dressed in a sharp dusty cedar silk blouse and white skirt.

"By the way, Adelaide, you look lovely today," Poppy said, smiling.

"I rarely have an excuse to get all dolled up so I figured I might as well make an effort, even if it's only for my pharmacist," she said, chuckling.

"Well, I'm sorry I can't help you today. . . ." Poppy suddenly stopped as a lightbulb seemed to pop on in her head. "Wait, I just remembered!" She reached into her purse and fished for her car key, which she then handed to Adelaide. "Here, take my car."

"But how will you get to the office? I don't want you to have to pay for an Uber."

"No, I completely forgot. I can take Sam's car. He left it in my garage while he's in New York."

"Are you sure it's not too much of an imposition?"

"Of course not."

"Oh, Poppy, thank you so much. I promise to be extremely careful driving your gorgeous Cadillac. And when you get home from work, I insist you come over for a glass of wine and some of my famous caramel shortbread on my patio."

"Sounds like a plan," Poppy said, waving as Adelaide scurried off toward Poppy's car, parked in the driveway. Poppy shut the door and raced past the laundry room to the door leading to the garage. By the time she pressed the wall button to open the garage door, Adelaide was already in Poppy's car, backing out of the driveway before speeding off.

Poppy jumped into Sam's SUV, had to adjust the seat for her shorter height, then started the vehicle. Before shifting the gear in reverse to back out of the garage, she quickly texted Violet her apologies, explaining she would be five minutes late.

As it turned out, traffic was light and Poppy managed to pull up in front of Iris's house at only two minutes past eleven. When she made her way inside the garage office, Violet was already handing a cup of coffee to their client, who was seated opposite Violet and Iris on the couch, while Violet's grandson, Wyatt, busily worked on his computer in the background, remote learning today, uninterested in anything else going on in the room.

The client was the owner of a high-end art gallery on the north end of Palm Canyon in downtown Palm Springs. She had recently hired a new employee to run the gallery while she would be laid up recuperating after her upcoming hip surgery, but almost immediately she began to suspect that her new hire was lying about her education, experience, and past. There were signs everywhere the girl was not to be trusted, and the owner was now worried about leaving her in charge of so many expensive paintings. She wanted Desert Flowers to run a routine background check quickly, before she was scheduled to be admitted to the Desert Regional Hospital for her operation.

Poppy assured the woman they could help. In fact, she had no doubt Wyatt could get a full report finished by the end of the day, although she had no intention of relating that fair assessment to the client and make it look too easy because she still wanted to make sure they received their full fee, no discounts.

The woman thanked the team and stood up to leave. "Will Mr. Flowers be personally handling my case?" Her eyes brightened at the mere mention of Matt's name. She had clearly seen a picture of his resoundingly handsome face on the company website.

"Mr. Flowers is not in the country at the moment, but we will be consulting him every step of the way," Poppy said.

It still rankled Poppy that many of their clients felt more comfortable with the young, masculine energy of Matt, as if women of a certain age were somehow not as effective in this line of work, which Poppy, Iris, and Violet had disproven time and time again. But as long as the checks cleared, Poppy was willing to accept that little dose of reality, at least for now.

After ushering the client out, Iris checked her watch. "I am starving. Where are we having lunch?"

Violet clapped her hands excitedly. "How about Wilma & Frieda's? They have the most delicious Strawberry Spinach Salad!"

"Fine with me, sound good to you, Wyatt?" Poppy asked, turning to the boy, who sat at his computer, transfixed. "Wyatt?"

Wyatt still didn't answer, his eyes glued to the screen.

"Wyatt, dear, would you like to join us for lunch?"

He slowly swiveled around in his chair, eyes focused on Poppy. "Aunt Poppy, did you drive here in your Cadillac today?"

"No, I drove in Sam's SUV."

"So your car is at your house?" Wyatt asked.

"No, I lent it to a friend. Why are you asking, Wyatt?"

"You'd better come over here," he said solemnly, spinning back around to face his computer screen.

Poppy, Iris, and Violet hurried over to the desk, hovering behind Wyatt as he played a live local news feed from a helicopter flying over the wreckage of a fatal car accident off Highway 74, a steep, mountainous road high above Palm Desert. As the camera on the chopper zoomed in on the burning white Cadillac at the bottom of a deep ravine, Wyatt pointed to the vanity license plate that was still visible at the crash site.

POPPYPI.

Poppy, Private Eye.

Sam had gotten it made for her as a joke.

It was definitely her car.

The reporter was breathlessly announcing one fatality, the driver of the vehicle, a woman in her mid- to late sixties.

Poppy gasped as she threw a hand to her mouth in shock.

It had to be Adelaide.

Adelaide Campbell was dead.

Chapter 12

Lynn Jordan was ecstatic to find Poppy standing on her front doorstep that evening. She had grown up watching *Jack Colt* reruns on TV Land back in her hometown of Jackson, Mississippi, and was an unabashed fan. But she had never imagined after moving to the Coachella Valley and marrying her husband, Detective Lamar Jordan, that Poppy Harmon herself would suddenly be in her orbit. Her husband was not nearly as enthusiastic about Poppy's regular presence, mostly because he found her constant poking around in his police business an unnecessary impediment. His wife, on the other hand, had grown rather fond of the ex-actress over the past two years, and Poppy was not above exploiting that copious amount of goodwill to her personal advantage when appropriate and necessary.

Which would explain why Poppy had shown up unannounced at the Jordan home bearing a German chocolate cake she had spent the late afternoon baking.

"I sincerely apologize for not calling first. I was planning to just drop this off by the door here, but then I noticed that you were home, and thought I would just ring the bell and say hello," Poppy said.

"Oh, I'm thrilled that you did! It's always a treat to see

you," Lynn gushed, beaming, as her eyes fell to the pink box Poppy held out in her hands. "What is this?"

Poppy handed the box to Lynn. "German chocolate cake, your favorite."

"How did you know?"

"I follow you on Instagram. You once posted that you have loved German chocolate cake ever since you were a little girl back in Mississippi. Your grandmother used to make it for you all the time."

"Gosh, yes! But I don't understand. What's the occasion?"

"Chic Boutique on El Paseo!"

"You heard about that?"

Poppy nodded excitedly. "Yes, it's very exciting! I actually know a world-famous fashion designer!"

Poppy may have been stretching that declaration just a tiny bit. Lynn Jordan was indeed an aspiring dress designer, and Poppy had learned through Lynn's social media accounts that she had recently sold a few of her creations to a small, upscale boutique in Palm Desert. It wasn't exactly a contract with a national department store like Nordstroms, but for a fledgling designer, it was still quite a big win.

"I just wanted to personally offer my congratulations," Poppy continued. "You're on your way!"

"Your timing is impeccable. Lamar and I are just finishing dinner. Why don't you come in and join us for dessert?" Lynn said, happily holding up the pink box.

"Oh, no, I don't want to intrude. . . ." Poppy said with the full confidence that Lynn would absolutely insist.

"I insist!"

Lynn grabbed Poppy by the arm with one hand while balancing the cake box with the other and excitedly pulled her inside the modest home in their quiet residential neighborhood in Cathedral City.

"Lamar, look who's here!" Lynn yelled, shutting the door behind them.

Detective Jordan wandered in from the dining room. The curiosity on his face gave way to a perceptible frown. "Hello, Poppy. . . ."

"Detective Jordan, you must be so proud of your wife's newfound success," Poppy said.

"Look at the lovely cake she brought to help us celebrate," Lynn said, popping open the lid of the cake box. "German chocolate! Isn't that thoughtful?"

"It's a very nice gesture, I suppose," Jordan said skeptically. "But you could have just mailed a card."

"Lamar . . . ," Lynn warned.

"Yes, but if I tried mailing this cake, it would have gotten all smooshed, so I thought it would be best to deliver it myself," Poppy explained, locking eyes with Jordan, fully aware he was catching on to her true motive.

Jordan nodded, then marched past her, opened the front door, and peered outside. "How are you getting around now that your car has been totaled?"

"I'm borrowing my boyfriend Sam's car while he's in New York. As for my own vehicle, I've been on the phone all afternoon with the insurance company. Adelaide Campbell was not on my policy, so there is a very good chance they won't honor my claim."

"Why don't we stop all this unpleasant talk and have some of this delicious cake, shall we?" Lynn suggested, glaring at her husband.

"Oh, I'm sure Poppy doesn't mind talking about poor Adelaide Campbell, honey, because as I have explained to you multiple times, this is Poppy's typical MO, charming her way into discovering information on any case that interests her, especially ones that she is personally involved in."

Poppy turned to Lynn. "I *really* am proud of you, Lynn."

"I know you are—thank you. Don't mind my overly suspicious husband. Now come, sit down, have some cake,"

Lynn said, half dragging Poppy into the dining room. She turned back and called out to her husband, "Are you joining us, Lamar? When have you ever said no to cake?"

Detective Jordan begrudgingly followed, sitting back down at the table as Lynn set the box down in the middle, cleared their dinner plates, and then returned from the kitchen with fresh dessert plates and a knife to cut the cake. After serving them, Lynn plopped down next to her husband and they all dug in.

"Oh, this is divine," Lynn moaned. "Poppy, you will have to send me the recipe."

Judging by the speed with which Detective Jordan was scarfing his own piece down, Poppy deduced he was enjoying the cake as well.

"If you show up with any more mouthwatering desserts like this, I may have to design a special dress just for you. I'm thinking a circle skirt dress, navy poppy print."

"You're making her a dress now?" Jordan exclaimed. "Come on, Lynn, she only showed up here because she wants information on the Adelaide Campbell case."

Lynn put down her fork and stared at her husband. "If that's what you believe, then go on and give it to her."

"You know very well I am not at liberty to discuss an active case—"

His wife interrupted him. "It was Poppy's car that was involved in the wreck. She has every right to know that you do not think it was an accident."

Poppy's ears perked up.

Detective Jordan sighed heavily, lowering his head. "Lynn, we've been over this a hundred times. What I tell you here in the privacy of our own home is not to be shared. With *anyone* and that includes Poppy."

"Nonsense. Poppy is practically a law enforcement officer herself. If it wasn't for her, you never would have busted up that home care crime ring. She and her team were totally responsible for that case getting solved, right, Poppy?"

Poppy had cake in her mouth but managed to get out, "Oh, I wouldn't go that far. . . ."

Lynn was done arguing with her husband. She sat back in her chair, folded her arms, and said quietly but forcefully, "Tell her, Lamar."

For the sake of his marriage, Detective Jordan decided to acquiesce to his wife's demand. From Poppy's perspective, it was either that or sleep on the couch for the foreseeable future.

Detective Jordan stuffed his last bite of cake into his mouth and chewed while he talked. "The tire marks on the road suggest Mrs. Campbell lost control of the vehicle, raising the possibility that someone deliberately ran her off the road."

The bearded man.

It was Poppy's first thought.

"But I am going to need a hell of a lot more evidence before I can classify this as a homicide. She was an older lady, those winding roads can be treacherous, she could have just somehow gotten flustered or confused," Detective Jordan said before noticing his wife's eyes blazing. "What? What did I say?"

"Your galling ability to make ageist and sexist comments never ceases to surprise me, Lamar," Lynn seethed.

"All I'm saying is, we don't know yet what did happen up on that highway, but we're working on it," Jordan said defensively. "Okay, honey? I didn't mean to sound offensive."

"I only met Adelaide a few days ago, but in my opinion, she was as sharp as a tack," Poppy concluded. "But I don't understand what she was doing all the way up on Highway 74 in the mountains. She told me she was just going to borrow my car to run a few errands in town. It doesn't make any sense."

Poppy stared at what was left of the cake in the middle of the table, deep in thought.

Detective Jordan studied Poppy. "Tell me what you're thinking, Poppy."

Poppy sat up and cleared her throat. "I believe that this mysterious bearded man who has been stalking me mistook Adelaide for me since she was driving my car. He was gunning for me. That was supposed to be me in that burning wreckage at the bottom of the ravine. . . ."

"That's a distinct possibility," Jordan agreed. "But there is also a chance that it was simply an accident, or if not, maybe *Adelaide* was the intended victim, but we can't be certain just yet."

"No, Detective, we can't," Poppy whispered.

But she was certain of one thing.

She was going to find out.

Chapter 13

Iris crinkled up her nose in disgust as she stepped inside Adelaide Campbell's house. "What is that rancid odor?"

Wyatt plugged his nose with two of his fingers. "Ew, gross!"

Violet pushed past them all and scurried ahead through the living room toward the kitchen as Poppy closed the door behind them, peering out the window to make sure none of the nosy neighbors had spotted them entering the house.

Violet called from the kitchen. "She left some hamburger out on the counter to thaw on the day she died, but she never made it home to eat it. I'll throw it out."

"I suppose it is safe to assume that suicide is out. Why in the world would she put frozen meat out to thaw for dinner if she was going to drive herself off a cliff and end it all?" Iris surmised.

Still pinching his nose shut, Wyatt turned to Poppy. "Are we breaking the law by sneaking in here, Aunt Poppy?"

"We most certainly did not sneak into this house, Wyatt," Poppy explained. "Adelaide gave me her security access code in case of an emergency, and I cannot think of a bigger emergency than her sudden death. I am confident she would want us to come over and look around to see if we can find some explanation as to exactly what happened to her."

Wyatt shrugged. "Where's her computer? I can probably get into her e-mails and see if she had any enemies we should know about."

"Good idea. Maybe there's an office down the hall. If not, try the bedroom," Poppy said.

Wyatt scampered off.

"This is a complete waste of time," Iris concluded. "We both know who it was who ran her off the road. It was the bearded man!"

"We cannot be sure just yet, Iris," Poppy said patiently. "The fact is, we know very little about Adelaide Campbell and the people in her life. I'm still confused about why she took my car so far out of town. Why did she lie to me about where she was going that day?"

Violet returned, waving a hand in front of her face while holding a brown paper bag out in front of her. "I'm going to take this rotten meat out to the garbage bin! Oh, the putrid smell is making my eyes water."

Poppy and Iris gave her a wide berth, covering their faces to avoid getting a whiff of the spoiled ground hamburger.

Violet disappeared out the front door.

Poppy began poking around the living area as Iris folded her arms and surveyed the room. "I will say one thing, she had terrible taste in home décor."

Poppy stopped to observe the jungle-motif-print wallpaper, botanical-inspired furniture and throw pillows, glass animal figurines on a wooden shelf, sheepskin area rug. "It's a little busy, but does seem, with all its bush and historical references, designed to remind her of her home back in Australia."

"All these bright colors and crazy patterns are making me dizzy," Iris huffed.

Poppy ignored her and began to inspect the framed photographs on the shelf just above the collection of figurines. Most were of Adelaide and her late husband throughout the years. A wedding photo taken probably in the mid-1980s, Poppy judged from Adelaide's puffed-up hairstyle. Her husband, blond, craggy faced, rough looking, reminded Poppy of the *Crocodile Dundee* actor Paul Hogan. They could have been brothers. There were several vacation photos from Greece, Morocco, China. There were no pictures of any babies or toddlers or teenagers, which led Poppy to assume the couple never had children.

Violet returned from outside. "One of the neighbors next door was sitting out on her porch in a rocking chair and just saw me fiddling around with the bins. I hope she doesn't call the police."

"Was she sipping from a martini glass?" Poppy asked.

Violet nodded. "Yes, and she kept waving her arms at me and saying, 'Shoo, Shoo.'"

"Don't worry, that's just Mrs. Stanton. Her happy hour starts every day around noon. It's almost four o'clock. I half expect she thought you were a large raccoon or stray dog foraging for food."

"Aunt Poppy, come quick!" Wyatt called from the main bedroom.

Poppy, Iris, and Violet rushed down the hall and into the bedroom, where Wyatt was seated at a small desk with a laptop computer open next to the queen-sized bed, which had a comforter with a loud, colorful jungle themed print that somewhat matched the living room wallpaper. Iris shook her head distastefully, but remarkably refrained from further comment.

Wyatt was scrolling down row after row of photos, all of them older men, ranging in age from midfifties to late seventies, some handsome, some not, most nondescript.

Violet leaned down and put her hands on her grandson's shoulders. "Wyatt, how did you ever figure out Adelaide's password to get into her computer?"

"I didn't have to," Wyatt said nonchalantly. "She had it written down on a yellow Post-it next to the computer so she wouldn't forget it."

"Who are all those men?" Iris asked as Wyatt continued to scroll through all the photos.

"I'm on a senior dating site called Prime of Life. Mrs. Campbell has a profile on it," Wyatt explained, tapping a key to bring it up on the laptop. The picture of Adelaide was very flattering, possibly air brushed. She looked happy and carefree, at least ten years younger.

"Well, it's nice to know that she hadn't given up on romance after the passing of her husband," Poppy noted.

"Hah, no way!" Wyatt exclaimed. "She was chatting with about a dozen different guys all at the same time. She was definitely getting around."

"Was there one in particular she seemed more serious about than the others?" Poppy asked.

Wyatt shook his head. "No, but on the day she died, she made plans to meet this one."

He clicked a key and brought up a photo of a man in his late sixties, a full head of silver hair, pleasant smile, glasses, a professorial type.

"Russell," Wyatt said.

"No last name?"

"Nope. They hadn't gotten that far yet. But they did arrange a coffee date, and Mrs. Campbell offered to come to him. He lives in Idyllwild."

"Idyllwild. That would explain what Adelaide was doing all the way up on Highway 74! It's the most direct route," Poppy said excitedly. "She had to either have been coming or going from her meeting with this Russell person."

"If you study the helicopter video from the crash scene, you can tell by the direction of the tire's skid marks on the road that she was probably going up the mountain, not coming down," Wyatt said as he furiously tapped the keys on Adelaide's computer. "Russell actually seems like a nice guy."

This got the attention of all three ladies.

"How do you know that, dear?" Violet asked.

"Because I'm chatting with him online right now," Wyatt said matter-of-factly.

"*What?*" Poppy gasped. "Does he think you're Adelaide?"

"Wyatt, you should not pretend to be someone you're not. That's fishcatting!"

"Catfishing, Violet!" Iris groaned.

"Relax, he knows it's not Mrs. Campbell. I just set up a profile for Aunt Poppy and sent him a direct message. It took him like thirty seconds to respond. He thinks he's talking to her."

"*Me?* Wyatt, no!" Poppy cried.

"I figured you'd want to talk to him, so I went ahead and set up a coffee date for the two of you for tomorrow around lunchtime in Idyllwild," Wyatt said with a sly smile. He turned around and gave Poppy a wink. "By the way, he thinks you're really hot."

Poppy moaned.

She wanted to scold Wyatt for going rogue, but how could she when she knew he was right? It was downright scary how smart and resourceful this kid was.

And like it or not, Poppy was now going on a coffee date with Russell from Idyllwild.

Chapter 14

"I must say, you are far lovelier in person than in the photo on your profile, and truth be told, I was quite taken with that already," Russell Hitchens said, eyes twinkling as Poppy shifted uncomfortably in her chair at the outside table next to the cafe in the town of Idyllwild.

"Thank you, Russell, that's very kind of you to say. I want to thank you for meeting me on such short notice—"

"I can't tell you how excited I was to get your message. I feel as if I'm always the one making the first move, reaching out to dozens of women on the website, feeling around to gauge their interest. What a nice change to have such a beautiful lady say hello first."

"The thing is, Russell . . ." Poppy felt awkward about dampening the man's obvious enthusiasm, but she had not driven all the way up the mountain to this nature lover's oasis for a date. But how was she going to explain that to Russell without hurting his feelings?

"What's your favorite food?"

Poppy sighed. "I am rather fond of Italian. . . ."

"Me too! But nothing too fancy, just put a heaping plate of spaghetti and meatballs in front of me and I'm a happy man!"

Poppy smiled. "I can never say no to pasta. I love it so much, I might as well apply it directly to my thighs."

Russell roared with laughter. "She's got a sense of humor, too!" He looked up at the sky. "God, how did an old geezer like me get so lucky?" Russell, who had ordered a pastry with his espresso, pushed the plate across the table toward Poppy. "Would you like some of my coffee cake?"

"No, thank you," Poppy said, shivering slightly, goose bumps forming on her bare arms from the chilly mountain air.

Russell noticed immediately. "You're cold." He started to pull off his red cashmere sweater. "Here, put this on."

"No, I'm fine, Russell. I just forgot there was going to be a significant temperature drop all the way up here."

"Yes, we're a mile high up from the valley."

Russell tried handing her his sweater, but Poppy politely waved him off. "Please. I don't want my new lady to catch cold."

Poppy cringed.

This was not going well.

She had to put the kibosh on this before Russell got down on one knee and proposed.

"Russell, I have something to confess—"

"Do you like to travel?"

"Um, yes, but . . ."

"I retired from my financial advisory firm in Omaha last year and moved up here, but they still hire me occasionally as a consultant, work I can do anywhere with a laptop and an Internet connection, so I am very eager to find that special someone who wants to see the world as much as I do. Have you ever been to Turkey? Istanbul is tops on my list."

"Yes, I have."

"Is it as beautiful and exotic as I imagine?"

"It was quite some time ago. I shot a movie there once, back in the nineteen eighties."

Russell perked up. "You're in the film business?"

"Not in years. But way back when, I was an actress."

Russell's jaw dropped open. "I knew you looked familiar. I said to myself when I saw your photo, 'Russell, you either know that woman from somewhere or you two were together in another life.' Either way, I felt strongly we were destined to meet again."

"You probably saw the television series I did for a few years during the eighties, *Jack Colt*?"

The name didn't seem to ring a bell with Russell. He shook his head. "I never saw it, I'm afraid. I didn't watch a lot of TV back then. I was too busy playing man about town in Omaha. I think I'm going to go with us meeting in a previous incarnation. It's more romantic, don't you think?"

Poppy took a sip of her espresso. She was going to need all the caffeine at her disposal to stay focused and get through this ordeal. "Russell, please let me explain why I'm here."

"I know. I bet I'm talking too much. I've had a few women tell me I tend to prattle on and on and don't allow them to get a word in edgewise. That's because I grew up in a family of seven, all us kids talking over each other constantly trying to get our parents' attention, and I was the worst one, so my sisters tell me. . . ." Russell stopped, noticing Poppy's thin, measured smile. "I'm doing it right now, aren't I?"

"Russell, you are a very sweet man, and I am sure you are going to meet the right woman very soon, but to be honest, I'm not her."

"Why? Am I not your type? I know I'm a little pudgy around the middle, but I'm working on that." Russell eyed his coffee cake and decided to shove another forkful in his mouth. "Starting tomorrow."

"Russell, it's nothing like that. You're very handsome and quite charming."

"I'm waiting for the inevitable 'but.' "

"*But* . . . I'm just not in the market for a male companion right now. The fact is, I'm currently seeing someone."

Russell appeared to deflate right in front of Poppy's eyes, like a punctured balloon at a children's birthday party.

"Then why did you agree to come all the way up here to meet me?" Russell asked curiously.

"Adelaide Campbell."

Russell gave her a puzzled look. "Who?"

"You met her on the same dating site. The two of you arranged to meet right here at this very cafe just a few days ago."

Russell appeared to be searching his brain, but came up with nothing, so Poppy decided to gently prod him along.

"She was Australian. From Melbourne. Recently widowed."

A lightbulb finally seemed to pop on in his head. "Addie!"

"Yes, her. So you know who I'm talking about?"

"Sure, we messaged each other back and forth a few times. I liked her profile, she seemed like a really nice, down-to-earth woman, but I never actually met her. She stood me up."

So Adelaide was on her way up to Idyllwild to meet Russell when she went over that cliff, just as Wyatt had suggested. She must have felt too embarrassed to tell Poppy that she wanted to borrow her car for a date with a man she had met online, and so she fibbed and told her she just had some errands to run.

"I admit, I was a bit disappointed. I thought we might have a spark, make good companions, but then she was a no-show, and so I said to myself, 'Russell, don't be down about this, just get back up on that horse and keep going.'

And a few days later, voilà, I got that message from you."

"I apologize if I misled you."

"Why are you so interested in Adelaide Campbell?"

"She was a friend."

Russell gave her a tentative look. "You keep saying *was*, like in the past tense."

"I'm afraid Adelaide died in a car accident on her way here to meet you that day."

Russell sat back, mouth agape, the wind suddenly knocked out of him. Once he managed to catch his breath, he leaned forward. "Is it safe to assume that you didn't arrange this date just to massage my ego by telling me Addie did not intentionally blow off our date?"

Poppy shook her head. "No, the circumstances surrounding her death are somewhat cloudy, and I'm trying to clear them up. Actually I'm a private investigator."

Russell's eyes popped open, full of surprise. "Wait, first you're an actress and now you're a detective? This is too much! Stop making me fall in love with you!"

Poppy downed the rest of her espresso. "Thank you for your time, Russell. You're going to make some woman very happy."

She stood up to go.

Russell gave her a flirtatious wink. "If you ever change your mind, you know where to find me!"

He blew her a kiss.

She nodded and smiled, but decided it would be best not to blow one back. As she walked toward her car, with Russell apparently in the clear, Poppy was growing more and more convinced that whoever forced Adelaide off that road believed that Poppy herself was behind the wheel.

Chapter 15

Poppy had only been home from Idyllwild for about ten minutes when her doorbell rang.

She froze in place, a sense of dread sweeping through her whole body.

She was not expecting anyone.

And she could not get the image of the bearded man in the dark sunglasses and the red cap out of her head.

She slowly crossed over to the front door, hesitating before opening it. "Who is it?"

"Lynn Jordan."

The tension drained from Poppy as she unlocked the door and swung it open to reveal the bright, happy face of Detective Jordan's wife. She was holding Poppy's cake tin in one hand and a black vinyl zippered garment bag over her right shoulder.

"Hello, Poppy, forgive me for dropping by unannounced, but I wanted to return your cake tin. Lamar and I devoured the rest of your delightful German chocolate cake. You're going to have to give me the recipe."

Lynn handed the tin to Poppy.

"I appreciate you returning it, but there was absolutely no rush. I have plenty more," Poppy said.

"I know," Lynn gushed excitedly. "But I was also eager to give you this."

She thrust out the garment bag toward Poppy.

"What is it?" Poppy asked curiously.

"I designed a dress, just for you."

"You what?"

"Designers are always trying to get celebrities to wear their creations on the red carpet, or in public, and . . . well, you obviously are the most famous person I know, so I thought, why not make one for Poppy Harmon?"

"I honestly don't see myself on a red carpet anytime soon, Lynn," Poppy said with an apologetic smile.

"Oh, I understand, but I figure you do get around in Palm Springs, and there are a lot of women, both locals and tourists, who might like what they see and ask who made it," Lynn said hopefully.

Poppy accepted the garment bag. "I don't know what to say, Lynn, thank you."

"My pleasure. If you're not too busy, I'd love to stick around for a few minutes and see you try it on. I'm pretty good at guessing measurements, but I want to make sure it doesn't need any minor alterations before I send you out in the world wearing it."

"Of course, please come in," Poppy said, stepping aside and welcoming Lynn into the house.

Poppy was flattered and touched by Lynn's gesture. It was not every day a fledgling clothing designer used her as inspiration for a frock.

"Can I get you something to drink while I go into the bedroom and put it on?" Poppy asked.

"No, I'm fine, I'm just dying to see you in it," Lynn replied, practically bouncing up and down. "I feel as if I really hit upon something with this one."

"Well, let's not keep either of us in suspense," Poppy said, winking at her. "Have a seat, and I will be right back." As she crossed to the bedroom, Poppy turned and called over her shoulder, "Does your husband know you're here?"

Lynn chuckled. "No, but I believe he is finally getting used to the idea that the two of us are friends. He came in and saw me sketching the dress in my studio, and I told him it was for you, and he just rolled his eyes, but shockingly he didn't complain."

Poppy entered the bedroom, leaving the door open a crack so she could still talk to Lynn.

"One of his detectives stopped by earlier today to discuss the Adelaide Campbell case. He took him into the den for some privacy while they talked, but our walls are so paper thin, I could hear everything they discussed."

Poppy did not want to appear too eager to hear the details so she feigned nonchalance. "Oh?"

"Yes, it turns out there was traffic cam footage all along Highway 111, before Adelaide turned onto Highway 74 and up the mountain toward Idyllwild, and you can plainly see a red pickup truck tailing her the entire way."

"A pickup truck? What was the make and model?"

"He didn't say. There's more, but it can wait. I'm dying to see you in my creation," Lynn said expectantly.

Poppy knew she was not going to get any more information from her new friend until she modeled her latest work of genius. Poppy unzipped the bag and opened it to reveal perhaps the ugliest dress she had ever laid eyes on. A hideous multicolored pattern of plum and some bland shade of red. A fuzzy fabric that reminded Poppy of Muppet fur. A metallic cummerbund. At first, Poppy considered this might be an elaborate prank. She had seen some of Lynn's other designs and they were quite lovely. But this one was without a doubt a resounding failure on every level. How was she ever going to tell her that she would not be caught dead in such a monstrosity?

The fact was, she could not.

"How does it look?" Lynn called from the living room.

Poppy knew she had no choice.

She had to put on a brave face and pretend not to hate the dress Lynn had worked so hard on.

"I'll be right out!"

Poppy quickly slipped out of her skirt and blouse and squeezed into the dress, hoping it might not look as bad when she had it on, but alas, no such luck. She stared at herself in the mirror, mouth agape, stunned that Lynn had come up with such an unmitigated misfire.

Poppy prided herself on her typical forthrightness and honesty, but she also loathed hurting anyone's feelings, and so she was not about to break Lynn's heart.

She took a deep breath, and marched out of the bedroom like Gisele Bündchen on a Paris runway during Fashion Week.

Upon seeing Poppy in her new creation, Lynn lit up like a Christmas tree and clapped her hands enthusiastically. "Oh, it looks better than I even hoped. Spin around so I can see the whole thing."

Poppy bit her tongue and twirled, already starting to sweat from the hot furry fabric, which was totally inappropriate for the desert. Not to mention a woman of her age. She could not for the life of her imagine where she could ever wear this ghastly outfit.

"You know, I was leaning toward something more conventional, but I decided to make a bolder statement. Lamar is always encouraging me to think outside the box, so I decided to just go for it, and I am *so* glad I did!" Lynn jabbered, basking in the moment.

Poppy tried pulling the dress down. The hemline was much too high for a sixty-something-year-old woman, as far as she was concerned.

"Do you think it's too short?" Lynn asked hesitantly, crinkling her nose.

"Perhaps a little," Poppy said with a forced smile.

"That thought did cross my mind for a moment, but you have remarkable gams, Poppy. You just make the whole thing work."

Poppy emphatically disagreed, but instead of voicing her opinion, she just nodded, accepting the fact that Lynn was not going to go back to the drawing board on this one. She said as off the cuff as possible, "So you said something about knowing more about the Adelaide Campbell investigation?"

"Yes," Lynn said, bounding over to Poppy to adjust the collar on her dress until she was satisfied. "Up along Highway 74 there was a family of tourists from Louisiana taking pictures from one of those turnouts that overlook the entire Coachella Valley. Apparently they saw what looked like a car chase racing by on the winding road. They said the first car was a white Cadillac. . . ."

A match for Poppy's car.

"And the second was a red truck, just like in the traffic cam footage, and it was right up on the Cadillac's bumper. The accident happened less than half a mile up the road from where they spotted the two vehicles racing by."

Lynn Jordan was a fountain of information, much more so than her gruff, frustratingly tight-lipped husband. So parading around in this grotesque Lynn Jordan original was a small price to pay. Poppy would just have to come up with a reason down the line why it was no longer in her wardrobe, maybe a small house fire, or a break-in where the burglar only made off with a few of Poppy's dresses. She would have to come up with something.

But there was no doubt in Poppy's mind.

The driver of the red truck had been deliberately chasing Adelaide in Poppy's Cadillac, and probably kept banging into her bumper, causing her to panic and lose control of the car, and that's when she went careening off the cliff to her death.

And whoever was driving that red truck, most likely the bearded stalker, left the scene that day believing he got away with murder.

The murder of Poppy Harmon.

Chapter 16

"Ladies, these are the women I was telling you about, the ones who saved me from bankruptcy," Cecile LaCrosse gushed to her two friends, while gesturing toward Poppy, Iris, and Violet, who stood next to their high-top table at the 19th Hole bar in the Palm Leaf Retirement Golf Club. When Poppy had called Cecile requesting a meeting, she was on the fifteenth hole, under par, and needed to concentrate, so she suggested Poppy and her associates swing by the bar for a drink when they finished. Poppy had picked up Iris and Violet in Sam's SUV, and they had headed to the private gated community. By the time they had arrived, Cecile and her golfing buddies were already on their second round of cosmos. All three were dressed in Pebble Beach short-sleeved polos and patterned skirts in a rainbow of fun, flirty colors.

Cecile, in bright green and yellow, continued, "Poppy, Iris, Violet, this is Inez and Carol Ann."

A flurry of pleasantries were exchanged.

Inez, a hefty woman with a dark tan and a shock of white hair, in purple, who could have been Iris's sister, gulped down her cosmo and said, "Cecile can't stop singing your praises, her master detectives, Miss Marple times three!"

Carol Ann, petite, much smaller than the others, with flushed cheeks that matched her red outfit, already buzzing from her first cocktail, added with a slur, "*The Golden Girls* fight crime!"

Poppy noticed Iris grimacing. She obviously was not inclined to compare herself to Beatrice Arthur, as she knew Poppy and Violet would, given her sharp tone and take-no-gruff demeanor. Poppy knew there was no mystery as to which one Violet most resembled, the ditzy Rose, played by national treasure Betty White. That would leave Poppy as the man-chasing harlot Blanche, which Poppy categorically refused to accept on any level.

"I have recommended you to all my friends who might require your services, and believe me, there are a lot of scheming grifters out there preying on older people, not to mention all the lying, cheating spouses in this valley who need to be held to account," Cecile huffed. "Have you three thought about renting a billboard to advertise your agency? Carol Ann's nephew is a vendor who rents them. I bet she can get you a discount."

"I would have to ask him, he can be very prickly when it comes to money, but he owes me—I helped put him through community college," Carol Ann said.

"Thank you, let us think about it," Poppy said politely before turning back to Cecile. "We were hoping to talk to you about Tanya Cook."

Cecile's face darkened. "I will tell you one thing, on the day that jury found that detestable girl and her two accomplices guilty as charged, I was finally able to get a full night's sleep for the first time in weeks."

"Yes, it is a relief knowing they will be behind bars for quite some time," Violet piped in.

"The nerve of her pretending to be some budding Florence Nightingale, this angel of mercy, worming her way into my life, my house, just so she could rob me blind! If it could happen to me, then it could happen to anyone. I am the least gullible person in the whole world!"

Inez and Carol Ann quietly sipped their cosmos, preferring not to comment.

"Can you tell us anything more about her?" Poppy inquired.

"Why? The case is closed. I have no intention of thinking about that deplorable scammer ever again." Cecile sniffed, before a thought suddenly struck her. "The case *is* closed, isn't it, Poppy?"

"Oh, yes, it's definitely closed. Tanya Cook will never bother you again. We're just trying to tie up all the loose ends, and we were wondering if she opened up to you about her life at any time, something that might have stuck in your mind?" Poppy inquired as Cecile sat back on her stool, going over the whole sordid caper in her mind.

"No, we spent most of the time talking about me. She was always buttering me up, saying how I had such exquisite taste in clothes, how beautiful my home was, how I didn't need antiaging cream because I already looked so young. . . ."

Inez snorted. "And that did not make you suspicious?"

Poppy caught Iris smirking.

It appeared Iris and Inez could be long-lost soul mates finally reunited after many years apart.

Cecile threw her friend an annoyed look. "No, Inez, at the time I thought she was just being sweet and had no nefarious agenda."

"She must have said something about herself at some point," Violet pressed.

Cecile thought it over carefully and then shook her head with an apologetic smile. "Nothing that I remember offhand. She seemed so trustworthy, I never even bothered to call any of the references on her resume. Big mistake."

Cecile noticed Poppy perk up. "I know your next question, and I'm sorry, Poppy, I don't have it. She gave me a paper copy instead of an e-mail, and I remember throwing the resume out after the police busted her. I have no clue what was actually on it, but I assume her credentials were as fake as she was."

Poppy's hopes of discovering any new clues were dimming, but she gamely pressed on. "So she never mentioned *any* close contacts, other than Bella and Kylie, any boyfriends or favorite relatives . . . ?"

"No . . ." Cecile paused, then suddenly sat up straight. "Wait, I do remember . . . she got a phone call once while she was giving me a sponge bath when I was at my worst after my knee surgery. . . . I remember she kind of lit up, and suddenly got all cutesy, like she was flirting with somebody."

Poppy fixed her eyes on Cecile. "A boyfriend?"

"I teased her about having a crush on a boy when she hung up, but she admitted nothing. She just gave me this playful smile and then quickly changed the subject. But I would see it plainly on her face—she was over the moon for whoever had just called her."

"You never heard her say his name, or saw a picture?" Poppy asked.

Cecile shook her head again, disappointed in herself. "I'm sorry, Poppy, I should have paid more attention."

"No, Cecile, you've been a big help," Poppy assured her.

"Now, if you're done with all your questions, why don't the three of you join us for a round?" Cecile suggested.

Iris and Inez, who were moments away from exchanging phone numbers and becoming fast friends, both smiled expectantly.

"I can't, Cecile; I need to follow up on this, but Iris and Violet, you two stay. You can take an Uber when you're ready to go home."

Iris wasted no time grabbing a stool and joining the three women, but Violet hesitated, not wanting to leave Poppy on her own. Poppy, however, was already out the door, racing to Sam's SUV, because she finally had something concrete to go on.

And she knew exactly whom she needed to talk to in order to get some answers.

Chapter 17

This was not Poppy's first visit to the California Institute for Women in Chino, which was about an hour-and-a-half drive from Palm Springs. No, she had been there many times over the course of the eleven months her daughter, Heather, had spent time incarcerated here. Poppy was intimately familiar with the long, tedious security process; the signing of endless forms; the trek down a dispiriting, drab hallway with chipped turquoise walls alongside the friends and family of other inmates.

Fortunately, this sad period of her life as well as Heather's was long over. Her daughter had bounced back from her troubled past, enrolled in NYU Law School, and was now thriving in Manhattan, halfway through her thirty-credit program for a law degree. Poppy was bursting with pride over Heather's dogged determination to turn her life around, and her fierce desire to help those in need of legal counsel but with limited resources. Her experience behind bars was what fueled her powerful empathy and her single-minded mission to champion the underdog.

A guard led the group into a drab room with a number of tables and chairs set up for the inmates and their visitors. Poppy was directed to a table near the back and was told by a gruff, no-nonsense female guard to have a seat and wait. Ten minutes later, a line of inmates were escorted in, who fanned out to find their loved ones and lawyers. Poppy scanned the cluster of inmates in their prison-issued tan jumpsuits, but didn't spot the woman she was here to see. Poppy knew there was a good chance that if she was told that her visitor today was Poppy Harmon, the inmate just might refuse to leave her cell.

But finally, the last to enter into the visiting room, Tanya Cook, looking bored and listless, shuffled in, glancing around. When her eyes settled on Poppy in the back of the room, alone, she frowned.

Poppy braced herself, half expecting Tanya to spin back around and march out in a huff, but she didn't. She just shrugged her shoulders and slowly walked over to the table where Poppy was waiting for her. Poppy surmised that meeting with *any* visitor, even Poppy, was preferable to passing the time, bored, locked in her cell.

"Thank you for seeing me," Poppy said.

"They didn't tell me it was you," Tanya spit out scornfully.

"Who were you expecting to see?" Poppy asked.

Tanya locked eyes with Poppy, but did not readily answer the question. After a brief moment of glaring, she dropped down in the chair opposite her. "What do you want?"

Poppy leaned forward, hands clasped in front of her. "How are you doing?"

"You can skip the small talk. It's not like you actually *care*," Tanya sighed, averting her eyes away from Poppy and down to the floor. "We both know you didn't drive all this way just to see how I'm coping with my wonderful new life in prison and to hear about all the amazing new friends I've met here. Just get to the point."

"All right," Poppy said coolly. "Someone ran my neighbor off the road and over a cliff and she was killed."

"Are you going to try to pin that on me, too?" Tanya asked contemptuously. "Because look around, I have an alibi."

"She was driving my car."

"So?"

"So I believe the person who slammed into her from behind and forced her off the road thought it was me."

"I'll be sure to send him a thank you card. Of course, it might take me some time working in the laundry room to buy a stamp. I get paid ten cents an hour."

"I never said the other driver was a man."

Tanya raised her eyes up again, a crooked, contemptuous, knowing smile on her face.

"Do you happen to know who it was, Tanya?"

Tanya shrugged. "Even if I knew, do you think I'd do anything to help you? You're the whole reason I'm even in here."

"No, I would argue that *you* are the whole reason you are in here. Listen to me, Tanya. If you know something, and you don't speak up, that's aiding and abetting, so don't think there won't be more charges coming your way."

"You don't scare me, old woman," Tanya sneered.

Poppy bristled.

Old woman?

Up to this moment, she had thought she was incapable of despising this insolent young woman any more than she already did, but she was dead wrong.

Poppy took a breath. "Are you covering for your boyfriend? Do you honestly think he's going to wait for you on the outside, Tanya? News flash. He probably won't, so perhaps you should start acting in your own self-interest."

Now it was Tanya's turn to bristle.

She paused, grimacing. "Who said I had a boyfriend?"

"Cecile LaCrosse heard you talking to him on the phone."

"Cecile LaCrosse is a hysterical, confused hag who doesn't know whether she's coming or going, which frankly was what made her such an easy mark."

"I swear, Tanya, if you are somehow directing this boyfriend of yours to stalk me and to try to terrorize me from behind bars, this will not end well for you."

Tanya folded her arms defiantly.

Poppy could feel her stubborn intractability from across the table, but took one last shot. "Just give me a name. . . ."

Tanya chuckled derisively.

Poppy slammed her hands down on the table. "Then I guess we're done." She stood up, and without saying good-bye, whipped around and started marching toward the exit.

She suddenly heard Tanya whistling behind her.

Twinkle, twinkle, little star.

Poppy shuddered and her whole body froze for a moment. Then she spun around and flew back to the table, where Tanya sat with a sick, self-satisfied grin on her spiteful face.

"Who is he, Tanya? Tell me *now!*"

"I've got nothing further to say to you," she grumbled before signaling to the guard. "We're done. I'd like to go back to my cell now."

The guard hustled over and led Tanya Cook out of the room, but not before she turned back to give Poppy a disconcerting wink.

Poppy stood there in the middle of the room, shaking. A few other inmates and visitors eyed her curiously.

A female guard approached her and gingerly touched her arm. "Ma'am, are you all right? You look a little pale."

Poppy snapped out of her reverie and said, "I'm fine, thank you."

But she wasn't fine.

By whistling that little tune, Tanya Cook had confirmed what Poppy had already feared.

Someone was out to get her and it was undoubtedly this mysterious nameless boyfriend of Tanya Cook's.

And he would probably not stop until Poppy was dead and buried.

Chapter 18

"Tell me honestly, did you really like the dress Lynn designed specially for you?" Detective Jordan asked with a sly smile, leaning back in his chair behind the desk in his cramped office at the detective bureau of the Palm Springs Police Department.

"It took my breath away," Poppy answered diplomatically.

Detective Jordan eyed her suspiciously, trying to assess whether Poppy was telling him the truth or not. "Lynn showed me the pictures. You looked . . ."

Poppy steeled herself for what was about to come.

Detective Jordan searched his mind for just the right word.

"Stylish?" Poppy offered.

Jordan shook his head. "No . . ."

"Splendid?"

"No . . ."

"Tasteful?"

"God, no . . ." Jordan seemed to catch himself. "I mean, Lynn has always had, shall we say, a more flamboyant style. Let's go with festive."

Words more akin to gaudy, excessive, and chintzy came to Poppy's mind, but she was hardly going to give any kind of hint to Detective Jordan that she hated his wife's original creation. She simply stated rather matter-of-factly, "It was a lovely gesture."

"My wife has grown rather fond of you as she's gotten to know you," Jordan said, almost annoyed by his own observation.

"The feeling is quite mutual. But I did not come here to discuss my friendship with your wife, or her avant-garde designing style," Poppy said emphatically, resting her purse on her lap as she sat opposite him.

"I know, I'm making small talk so I don't suddenly blow up at you for going behind my back and visiting Tanya Cook in prison," Detective Jordan said sternly.

"What was I supposed to do, just wait around for this mysterious boyfriend of hers to strike again since he missed the first time around and got poor Adelaide Campbell instead of me?"

"Look, I understand you're frustrated. . . ."

"I'm not frustrated, Detective, I'm *terrified*! And I will not just sit idly by while some dangerous psychopath is busy plotting my demise!"

"What did you expect to happen when you went to see Tanya Cook? That she would just offer her full cooperation, give up the name of her boyfriend, who might be stalking you, out of the goodness of her heart?"

Poppy hesitated, not sure how to answer him.

"She was *never* going to do that," Detective Jordan barked.

"Perhaps, but I had to at least try," Poppy sighed.

"We might have a much better shot with her two accomplices," Jordan added.

"Bella and Kylie?"

"I sent two of my detectives, Lasky and Drummond, over to the jailhouse this morning. I'm waiting to hear back from them. If the district attorney agrees to cut the girls a deal for a lighter sentence on the condition that they cooperate, maybe they'll cough up the name of Tanya's boyfriend."

"That's an excellent idea," Poppy concluded.

"Yeah, sometimes I actually come up with one. It's rare, according to my wife, but sometimes I do," Jordan joked with a smirk.

Poppy stood up. "Will you keep me informed?"

"Cross my heart," Jordan said, miming an *X* across his chest.

The phone on his desk rang.

Jordan checked the caller ID and held up a hand. "Hold on, it's Lasky." He picked up the phone. "What have you got, Don?" As Jordan listened, he glanced up at Poppy and gave her a quick nod and an encouraging smile. Then he grabbed a pencil and began jotting a name down on a pad of paper. "Uh, huh . . . And they're sure? Excellent work. Okay, see you back here." He hung up and finished scribbling a few details before standing up from his desk. "Bella and Kylie took the deal. According to my detectives, they didn't need much convincing. They're both scared and remorseful and regret ever getting mixed up with Tanya Cook."

"Did they know about Tanya's boyfriend?"

Jordan nodded. "We got a name. Let us check it out and I will call you later."

"Well, who is it?"

"No, Poppy, you don't get to play in my sandbox. I need you to allow me to do my job."

"But don't you think it's in my best interest to know the name of the man who wants to kill me?"

"I think it's in your best interest to keep a low profile until we can pick this guy up for questioning," Jordan said. "I already have a unit watching your house, so that's the safest place you can be right now, okay?"

Poppy set her purse down in the chair as Detective Jordan tore the piece of paper off his pad and pocketed it.

Then he circled around his desk to escort her out of his office. Halfway to the door, Poppy shook loose from his light grip. "I forgot my purse." She spun around and walked back toward the desk. As she reached for her purse in the chair, her back to Jordan, she managed to tear the top piece of paper off the writing pad and slip it into her pocket before turning around with a bright smile and walking out again.

Once she was back in her car, she retrieved the blank piece of paper, reached into her glove box for a pencil, then quickly rubbed the tip across the paper. The pencil lead shaded the imprint of the notes Jordan had written down until they were legible.

Patrice Marceau.

French computer programmer from Lyon.

In U.S. for two years.

It was a good start.

And for the record, Poppy could tell herself she had not made any kind of promise to Detective Jordan to stand down.

Although she appreciated the police department keeping a watchful eye on her house, she knew she could never just go into hiding.

No, Poppy Harmon was far more proactive.

If the detectives could not find Patrice Marceau, then she most certainly would.

Chapter 19

Mr. Duffy, the landlord at the Desert Cactus Apartments on North Sunrise Way, trudged up the steps to the second level with Poppy close on his heels. He was a portly, white-bearded man with a bulbous nose and splotchy red skin, looking as if he were Santa Claus exiled from the North Pole who had incredibly landed his sleigh in the summer heat of the Coachella Valley.

"You say you're Patrice's grandmother from Paris?" he asked, already out of breath halfway up the stairs.

"*Oui*," Poppy answered in her best French accent. "Fanny Marceau. I just arrived this morning."

She was counting on the landlord not knowing how to speak French since her own knowledge of the language was rudimentary at best. But she was certainly dressed for the part. A Pierre Cardin midlength dress. Christian Louboutin patent leather pumps. Louis Vuitton handbag. She had combed her closet for anything that reeked of the French. She even had dabbed a Chanel fragrance behind her ears and carried a pink box of pastries she had purchased at a French-owned bakery in the mini-mall next to the studio where she occasionally took a Pilates class whenever she felt bloated.

"I'm pretty sure Patrice isn't home right now. I saw him leave earlier this morning," the landlord said.

"*Oh mon Dieu, j'avais peur de ça. J'ai oublié de l'appeler de l'aéroport pour lui dire que mon vol est arrivé tôt*," Poppy managed to spit out.

Mr. Duffy gave her a blank look.

"I am sorry, I was just saying I should have called Patrice from the airport to tell him my flight arrived early."

They reached the door of Patrice Marceau's apartment. It had taken Wyatt roughly ten minutes to work his magic back at the Desert Flowers office and come up with a home address once Poppy had provided him with a name.

The kid was inarguably a genius.

Mr. Duffy banged loudly on the door.

There was no answer.

Poppy had not expected one since there had been no sign of the red truck in any of the parking spaces on the property.

Mr. Duffy tried again.

After waiting a few seconds, Mr. Duffy turned to Poppy. "Were you planning on staying here with your grandson?"

"Oh, no, I have booked a room at the Parker. In hindsight, I should have gone there first before just showing up here unannounced," Poppy sighed. "Poor planning on my part."

Mr. Duffy gave her a sympathetic smile before his eyes fell upon the pink box she was holding.

On cue, Poppy opened the box to reveal a cluster of delicious-looking pastries, two eclairs, three macaroons, four croissants. "Please, Mr. Duffy, help yourself."

Mr. Duffy lit up, anxiously perused the selections, then plucked one of the macaroons and popped it into his mouth. "Oh, man, that's delicious," he moaned.

"I made them myself," Poppy fibbed.

Mr. Duffy chewed and swallowed as Poppy closed the box and glanced around. "It would be silly of me to call a taxi and go to my hotel, and then have to come all the way back here when Patrice returns home. I suppose I can just wait here." She stared sullenly at her pink box of pastries. "I just hope the eclairs don't melt in this stifling heat."

"I don't think Patrice would want me leaving his lovely grandmother standing outside his apartment on a scorching day like this. He'd never forgive me if you got heatstroke." Mr. Duffy shoved his hand into the front pocket of his Bermuda shorts and yanked out a set of keys. He inserted the master into the lock and opened the door, then ushered Poppy inside.

The air conditioner mounted in the window had kept the small apartment cool. The studio space was relatively bare, but well kept. Not a lot of thought went into the decorating. No pictures on the walls. A couple chairs and a TV but no couch or dining table. It was as if this was just a temporary residence.

Mr. Duffy bowed slightly to Poppy. "Make yourself at home, Mrs. Marceau."

"Please, call me Fanny," Poppy said, playing up the French accent so much it almost bordered on ridiculously over the top, like Pepé Le Pew, so she tried pulling it back a bit. "Tell me, does my grandson have many visitors? I want to know he is making friends in America."

"Not that I can tell," Mr. Duffy said. "He's pretty quiet, keeps to himself mostly. There was a girl who came around sometimes, but I haven't seen her lately."

"Ah, yes, he sent me a picture of the young woman he was dating," Poppy said, rummaging through her handbag and pulling out a candid photo of Tanya Cook that Cecile LaCrosse had provided when she first hired the team.

She handed it to Mr. Duffy, who studied it.

"Yeah, that looks like her," he said, handing the photo

back. "I also saw some guy coming and going the last few days, never seen him before. I thought he might be a room-mate, but when I asked Patrice about him, he told me it was his cousin Pete. They did kind of look alike, but he didn't strike me as French, he had no trace of an accent, so I figured he was an American cousin from around here somewhere."

"Must be from his mother's side of the family," Poppy said, pouring on some disdain.

Mr. Duffy's phone buzzed. He appeared annoyed to be interrupted while chatting with Poppy, or Fanny, and an-swered the call gruffly, "Yeah?" He listened for a few sec-onds, then rolled his eyes. "Okay, let me get my toolbox and I'll be right down." He ended the call and stuffed his phone back in his pocket. "I have to go. One of my ten-ants has a leaky shower. Yesterday it was her ice cube maker. Every day it's something else. I swear she's just lonely."

"Well, who can blame her wanting the company of such a charming man? I appreciate all you have done for me, Mr. Duffy," Poppy cooed before opening the pastry box again. "Please, take a croissant with you."

He didn't have to be told twice. He snatched one from the box, then took Poppy's hand and kissed it several times. "I've seen French men do this a lot in the movies."

"You are enchanting, Mr. Duffy. I do hope our paths cross again," Poppy said breathlessly, nailing the accent this time.

She thought Mr. Duffy was blushing, though it was hard to tell from all the red splotches that populated his face, but he did appear smitten with the glamorous French woman before him who was roughly the same age as him.

"You can bet on it," he said with a wink as he sauntered out, shutting the door behind him.

Poppy's French grandmother ruse had worked bril-liantly. She grabbed her phone and hurriedly texted Iris and Violet, who were parked outside waiting in Violet's Buick Lucerne. Within two minutes, they had joined Poppy in Patrice Marceau's studio apartment, and the three of them began fanning out to search for any clues or evidence that would conclusively connect him to Adelaide Campbell's murder.

Violet was the first to stumble across something interesting. On the small nightstand next to the lumpy single bed was a stack of photos, mostly professional posed shots, featuring a gorgeous young woman in her mid- to late twenties, with flawless alabaster skin, luxurious blond hair, and stunning blue eyes.

"Oh my, he seems to have a terrible crush on this one," Violet noted, drawing Poppy over to the night table.

"That's definitely *not* Tanya Cook. Who do you suppose it is?" Poppy said, studying all the photos.

Violet shook her head. "I have no idea, but judging from the amount of shots he has of her, it's safe to say he's somewhat obsessed with her."

Violet began scanning pictures of the photos with her phone.

Poppy crossed the room to Iris, who was rifling through a chest of drawers. The first few drawers were filled with shorts, T-shirts, and underwear, but near the bottom, Iris opened one stuffed with a treasure trove of clues. She sat down on the floor and pulled out folders and papers and started spreading them out on the floor, carefully inspecting them.

"Anything interesting?" Poppy asked.

"Passports, credit cards, financial documents, all in different names. Look, this French passport belongs to Patrice Marceau."

Poppy stared at the photo.

It definitely looked like the shaggy-haired bearded man who had been following her around. But she could not be 100 percent certain.

Iris handed her a second passport. "This American one belongs to Pete Chambers, but look at the picture. The hair is close cropped and the beard is trimmed, but you can tell it's the same man."

It instantly became obvious to Poppy that Mr. Duffy had not actually seen Patrice Marceau's American cousin because Patrice and Pete were one and the same.

Iris flipped open a third passport. "This one is German. Hans Kirsch. His hair is blond, his eyes are hazel, his goatee is lighter, but look at the angular features, again they're the same. They're all the same. He has multiple identities, either made up or real people whose identities he has stolen."

"He's changed his appearance so many times, with facial hair, wigs, colored contact lenses, even skin tone, it's impossible to know what he actually looks like," Poppy noted.

Iris pointed to the stack of bank statements she had piled up on the floor. "And each name he's used has a detailed financial history with cashed checks and large deposits."

"He's a straight-up Mr. Ripley," Poppy said.

Iris examined the numerous passports. "I don't see the name Ripley on any of these passports. . . ."

"No, Iris, I'm talking about *The Talented Mr. Ripley*," Poppy explained. "It was a novel by Patricia Highsmith, and a movie starring Matt Damon, about a devious young man who co-opted the identities of his victims to defraud them of their finances. Patrice Marceau, or whatever his real name is, seems to be duplicating the plot line from the book."

"Well, if he thinks he is going to outfox us, he has another thing coming," Iris huffed.

"I'm beginning to suspect that this clever young man, not Tanya Cook, was the real brains behind the home nursing care scam, and that the girls were working for him," Poppy said.

"Like Charlie dispatching his evil Angels!" Violet gasped from across the room.

Suddenly the door to the apartment burst open, startling Poppy, Iris, and Violet. It was a man and a woman, both in casual business attire, both wearing visible gun holsters. They charged inside.

"All right, stop what you're doing right now!" the woman ordered.

Poppy did not recognize either of them. "Who are you? What are you doing here?"

"We could ask you the very same question," the man growled. "I'm Detective Lasky, this is Detective Drummond."

The blood drained from Poppy's face.

She had heard those names before.

Out of the mouth of their superior.

Detective Lamar Jordan.

"Do you have a warrant?" Iris asked haughtily.

"No, we don't have a warrant," Detective Drummond, an attractive dark-haired woman in her early thirties, scoffed. "We were tasked with staking out Patrice Marceau's apartment until he showed up and we could bring him in for questioning, so imagine our surprise when we witnessed you three, none of you officers of the law, break into our suspect's apartment!"

Poppy stepped forward sheepishly. "Actually, the landlord, Mr. Duffy, let me in here of his own accord, so technically no laws were broken."

Detective Lasky, a few years younger than Drummond, boyish, intense, by the book, glared at Poppy. "Do you think this is some kind of scavenger hunt at the senior center? You are interfering with police business, ma'am!"

"I find his arrogant, ageist tone insulting!" Iris snapped.

Poppy knew better than to argue. She signaled Iris and Violet that it was time to depart the scene pronto. On their way out, Poppy swung back around and said politely to Detective Drummond, "Would you be a dear and *not* mention this unfortunate incident to Detective Jordan, as a personal favor to me?"

"That would be a hard no," Drummond barked.

Poppy chose not to press the matter any further and fled the apartment.

The three women scurried down the steps back to Violet's Buick.

"I thought they were going to arrest us," Violet wailed with a sense of dread.

"They still might," Poppy muttered.

As Poppy reached for the door handle on the passenger's side of the Lucerne, she suddenly noticed a red truck pulling into one of the empty covered parking spots adjacent to the building.

The driver hopped out.

He was a bearded man with a red ball cap pulled way down, shadowing his face, and he was wearing dark glasses.

It had to be him.

The stalker.

Patrice Marceau.

Or Pete Chambers.

Or whatever name he was going by now.

Chapter 20

Marceau slammed the door of his truck shut and as he started walking toward the building he suddenly spotted Detectives Lasky and Drummond emerging from his apartment building. He froze in place, then swiveled around, and hurriedly made a beeline back to his truck, trying not to break into a run and arouse suspicion.

The two detectives were busy conferring with each other and failed to see their suspect in the midst of getting away.

Poppy considered calling out to the detectives but didn't want to alert Marceau, who had already jumped back into his truck and was backing out of his parking spot to take off again.

"Quick, Violet, follow that red truck!" Poppy yelled as she scrambled into the Lucerne.

Violet gazed around, puzzled. "What red truck?"

Poppy pointed ahead. "That one! Hurry! We're going to lose him!"

Iris climbed into the backseat as Violet took the wheel, slowly turned the ignition, and carefully checked her rearview mirror before lightly pressing her foot down on the gas pedal and cautiously pulling away from the curb.

Poppy sighed, frustrated. "Faster, Violet, faster!"

"I have been a licensed driver for over fifty years without ever having one traffic ticket or accident, Poppy, so I am not going to ruin that stellar record today."

Poppy strained to see the red truck swerve onto a side street, tires squealing. "Take the next right, Violet!"

Violet, slowing the Lucerne down, flipped on her turn signal and judiciously kept her eye out for any pedestrians crossing the street before making the same turn as the red truck had moments before.

"This is not some leisurely Sunday drive, Violet!" Iris barked from the backseat. "We're trying to tail a suspect!"

"I know, I know, stop yelling at me, you're making me nervous!" Violet sputtered, hands gripping the wheel. She sped up a little, but the red truck was now far ahead of them with about four vehicles between them.

"I probably should have driven," Poppy muttered.

"Oh, I couldn't have allowed that. You're not on my insurance policy," Violet said matter-of-factly.

Up ahead, a traffic light turned red before Marceau had a chance to speed through the intersection, allowing Violet to catch up.

Poppy kept her eyes glued on the truck. "Violet, if you change lanes now, you can get up alongside him."

Violet flipped her blinker on again.

"Hurry, before the light changes!" Iris howled.

Startled by Iris's bellowing tone, Violet cranked the wheel and veered the car into the next lane, but didn't see a silver Rolls Royce coming right up behind them. Violet's car nearly sideswiped it before the Rolls swerved into the emergency lane to avoid a crash, the irate driver slamming on the horn.

"See, all this yelling is making me flustered! I can't think clearly!" Violet exclaimed as she waved apologetically to the driver of the Rolls, who turned out to be a woman in her late eighties with Coke-bottle glasses, who was angrily giving Violet the middle finger.

The light turned green and the truck peeled away just as Violet managed to get closer. She sped up a little, but not enough to keep up with the truck.

"The speed limit's fifty, Violet, you're only going forty-six!" Iris huffed.

Violet huffily pumped the gas some more, enough for the Lucerne's speedometer to inch up closer to fifty miles an hour. When it was hovering around fifty, Violet let her foot up slightly off the pedal.

"Just so you know, Violet, the police usually don't pull you over for speeding if you're only going seven or eight miles over the speed limit, so it's okay if you go a little faster," Poppy suggested gently.

Violet shot her an annoyed look. "That's a myth, Poppy. My sister Jean got a ticket once and she was only going twenty-eight in a twenty-five-mile zone."

"You told me that story, and it wasn't that she was speeding, she passed a stopped school bus when the red lights were flashing, that's why she got the ticket!" Iris shouted.

The truck was now far ahead, zipping from lane to lane, passing cars, almost as if the driver was suddenly aware that he was being followed.

Poppy tapped her foot impatiently on the floorboard, trying desperately not to distract Violet from her driving, but fearing they were going to lose Marceau, and then they would never be able to find him again if he was on the run.

The truck suddenly slipped into a turn lane and screeched onto a side street.

Poppy cranked her head around. "Violet . . . ?"

"I see him! I see him!" Violet wailed, twisting the wheel.

The Lucerne swung into the turn lane in hot pursuit, tailing the truck down the side street.

Up ahead, the truck sped up, flying through a stop sign.

Violet was gaining ground but would no doubt lose him if she braked for the stop sign.

Poppy wanted to scream for her not to slow down, to keep going, but she also didn't want to strong-arm Violet into breaking the law, so she reluctantly remained mum.

True to form, Violet hit the brake and the Lucerne rolled to a quiet, peaceful stop.

Iris heaved a loud, defeated sigh in the backseat.

Steaming mad, Violet glared at her through the rearview mirror. "All right, Iris, you want a car chase, I will give you a car chase!"

Violet banged her foot down on the accelerator and the Lucerne shot forward, just as a Chevy Malibu came barreling around the corner. Violet screamed, unable to stop in time, and the Lucerne slammed into the back side of the Chevy, smashing the taillight and puncturing the left rear tire.

Violet stared at Poppy, eyes blinking, in a state of shock. "Is anyone hurt?"

Poppy shook her head. "This was *all* my fault, Violet. I never should have pressured you to chase after that truck."

"Look on the bright side," Iris said. "At least you don't have to worry anymore about maintaining your perfect driving record."

Violet couldn't help but throw another exasperated look Iris's way through the rearview mirror. "I'd better check to see if the other driver is okay."

Violet shoved open the driver's-side door and got out. She was joined by Poppy. They could hear a hissing sound, which Poppy surmised was the Chevy's back tire rapidly deflating.

The doors to the Chevy were swung open, and to Poppy's surprise, Detectives Lasky and Drummond clamored out. Both of them were red faced and furious.

"Oh, dear . . . ," Poppy whispered.

"What the hell do you think you're doing?!" Lasky shouted at Violet, who shrank like, well, a shrinking violet.

Poppy stepped protectively in front of Violet. "We saw Patrice Marceau arrive just as we were leaving. We figured you didn't see him so we decided to—"

"Chase after him on your own?" Lasky snarled, shaking his head in disgust.

"We saw him, too," Drummond growled. "We had him in our sights, we were closing in on him, that is, until you and your little knitting circle came out of nowhere and sideswiped us!"

Violet shakily reached inside the car for her purse. "We should probably exchange insurance information. That is the proper thing to do, correct? This is my first accident."

Lasky stared at her, dumbfounded.

Poppy meekly walked over to the two detectives and said softly, "I don't suppose we could keep this unfortunate incident to ourselves and not share it with Detective Jordan?"

Detective Drummond scowled. "Once again, that would be a hard no!"

Chapter 21

"I will just die if I have to go to prison!" Violet wailed, in a frantic state at the Desert Flowers garage office.

"You are not going to prison, Violet, I can assure you," Poppy promised.

"I don't know, Aunt Poppy," Wyatt said, sitting in his chair, swiveling it around in circles next to his computer. "Reckless driving isn't like a speeding ticket. You can't just pay the fine and move on with your life. You can actually go to jail for up to ninety days."

Violet gasped, horrified.

Poppy threw him an admonishing look. He was clearly not helping the situation.

Wyatt shrugged. "What? I looked it up online."

Violet nervously paced back and forth, waving her arms around. "I asked my insurance agent when I filed the claim if my premiums were going to go up, and she said absolutely yes, plus all my good-driving discounts I got from years of no accidents will also now go right out the window!"

"Violet, please, we understand you're upset, but the most important thing we have to deal with right now is finding this madman, this two-bit 'Talented Mr. Ripley' wannabe, who has it out for our poor Poppy!" Iris barked.

Violet nodded repeatedly, turning to Poppy. "I know, forgive me, Poppy, I am just so traumatized by what happened today, I keep reliving it over and over in my mind."

"At least nobody got hurt, Maw Maw," Wyatt offered.

"That's right, dear, and I am incredibly grateful for that," Violet said with a forced smile, but still shaken.

Iris marched to the kitchenette. "Perhaps we should have a cocktail to take the edge off and calm us all down?"

"It's not even noon," Poppy said.

"It's Palm Springs, happy hour runs twenty-four hours a day," Iris said defensively. "But if you think alcohol at this hour is unseemly, I can make mimosas so you will feel less guilty. There is a bottle of champagne in the fridge."

"Where do we go from here?" Wyatt asked.

"I'm afraid we're back to square one," Poppy sighed. "Now that Patrice or Pete or whatever his real name is knows the police are on to him, I am sure he has gone into hiding, or changed his identity and appearance again, so now we'll never be able to locate him. He must have had a dozen fake passports to choose from in his apartment, and who knows how many different bank accounts."

"At least if he's on the run that probably means you will finally be safe from danger. He will not be thinking about you," Iris said, popping open the cork on the champagne bottle and holding it over the sink as some fizz oozed out. Then she set about grabbing some glasses from the cupboard and a carton of orange juice from the refrigerator.

"Let's hope so," Poppy said, although she was still struggling with a sense of dread. She had a disturbing feeling that this arduous ordeal was far from over.

Iris finished making two drinks and carried them across the room, then handed one to Wyatt. "You get just orange juice." She passed by Violet. "I will give this one to Poppy since I know you are a teetotaler until at least five o'clock, Violet."

Violet reached out and snatched the mimosa away from her. "Not today."

She gulped it down.

Iris raised an eyebrow before returning to the kitchenette to pour two more for herself and Poppy.

"Aunt Poppy, did you take any pictures of the passports with your phone? Maybe if I Google a few, something might turn up that could help us find him."

"That's an excellent idea," Poppy said, unlocking her phone and walking over to hand it to Wyatt. "Violet, you took photos, too. We all did."

Violet pulled her phone out and scrolled through the photos she had taken. "Mine are mostly of that pretty girl."

Wyatt perked up. "What pretty girl?"

"He had a whole stack of photos on his nightstand of a young woman in all kinds of poses. He seemed to be quite taken with her," Violet said.

Wyatt jumped down off his chair and scurried over to his grandmother with his hand out. "Let me see."

Violet handed him her phone.

Wyatt took one look at the first picture and his eyes widened in surprise.

Violet bent down to his eye level. "Wyatt, dear, what is it?"

"It's Jessie Walters!" Wyatt cried, a big, wide, excited grin on his face.

Poppy, Iris, and Violet all exchanged puzzled looks.

"Who?" Poppy asked.

"Oh come on," Wyatt cried. "She's *hugely* famous!"

"Is she an actress?" Iris asked.

"No! She's a reality TV star!"

Iris rolled her eyes. "I forget we live in a time when someone with no discernible talent can become rich and famous."

"She's so hot!" Wyatt noted with a libidinous grin.

Violet snatched the phone back from him. "I think you have seen enough."

"She was one of the contestants vying for Hank Tibbets on *Finding Mr. Right* this past season," Wyatt said.

"And who is Hank Tibbets?" Poppy asked.

Wyatt sighed, frustrated. "Oh come on, Aunt Poppy, he's, like, a big-deal NFL quarterback for the Pittsburgh Steelers. He was the new Mr. Right, looking for love, and something like twelve beautiful girls competed for the chance to date him. Jessie made it all the way to the final two, and everybody thought Hank was going to pick her, but in the end he went with Lou Jean Farley, a Dallas Cowboys cheerleader. Jessie was heartbroken. She was a real fan favorite."

"Obviously Poppy's stalker was a big fan as well," Iris remarked.

"Judging from all the photos of her in his apartment, I would say obsessively so," Poppy suggested. "I think the prudent thing for us to do is to somehow locate her and warn her."

"That shouldn't be too hard," Wyatt said. "She's in Los Angeles preparing for a new show. Jessie was so popular and has, like, this massive social media following, and everyone's rooting for her to find true love, so they're giving her her own show called *My Dream Man*. This time she's the one who gets to pick a winner from five different bachelors competing for her affections. I read all about it online. Normally I wouldn't waste my time watching just one pretty girl—I like the shows with ten or fifteen girls—but Jessie is so hot!"

"Yes, you have mentioned that fact before, dear," Violet said. "We get the point."

Wyatt had already clicked on a photo of Jessie in a tiny

white bikini that left little to the imagination, which caused Violet to cover her grandson's eyes with her hand.

Poppy stared at the photo on Wyatt's computer screen.

The bright, happy eyes. The warm, carefree smile.

The young woman was indeed strikingly beautiful.

And she was probably oblivious to the fact that her life, just like Poppy's, could be in grave danger.

Chapter 22

Jessie Walters tucked her luxurious long blond hair behind her ear as she studied the photo of the bearded man on Poppy's phone. She bit her bottom lip, her eyes fixed squarely on the man's face and features, which were obscured by the dark sunglasses and red ball cap. Finally, Jessie shook her head and handed the phone back to Poppy, who sat across from her in the spacious office on the fourteenth floor of a high-rise in Century City in West Los Angeles. Next to Poppy on the plush leather couch was Wyatt, who was dumbstruck and had a goofy grin on his face as he stared at the beautiful reality TV star.

"I'm sorry, I don't recognize him," Jessie said.

"Are you absolutely sure?" Poppy pressed.

"Yes. I mean, it's hard to tell, because I can't see his eyes or hair color, but he doesn't strike me as familiar at all."

Poppy scrolled to another passport photo. "What about him?"

Jessie, who already appeared bored with this last-minute meeting, reluctantly reached out and took the phone again. This time she took only a cursory glance at the picture before handing it back. "No, I don't know him, either."

"We believe it is the same person," Poppy said.

"What? No, they look nothing alike," Jessie scoffed.

"The man we're trying to find appears to be some kind of chameleon, constantly changing his looks and identity."

When Poppy had decided to warn Jessie Walters about her potential stalker, Wyatt had quickly come up with the talent agency that represented Jessie's TV endeavors, and found the name of her manager, Ginger Kaplan. Poppy had tried calling several times, insisting that it was an emergency, but only when she strongly suggested that Jessie's life was in imminent danger did she get a call back from Ms. Kaplan's obviously annoyed assistant. After Poppy forcefully explained the situation and how serious it was, Ginger Kaplan finally agreed to call Jessie and summon her to her office and grant Poppy a five-minute meeting to make her case.

Although Poppy had planned to make a solo trip to LA to meet with Jessie and her manager, Wyatt had insisted on tagging along, this being his one chance to meet this heaven-sent angel he worshipped so much.

Jessie had made a big production of introducing herself to the thirteen-year-old boy, hugging him and pretending to be interested in what grade he was in and what movies he liked, but it was crystal clear to Poppy that Jessie wanted to be in and out of this slog of a meeting as quickly as possible.

And Ginger's job was to facilitate her wishes.

"Is that all, Ms. Harmon?" Ginger said brusquely in a distinct, gravelly smoker's voice, making up for her petite frame with a booming volume. "Are we done? Jessie is very busy prepping for the start of production on *My Dream Man.*"

"Yes, but I urge you to be on the lookout for this man," Poppy warned. "I cannot stress enough how dangerous he might be."

Jessie nodded amicably, trying to placate Poppy, but it was clear she was not taking the threat seriously.

"I can assure you, we have tightened security at the house in Los Feliz where we will be shooting. Nobody is going to get in who is not authorized to be there," Ginger promised.

"I have complete faith in Ginger to make it a priority that I stay safe, Ms. Harmon."

Poppy was growing frustrated at their infuriating lack of urgency. She leaned forward, hands clasped in front of her. "I just fear, based on what we know, that this man is not your average stalker. He's smart and sophisticated and manipulative and unpredictable, and I just want to make sure you understand what you could be dealing with—"

Ginger had heard enough. "We understand. Thank you for coming to see us with this information, Ms. Harmon." She stood up and with a tight smile added, "The receptionist will validate your parking ticket."

Poppy knew she had worn out her welcome. She turned to look at Wyatt. "Ready to go?"

Wyatt slid off the slippery leather couch, his eyes still glued to Jessie, beside himself, totally smitten with seeing this stunning woman he had coveted for so long, up close and in the flesh.

Acutely aware of how in awe he was, Jessie made a point of reaching out and shaking his hand while dazzling him with her winning smile. "It was lovely to meet you, Wyatt."

Wyatt tried to reply but was utterly tongue-tied.

Jessie chuckled and rubbed the top of his head. "You're going to be a real heartbreaker when you grow up, you know that?"

"Yeah, I do," Wyatt finally managed to spit out.

Jessie laughed heartily.

Ginger opened the door to the office to usher them out. She scrutinized Poppy as she passed by her. "You know who you remind me of? Remember that old private eye show from the eighties, the one with Rod Harper, what was it called?"

Poppy had no desire to engage with Ginger Kaplan after being so summarily dismissed.

Ginger turned to Jessie for help, but of course, the girl had not even been born yet in the eighties, so she was useless and just stared at Ginger, confused.

"*Jack Colt*," Wyatt muttered under his breath.

"Yes!" Ginger cried, pointing a finger at Wyatt. "That's it! How do you remember that show? You're like . . . ten years old."

"Thirteen," Wyatt muttered, not wanting Jessie to think he was *that* young.

Ginger stared at Poppy. "You're the spitting image of the actress who played Rod Harper's secretary, what was her name, Debbie? Donna?"

Wyatt sighed. "Daphne."

Ginger pointed at Wyatt again. "Daphne." Then she went back to Poppy. "You do. You look just like her. Although much older, of course."

Poppy bristled.

Wyatt snickered.

"I get that a lot," Poppy remarked, not about to give Ginger the satisfaction of being right.

Poppy then swept out of the office with Wyatt scampering behind her, worried more now than ever that her stern warning had simply fallen on deaf ears. That no serious steps would be taken to prevent this "Talented Mr. Ripley" from pursuing his obvious obsession. And that it would ultimately, especially for Jessie Walters, prove to be a very costly mistake.

Chapter 23

Poppy groaned, exasperated.

This could not be happening.

Just to be certain, she stood underneath the air vent in her hallway and raised her arms in the air.

Sure enough, her brand-new seven-thousand-dollar air-conditioning unit was at the moment blowing heat through the vents in her home.

And it was ninety-two degrees outside.

She had just arrived home from LA as the sun descended behind the San Jacinto Mountains, and, after parking Sam's SUV in the garage, entered her sweltering hot box of a house and turned the temperature down to a more comfortable seventy-five degrees.

But almost instantly she felt something was wrong as she began to sweat profusely. It appeared to be getting hotter, not colder. Poppy sighed as she marched back to the Nest thermostat and brought the temperature farther down to sixty-eight degrees. After waiting another five minutes with no change, she grabbed her phone and called Atlas, the air-conditioning company that had installed the new unit. She got a voicemail recording and left a very stern, detailed message about her current situation, pointedly reminding them that the unit was not even a week old, and that given the stifling heat she would consider this an emergency situation.

Luckily, within the hour, an Atlas truck pulled up in front of her house and a technician hopped out.

Poppy peered out the window to see who had answered the call. He was young, had a lanky build, a scruffy face, and a blue ball cap pulled down over his head that shielded his eyes, which Poppy found odd given that the sun had just gone down.

It looked like Rusty, the technician who had been present when the unit had been initially installed, the one who said he lived in Desert Hot Springs with his girlfriend and young daughter.

Yes, it had to be him.

Poppy knocked on the window, startling him as he headed around the house toward the unit in the backyard.

He barely looked up as Poppy waved at him.

He gave her a tip of his cap and kept going.

Why hadn't he come to the front door first?

Poppy found that odd, too.

But then again, she had explained the situation over the phone to the company's answering service, so Rusty probably knew what he needed to do in order to get it running properly again.

Still, he had been friendlier before.

Poppy crossed through her living room to the sliding glass door that led outside and opened it. She could see Rusty bent over, checking the unit, his toolbox next to him.

"Rusty, would you like something to drink?" Poppy called out.

His back to her, he waved and responded, "No, thank you, I'm good."

"Well, let me know if you change your mind," Poppy said before retreating inside and sliding the door shut again.

He was out in her yard working for almost an hour.

During that time, Poppy managed to grow more and more concerned. It was a fact that Rusty closely resembled the stalker, Patrice or Pete, at least from a distance.

What if, in fact, this was *not* Rusty?

What if it was actually Patrice?

She could feel the panic rising inside her before she caught herself. It couldn't be the stalker. How would he have known her new air-conditioning unit was going to break down? Unless he had arranged for it to blow heat instead of air while she was away in Los Angeles? But for what purpose? And how would he know she would call Atlas for service?

She looked out the front window again.

The Atlas truck appeared to be legitimate.

Poppy decided she was working herself up into a tizzy for no reason.

That was Rusty in her backyard.

Not the stalker.

Suddenly the air conditioner kicked to life, and mercifully, cool air began pumping through the vents. Relieved, she went back outside but Rusty was no longer there. By the time she was back in her living room and looking out the front window, she heard a door slam shut and saw the Atlas van pulling away.

He hadn't even bothered to come and explain to her what the problem had been. The unit was still under warranty, so it wasn't like he needed to hand her a bill. But she had been used to more friendly service.

As Poppy's house became more bearable and she started preparing vegetables for a nice, cool summer salad, she stopped slicing an English cucumber halfway, her mind preoccupied.

The sense of dread was not going away.

She had to know if that had been Rusty or someone else.

Poppy reached for her phone when the screen lit up.

It was Detective Jordan.

Poppy scooped it up and quickly answered the call. "Yes?"

"It's Detective Jordan. I'm calling with some news."

"What is it, Detective?" Poppy said, bracing herself.

"We got him."

"Who?"

"The bearded man who has been stalking you. Patrice, or as of today, Pete, according to his current driver's license. A couple of officers in Cathedral City just pulled him over for a rolling stop, and after running a check on the red truck he was driving, they discovered there was an APB out on him."

"Where is he now?"

"In jail down at the Palm Springs precinct. I'm on my way there now to question him," Jordan said.

"Thank you," Poppy said quietly as she set down the phone. She felt as if she was able to breathe for the first time in a couple of weeks.

Chapter 24

"His driver's license identified him as Pete Chambers," Detective Jordan said as he ushered Poppy into his office.

Poppy suppressed a yawn as Jordan closed the door behind them, which the detective noticed.

"Can I get you some coffee?" Jordan asked.

Poppy shook her head. "No, I just haven't been able to get much sleep lately."

"Understandably," Jordan said, circling his desk and sitting down behind it.

Poppy took a seat in a hard metal chair facing him. "Pete Chambers, that's one of the names we found in Patrice Marceau's apartment."

"Right, one of the many aliases he's been using. But this guy swears he actually *is* the real Pete Chambers, and that he has no clue who Tanya Cook is. He's also vehemently denying that he forced Adelaide Campbell off Highway 74. When we pointed out the slight damage to his front bumper, which is consistent with him ramming the back of your car, he claims he was just seeing those dents for the first time."

"But if the truck does indeed belong to him, then who else could have done it?"

Jordan reached into his desk drawer and pulled out a bottle of whiskey. "It's been a long day, care to join me?"

Poppy gave him a thin smile. "I'm fine, thank you, Detective."

Jordan shrugged. "Suit yourself." He poured some liquor into a ceramic coffee cup, then downed it in one gulp. "Chambers told us he had regularly lent his truck to a buddy of his, guy by the name of Bobby Doyle."

Poppy rolled the name around in her head. "Bobby Doyle, Bobby Doyle . . ."

"There was another passport at the apartment belonging to a Robert Doyle, so we can assume it's yet another alias. Doyle told Chambers he had crashed his motorcycle and it was still at the mechanic's getting repaired, so Chambers let him tool around in his truck while he was working at Home Depot in customer service. That's where the two of them met. Chambers waited on Doyle, helped him find some supplies he was looking for, and the two hit it off. They started to hang out together and became drinking buddies. Now here's the unsettling part. Chambers said he didn't think too much about it at the time, but on the day the two men met, Doyle was purchasing a bunch of steel metal pipes, brass caps, fuse wire, nails, glass, and other shrapnel."

"But that sounds like materials for a—"

"Pipe bomb," Jordan said, glowering. "When I pressed Chambers about that, he swore on his mother's life that he knew nothing about any kind of attack Doyle might be planning. It never crossed his mind to ask him about it. He and Doyle just talked about sports mostly, or so he claims."

"Do you believe him?"

Jordan shrugged again. "If we know one thing, it's that this guy is one hell of an actor. He could be playing us like a fiddle. But my gut tells me the Chambers I've got in my interrogation room is being sincere and honest, but then again, I can't be totally positive."

"Does Pete Chambers know where Bobby Doyle is now?"

"No. In addition to lending him his truck, he also let him crash on his couch the last couple of nights. He obviously had to ditch his apartment after you and my detectives showed up there. But this morning, when Chambers woke up, Doyle was packed up and gone and didn't leave a note saying where he was heading. And today, right before he was pulled over and arrested, Chambers tried using his ATM card only to discover that his entire checking account had been cleaned out. He figured it had to be Bobby. He was the only one with access to Pete's apartment, where he could have found his PIN written down somewhere."

"So for all we know, Bobby Doyle could be in Mexico by now," Poppy sighed.

"If we believe Pete Chambers," Detective Jordan added before leaning forward, clasping his hands in front of him on his desk. "You're the only one who actually saw Bobby Doyle in person, which is why I would like you to take a look at a lineup, see if you recognize him. It's the only way we'll know if he's lying to us or not."

"Of course," Poppy said, her stomach flip-flopping. She was hardly looking forward to possibly coming face-to-face with the bearded man who had been stalking her.

Detective Jordan made a quick call, and within minutes, he was leading Poppy down a hallway to a giant two-way mirror where she saw five men being escorted into the room on the opposite side, taking positions underneath numbers from one to five. All of them were stone faced, lethargic, and similar in height and build. What struck Poppy was that all of the men were clean shaven. Two had buzz cuts. One had wavy brown hair. The other two were dirty blondes, one with shoulder-length hair, the other cropped shorter. Poppy went down the line, studying each one quickly before Jordan began ordering each one to step forward one at a time and introduce himself as Pete Chambers.

They all did as instructed.

When they were finished, Poppy felt a tremor of anxiety over the fact that she was completely stumped. She didn't recognize any of them. The stalker had sported a scruffy beard and shaggy hair. All of the men standing there resembled him somewhat, but she had not been able to register any prominent, distinctive physical features.

It could be all of them, or none of them.

"Do you recognize any of them?" Detective Jordan asked hopefully.

Poppy hesitated, carefully studying the five men again, but then, after struggling some more, she sighed, defeated, and shook her head. "No, Detective, I'm sorry. I never really got a good look at the man's face."

Detective Jordan put a reassuring hand on Poppy's arm. "It's okay, you did your best."

"Which is clearly not good enough since it means he is still out there somewhere, ready to strike again without warning."

"We'll get him," Jordan said confidently.

She wanted to believe him.

But this stalker was such a chameleon.

Popping up and disappearing whenever he pleased.

Elusive and dangerous.

"I'm going to keep that patrol car watching your place until we find him. You will be safe, I promise you," Jordan said.

Poppy prayed the detective was right.

Because right now she was more frightened than ever.

Chapter 25

Poppy checked the heated milk in the saucepan on her stove, making sure it had not come to a boil, and then opened the microwave oven and pulled out the bowl of melted chocolate and slowly added it to the milk, stirring gently until it was smooth and creamy. She tested it by dipping her finger into it a little and licking it off.

Delicious.

After pouring the hot chocolate into two paper cups and adding a couple of marshmallows since she was out of whipped cream, Poppy snapped two plastic covers over the cups and set them down on a tray that had two pieces of her homemade mango key lime pie cheesecake on a pair of paper plates with some plastic forks.

"Oh, napkins," she muttered to herself while snapping her fingers. She opened the cupboard, grabbed two white paper napkins, folded them, and slid them under the plastic forks. Then she picked up the tray and walked out of the kitchen and through the living room to the front door. Balancing the tray with the palm of one hand, a trick she had learned while waiting tables in college, Poppy opened her front door and headed outside.

Parked across the street was a police patrol car. The two officers inside were too engrossed in some kind of conversation and did not see her approaching. When she reached the driver's-side window, she stood there waiting for them to notice her but they were laughing at something one of them said and still had not seen her. Finally, Poppy balanced the tray again and knocked on the window, startling both of them.

The officer in the driver's seat, baby faced and a little hefty, spun around, wide eyed, and then breathed a sigh of relief at the sight of Poppy. He pressed a button and rolled down the window.

"Good evening, Ms. Harmon," the officer said.

The muscular, even younger officer in the passenger seat nodded to her politely.

"Hello, officers, I just wanted to let you know how much I appreciate you staying out here all night and keeping watch over my house. It gives me such a sense of peace and security. What are your names?"

The officer behind the wheel pointed to himself. "I'm Officer Radditz," he said, then indicated his partner. "And this is Officer Diaz."

Poppy held out the tray. "I thought you might enjoy some hot chocolate and a piece of my world-famous Mango Key Lime Pie Cheesecake. It's not really world famous, I just like to say it is, but my friends tend to rave about it."

"That's awfully kind of you, ma'am," Officer Radditz said, reaching out to take the tray.

"I was going to invite you in, but I suspect that would be against the rules," Poppy said.

"Yes, ma'am," Officer Radditz said.

Officer Diaz eagerly grabbed one of the hot chocolates while perusing which piece of cheesecake was bigger before grabbing the one he wanted.

"If you need anything else, a sandwich or something, please do not hesitate to call me. I assume you have my phone number?"

"We do, ma'am. But we will not be bothering you," Officer Radditz said, eyeing the slightly smaller portion of cheesecake his partner had left him.

"Well, good night," Poppy said, saluting them, and then wondering if it was inappropriate to salute an officer of the law, or was that just for people in the military? Poppy shrugged, too tired to have a debate with herself, and scurried across the street and back inside her house.

She had just slipped out of her clothes and into her silky, pleated sleeveless nightgown and was turning down the covers on her bed when she noticed her phone buzzing on the nightstand. She crossed over to look at the screen.

It was Sam calling from New York.

She quickly answered the call. "It's something like two in the morning back east. What are you doing up so late?"

"Worrying about you," Sam said.

"Don't be silly, I'm fine."

Poppy had decided to downplay recent events after Sam's departure for New York. She saw no reason to divulge everything that had happened since Sam obviously could do nothing from three thousand miles away.

"So the cops still haven't found this guy?"

"They made an arrest, but unfortunately it turned out it wasn't him. It was just a friend whose identity he stole before draining the poor man's checking account."

"Some friend."

"But you should know, at this very moment, there are two strapping police officers parked in front of my house who will be here to protect me until this man is finally located and put behind bars."

"That puts my mind at ease a little, Poppy, but you need to remain vigilant. Do not take any chances. No new cases. No unnecessary errands where you might be exposed. You need to stay home with the door locked, and do not answer it for anyone."

"Sam, I refuse to allow this man to turn me into an agoraphobic, afraid to ever leave the house. That's giving him just what he wants. He wants to terrify me."

"No, he wants to kill you, so don't make it easy for him," Sam said, trying to stay calm, although Poppy could hear in his voice that he was becoming upset.

"Okay, Sam," Poppy said, grateful he cared so much. "Now, tell me about New York. How's it going?"

"Rod can be difficult and grouchy, especially with the younger co-stars who play his sons, but he's been fine with me, probably because he knows if he gives me any gruff, I'm on the next plane back to California."

Poppy chuckled.

Her former *Jack Colt* co-star whose career had fallen far from the heights of his fame in the 1980s was enjoying a steady comeback after all these years on a popular police procedural that continued to win its time slot every Thursday night even amidst the flood of streaming options available now. There were still a lot of viewers who preferred the old-fashioned network TV schedule, and a meat-and-potatoes-type television series, nothing too fancy or complicated, just simple, straightforward good guys versus bad guys storytelling.

"Rod and I grabbed a beer after shooting wrapped the other night," Sam continued. "And he spent the whole time asking about you. It's obvious he still wants to make that happen."

"Did you tell him I'm taken?"

"Oh, he knows, but he's pulling down a hundred grand an episode so he's kind of used to getting what he wants," Sam said, laughing. "I can see in his eyes how inexplicable it is to him that you chose me over him."

Suddenly the air conditioner shut down.

"Oh, no, not again . . . ," she muttered.

"What's wrong?"

"I've been having trouble with my new air conditioner. They've already been out to fix it once. Hold on, Sam."

Still holding the phone in her hand, Poppy walked down the hall to the thermostat.

The temperature on the control had been set at seventy-two degrees.

But the house was still at seventy-eight.

The unit should not have stopped.

Poppy turned the dial to lower it even farther.

All the way down to sixty-five.

Nothing.

But then, she heard a loud clicking sound.

"Poppy?" she heard Sam calling from the phone.

Ignoring him for the moment, Poppy followed the clicking sound, sliding open the glass door to the backyard. It was coming from the unit.

"What on earth . . . ?"

Her stomach began twisting in knots.

Something was seriously wrong.

And then, there was a deafening explosion.

Glass flying everywhere.

And everything went black.

Chapter 26

Matt Flowers stood resolutely behind the lectern at the Palm Springs Presbyterian Church, eyes wet with tears, grief stricken. He had just flown in from Europe for Poppy's funeral the night before, although he had been alerted of her tragic death just hours before boarding the plane. The pews of the church were filled with friends and acquaintances of the beloved late actress. Her core group of confidantes, Iris and Violet, huddled together in the front row, holding on to each other for emotional support. Poppy's daughter, Heather, sat at the end of the row, dabbing her face with tissues, having just arrived from New York, where she attends law school, early that morning. Across the aisle sat Detective Jordan and his wife, Lynn, heads bowed, grieving.

Matt, who was halfway through with his remarks, stopped speaking and gazed over at the closed casket with a copper finish, rather pricey, but Matt had insisted that no expense be spared. "Many will remember Poppy for her work in television as an actress. Through her portrayal of Daphne in the *Jack Colt* show, millions of Americans and people around the world welcomed her into their home every week, they felt as if they knew her personally, that she was one of the family. The character of Daphne was warm, friendly, empathetic, loyal to a fault, willing to do anything for her employer, like go undercover as a go-go dancer to catch a strangler in one memorable episode, or risk her own life protecting a battered child from his abusive father in an episode that garnered a Golden Globe nomination for best supporting actress in a television series for the actress who portrayed her. And like her indelible role of Daphne, Poppy Harmon, the actress, the person, was also warm, friendly, empathetic, and loyal. And she was so much more. . . ." There was a catch in his throat as he choked up. He paused, waited until he managed to get himself under control, and then slowly continued. "Most people who discover their late spouse left them penniless might give up, wallow in the hopelessness of her wretched circumstances, but not Poppy. She got back up, brushed herself off, and reinvented herself as a private investigator. And a truly successful one at that. That is how she touched so many lives, beyond her acting career, with her innate kindness, her unshakable sense of justice, her tenacious drive to help people who have been wronged. She was my role model. . . ." Matt sniffed. He reached into the pocket of his suit coat for a handkerchief and rubbed his runny nose. Matt peered out at the grim-faced, solemn crowd of mourners dressed in black, and squeaked out, "I will miss her every day for the rest of my life."

And then he lost it. He covered his face with the handkerchief, his whole body heaving as he wept, and then he stepped down, squeezing in between Iris and Violet in the front pew as they comforted him like two overprotective aunts.

The minister, who had been sitting in a tall hard-backed chair on the opposite side of the lectern away from the casket, stood and took Matt's place at the lectern, adjusting the microphone for his shorter height. "Thank you, Mr. Flowers, for that lovely tribute to Ms. Harmon. And now let us bow our heads in prayer." The minister cleared his throat before continuing. "God of peace, as we end this time of gathering and bid our last farewell to our departed loved one, Poppy Harmon, we ask for your comfort upon every friend and family member. Be with them each and every day. Let them feel your loving and strong presence in their hearts. . . ."

Sitting in the back of the church, watching everyone sniffling and drying their eyes with Kleenex, was a woman in a black dress and a black hat with a veil hanging down covering her entire face. She had arrived late and made a point of not calling any attention to herself. She had slid into the last pew, on the end, and observed the proceedings in utter silence.

No crying or carrying on.

Just a stiff upper lip.

It was Poppy Harmon, alive and well. Although Detective Jordan had discouraged her from showing up and possibly risking exposure, Poppy had firmly declared that there was no way she was going to miss her own funeral. She had managed to keep a low profile throughout the entire service, and as the minister wrapped up and the mourners slowly began to file out of the church, Poppy deliberately hung back, waiting for everyone to be gone until she could join Jordan, Matt, Heather, Iris, and Violet in the church parlor, where they had prearranged to meet directly after the service.

"Excuse me," a woman said, trying to get by Poppy.

"Oh, I'm sorry," Poppy said in a gravelly, low voice to disguise her true identity.

As Poppy stood up, she realized the woman was Serena Saunders, appropriately in black but with a white corsage pinned to her ample cleavage. Poppy wasn't sure what statement she was trying to make with that. She was just surprised that Serena had bothered to show up at her funeral. The two had hardly been close pals.

As Serena slid by Poppy, she stopped and turned back around. "Were you a friend of Poppy's?"

Poppy nodded.

"Poor Poppy," Serena sighed. "She was such a dear. We were the best of friends, but truth be told, I always worried about her trying to be a detective. I mean, it's one thing to play one on TV, but it's quite another to try your hand at it in real life. And look where it got her. Such a tragedy."

Serena shook her head sadly.

Poppy could feel her cheeks flushing behind her thick black veil. She bit her tongue, trying her best not to respond.

Best friends?

The two women could barely stand each other.

But it was no surprise Serena would play up their relationship in order to make herself feel more important on this sad, somber day.

"It's clear now that she was in way over her head. You know, I heard she was just an assistant at the Desert Flowers Detective Agency, not a real, bona fide investigator, but her pride got in the way, and she was trying to solve a case while her boss, Mr. Flowers, was regrettably out of the country, and well, the rest, as they say, is history. . . ."

Poppy clenched her fists, resisting the urge to rear back and sock the insipid, trash-talking Serena Saunders right in the nose. Instead, she decided to just turn the other cheek and join the others in the parlor as quickly as possible. Before she got to her feet, she felt a hand on her arm.

It was Serena, refusing to allow her to go. "Quick question. Matt Flowers. Do you know if he's single?"

Poppy was appalled.

She was hoping Serena might be asking for a much younger niece or the daughter of a family friend.

"I just find him so dreamy. I wonder if he likes women a few years older than himself?"

A few years?

"I wouldn't know," Poppy whispered in the same gravelly, low, unidentifiable voice.

Poppy also wondered what had happened to the younger boyfriend Serena had been so shamelessly bragging about just a few weeks earlier.

Serena crinkled her nose. "Who did you say you were again?"

"I didn't," Poppy snapped gruffly, pushing past Serena and down the aisle toward the empty casket, veering right to the door that led to the parlor. She could feel Serena's eyes watching her as she made a hasty exit.

Once she was inside the parlor, cheeks still burning from her encounter with the odious Serena Saunders, Detective Jordan closed the door behind her and locked it so no one else could wander into the room unannounced.

As Poppy removed her veil, Matt bounded over and enveloped her in a big bear hug. "I know this whole funeral was all just a ruse, but it still makes me feel better to see you in the flesh and know you're still with us!"

"That was a lovely eulogy, Matt," Poppy said, gently patting the back of his head. "I think you should save it for when I actually do kick the bucket."

He still held Poppy tightly in his arms.

"Matt?" Poppy whispered.

He made no move to let her go.

"Matt?"

"I've missed you so much!" Matt declared, squeezing her even tighter.

"Matt, I can't breathe . . . ," Poppy wheezed.

He finally got the message and released her.

Heather stepped forward. "I still don't quite understand why we had to go through with this whole charade."

"Because we have a very dangerous killer on the loose, and apparently he was not going to stop until he succeeded in bumping off your mother," Detective Jordan explained. "Once he discovered the woman he ran off the road was not Poppy, he tried again by rigging her air conditioner with a pipe bomb."

"I got lucky that his homemade bomb wasn't wired correctly and only caused a small explosion. Otherwise you wouldn't just be going through the motions, you would have been planning my funeral for real," Poppy said, relief in her voice. "But thankfully I walked away with just a few scrapes and bruises and a mild concussion."

"What about your new house?" Heather asked.

"The back side of the house where the air-conditioning unit was located was badly damaged, but fortunately the rest of the house is still intact."

"I know it was all fake," Violet cooed breathlessly, "but I must say it was a lovely service, Poppy. When I go, I hope mine is as special."

"I do not need all that pomp and circumstance," Iris huffed. "When I die, just wrap me in a Hefty bag and set me out on the street for the garbage collector."

"If that's your final wish, Iris, you can count on me to carry it out," Violet promised.

"I am just grateful you all kept me in the loop on what was happening," Heather said. "If I had read online my mother blew up in her own house, I would have probably keeled over myself from a heart attack!"

"It's all over social media now," Matt said.

"Which is good," Detective Jordan said. "We're counting on the killer to think he got away with it. We want him feeling cocky so maybe he gets a little sloppy as he moves on to his next identity and whatever game plan he's got in his head."

Heather stared at her mother with worried eyes. "So what happens now?"

"I hide out at the garage office out of sight until we can figure out the killer's next move," Poppy answered. "And you go back to NYU and continue with your studies."

"I hate leaving you, especially now," Heather sighed.

"If you stick around here, you might raise suspicion. It's best you go back to New York," Jordan said firmly.

"Don't worry, Heather," Matt said. "I will make it my personal mission to make sure your mother stays safe."

"Thank you, Matt," Heather said with a warm smile, almost as if she were noticing Matt for the first time. "By the way, how have you been, are you seeing anyone?"

There was an awkward pause in the room.

"I'd better go check on my wife," Detective Jordan said, having no interest in the interpersonal dynamics of anyone in this room, especially the past romantic entanglements of Matt and Poppy's daughter. He unlocked the door of the parlor and hurried out.

Iris scurried over and locked the door behind him.

"No," Matt said quietly. "Not at the moment. You?"

Poppy could detect a hopefulness in his voice.

Heather nodded slightly. "A fellow law student. Jim. From Alabama. I can barely understand him, he's got such a thick Southern accent. It's still early, though, so who knows?"

Matt smiled. "I'm happy for you."

Poppy could see he genuinely was pleased, although she suspected he was feeling at least a little disappointment over the fact that Heather had just put the kibosh on any lingering hope for a rekindled relationship. She knew Matt had been hit hard by the breakup a couple of years back and in some ways was still trying to get over it.

Poppy was just relieved that Matt was finally home.

And here to help her find the man who was so determined to see her dead.

Chapter 27

"What a relief it is to hear your voice," Sam said on the other end of Poppy's phone.

"Well, reports of my death have been greatly exaggerated," Poppy said from the Desert Flowers garage office, where she was holed up until further notice. A few feet away, Matt hovered over Wyatt in front of the desktop computer sifting through all the photographs Poppy, Iris, and Violet had taken at the apartment of the stalker, whom now they simply referred to as Mr. Ripley since they still had no clue what his actual name was, given his multiple aliases.

"I know you prepared me, but it was still a real punch to the gut to see all the stories online about your passing," Sam said. "How long is this going to go on?"

"Until we can finally locate this rather elusive killer," Poppy sighed. "Hopefully, it will all get resolved soon."

"I'm worried about you, Poppy," Sam said somberly. "I mean, investigating missing relatives or cheating spouses is one thing, but this guy has killed once and doesn't seem to have any hesitation about trying again and again until he gets it right."

"The good news, Sam, is that as long as he thinks I'm

dead, I'm no longer a target. With all the obituaries float-ing around online, Poppy Harmon should officially be off his radar," Poppy said, trying to be reassuring, but the un-ease in her voice was noticeable, and Sam knew her well enough to pick up on it.

"Still, I want you to be extremely careful," Sam said. "I know I'm starting to sound like a broken record, but please, don't take any chances. . . . I hate that I'm not there to look after you."

"That's very sweet, but in addition to the police, I have a whole team of detectives watching over me now. I will be fine."

Poppy hoped that if she said it enough times, she would convince herself that it was true. But she had been seri-ously rattled by the explosion at her house and could not stop reliving it over and over in her mind.

"I love you," Sam whispered through the phone.

"I love you, too," Poppy said, smiling.

She never tired of hearing him say it.

She hung up and wandered over to Matt and Wyatt at the computer. "Any luck?"

Wyatt intently scrolled through the digital photos on the screen as Matt turned to her and shook his head. "We must have gone over the photos you took a dozen times. Other than a handful of fake passports and bank ac-counts, there's nothing that points to what name he might be going by, or where he could be now. For all we know, he may not even be in the Coachella Valley anymore."

"Why would he stick around here now that he got his revenge for me putting his girlfriend away?" Poppy said. "What if we never find him? I can't stay dead forever."

Matt put a hand on her shoulder. "Stay positive, Poppy. We'll dig him up."

Poppy's phone dinged with a notification.

At first glance, she thought she had misread it.

She blinked and looked again. "I don't believe it. . . ."

Matt glanced at her phone. "What is it?"

"Serena Saunders . . ." Poppy sighed. "She just tweeted that in the days before my death, I was trash-talking her to a famous director she won't name, trying to persuade him to cast me instead of her in his new movie for Hulu. That's a bald-faced lie!"

"That's nothing, you should have heard what she said about you on Facebook," Wyatt remarked, eyes still glued to his computer screen.

"*What?*" Poppy gasped.

"She's all over social media playing up your so-called famous feud and bad-mouthing you. She's getting lots of attention, too. She just doubled her followers on her fan page," Wyatt said.

"That's outrageous," Poppy wailed. "She is using my death to elevate her own profile in a desperate attempt to jump-start her career! Well, I won't have it! She will not get away with this!"

"What can you do? I mean, you can't exactly come out and refute her claims," Matt said. "Given that you're supposed to be dead and all."

"There is that," Poppy sighed. "I just cannot believe the gall of this woman. I haven't seen her in over thirty years until recently, and now suddenly she pops back into my life to slander and belittle me. How am I supposed to fight back? It's infuriating!"

There was a knock at the door.

Everyone froze.

Matt gestured for Poppy to get out of sight.

She scurried over to the right of the door where she would be unseen by whoever was standing outside.

Matt marched over to the door. "Who is it?"

"Detective Jordan."

POPPY HARMON AND THE BACKSTABBING BACHELOR   147

Matt exhaled, relieved, and then opened the door. "Come in, Detective."

Jordan entered in time to see Poppy come out of hiding. "How are you holding up?"

"Fine, but I will feel a lot better when this horrible ordeal is finally over," Poppy said quietly.

"We may have a lead," Jordan said.

Poppy perked up. "What is it?"

"Lasky and Drummond combed the apartment of Pete Chambers, whom our perp was crashing with before he disappeared, and they came across an application for a reality dating show called *My Dream Man*."

"Yes, we found a shrine to the young woman in the show they're about to start shooting. He was obviously laser focused on her. I tried to warn her, but unfortunately she was unreceptive to me," Poppy explained.

"Chambers confirmed his friend Bobby Doyle was obsessed with this Jessie Walters and was determined to meet her. He applied to be on the show with her, and Chambers even lent him his truck to drive to LA for an in-person interview. We contacted the show's producers and were told that he had been rejected after a psych evaluation."

"No surprise there," Matt cracked.

Jordan nodded in agreement. "Chambers said Bobby was livid, and was hell-bent on getting on that show no matter what, intimating that he would apply again using a different name, a new backstory, the works, and this time try to fool the psychiatrist in charge of weeding out the crazies. Chambers at the time thought he was joking, but given the intensity of his obsession, it looks like that might be his next goal."

Poppy was skeptical. "Do you honestly believe he has managed to con his way onto a reality TV show?"

"The producers have narrowed the list of bachelors to

four. All of them checked out, but their vetting process isn't exactly on the level of a government security clearance, so he could have slipped through the cracks."

"So you're saying the killer could be one of those four finalists?" Matt asked, eyes wide.

"I tried convincing the producers to halt production, but they're on a schedule. It would cost millions to stop now, and they're not convinced we're even right about this, so the most they would agree to is to allow me to put a man in there to quietly investigate. Detective Don Lasky is going to be the fifth bachelor." Jordan noticed their dubious faces. "What?"

Poppy crinkled her nose. "He's so . . ."

"So what?" Jordan barked. "He's a damn good detective."

"I am sure he is, but he's so boyish and . . ."

"And what?" Jordan demanded.

"Goofy," Poppy sighed. "I just don't see him flourishing as a suitor for Jessie Walters. I can see her sending him home before he's even had a chance to question the other bachelors."

"What are you talking about? Lasky's a good-looking guy!" Jordan argued.

"Yes, I am sure any girl would be lucky to have him, he's very cute, but what you need is someone striking, who looks good in a tuxedo, who possesses a natural charm that will certainly win over Jessie and convince everyone connected to the show that he's there for the right reasons."

"Look, I don't run a male modeling agency. I don't have someone like that to send in undercover."

"No, but fortunately we do," Poppy said, eyeing Matt.

Detective Jordan glanced at Matt, who smiled at him expectantly. "No way . . ."

"He's perfect for the show!" Wyatt piped in. "And he's a trained detective!"

"That's a stretch, kid," Jordan scoffed.

But Poppy instinctively knew this was a brilliant idea, and with a little nudging, Detective Jordan would also see that Matt Flowers was born to be one of the impossibly handsome, charming bachelors on *My Dream Man*.

Chapter 28

Iris stared curiously at the elderly woman standing on her doorstep next to Matt. "Who is this?"

Matt put an arm around the gray-haired woman with thick black glasses, a rosy complexion, and a colorful print blouse and white capri pants and matching espadrilles, and a cane. "Iris, I would like you to meet my aunt Beatrice."

Iris studied the old woman, who had to be well into her eighties. "You never mentioned having an aunt before."

"I'm sure I have," Matt insisted. "Aunt Beatrice raised me ever since I was a little boy."

"What about your parents?" Iris asked.

"They weren't around much. Soon after I was born, they came to the conclusion that having a child cramped their freewheeling lifestyle. They were more into hiking to the top of Machu Picchu than raising a kid, and so they dropped me off to stay with Aunt Beatrice."

"Hello. Iris, is it?" Aunt Beatrice asked in a sweet but scratchy voice.

"That's right. Nice to meet you," Iris said gruffly.

"Aren't you going to invite us in?" Matt asked.

"I am afraid now is not a good time," Iris said. "Violet is here. She is in my kitchen making lunch for . . ." Iris leaned forward and whispered, "You know who . . . out in the garage office."

She was referring to Poppy in her current hideout.

Matt pushed his way inside. "Well, don't worry, we'll only stay a minute. I want Aunt Beatrice to meet Violet, too."

Iris balked, but Matt was already in the house leading his aunt by the hand toward the kitchen.

"Violet! Can you come out here for a second? There's someone I would like you to meet."

Violet rushed out, an apron tied around her waist, carrying a turkey sandwich, pickle, and side salad on a turquoise Fiesta plate. "Oh, hello, Matt," she said, then smiled pleasantly at Aunt Beatrice. "And . . . ?"

"This is my aunt Beatrice," Matt said, smiling.

Violet wiped her hand on her apron and stuck it out for Aunt Beatrice to shake. "It's lovely to meet you. I'm Violet. And this is Iris."

"We met at the door. I told them this was not a good time," Iris huffed.

"Don't be silly, it's never inconvenient to meet a relative of Matt's. Where are you visiting from, may I ask?"

"Bar Harbor, Maine," Aunt Beatrice answered.

"It's been a dream of mine to go there one day and see Acadia National Park. I hear it's spectacularly beautiful."

"It most certainly is," Beatrice said. "I was born and raised there, but I had no idea just how gorgeous it was until I got out and saw the rest of the world. Nowhere else on the planet can even compare to it."

"I beg to differ. I can show you a number of places in Bavaria that I am sure are just as beautiful," Iris snorted.

Aunt Beatrice studied Iris's face. "You look so familiar to me, are you sure we have not met before?"

"Yes, I have never seen you before in my life," Iris said.

"My late husband, Cecil, and I traveled through Europe when we were younger, and you remind me of a lovely singer we saw once in Munich. . . ."

Iris's eyes popped open. "That could have been me. I was quite a popular chanteuse back in the day."

"This woman was so talented, I remember her enchanting us with her heaven-sent voice," Aunt Beatrice gushed.

"Yes, that was me! I received so many flowers after every performance I had to donate most of them to the local funeral parlor," Iris said.

Matt snickered.

Annoyed, Iris gave him a little side-eye before turning her attention back to the sweet little old lady she was quickly growing fond of. "Would you like some coffee, Bea? Can I call you Bea?"

"Of course, all my friends do," Aunt Beatrice said.

"She's really warming up to you now," Violet said, grinning. "Usually all it takes is a healthy dose of flattery."

"Nobody was talking to you, Violet," Iris snapped. "Now, why don't you take Poppy her lunch? I'm sure she's starving."

Violet froze, her eyes widening in horror, as she tightly gripped the lunch plate in her hand.

Iris instantly noticed Violet's sudden change in demeanor. "What's wrong with you?"

With her free hand, Violet pulled Iris aside and whispered frantically, "You just said her name."

"Whose name?"

Violet mouthed, "Poppy."

"What? When?"

Violet leaned in closer and whispered almost inaudibly, "Just now."

Iris, realizing her mistake, spun around to Matt and Aunt Beatrice, and, wringing her hands, managed to spit out, "I meant Polly, my dear friend Polly, who is staying with me, here for a few weeks from . . . from . . ." Iris was drawing a blank.

"Kansas City," Violet piped in. "The Paris of the Prairie, as they say."

"Do they?" Matt asked, smirking.

"I . . . I didn't mean to say Poppy, I got confused. Poppy was on the tip of my tongue because sadly that's the name of another close friend, who recently died. You . . . you may have read about it in the papers," Iris fumbled to explain.

Matt held up a hand. "Iris, it's okay. You don't have to worry about Aunt Beatrice. She won't say anything about Poppy still being alive."

Iris gasped. "You *told* her? We agreed not to say anything to anyone!"

"I didn't have to say anything," Matt said. "Aunt Beatrice already knows everything that's going on."

Aunt Beatrice reached up and pulled the gray wig from her head and then removed her glasses.

Iris reared back. "What on earth . . . ? Is that you, Poppy?"

Violet stepped up close to Beatrice, still not understanding what was happening. "It's not Poppy! Poppy has blue eyes, this woman has brown eyes."

"They're colored contacts, Violet," Poppy said.

"What is going on? Why are you wearing this disguise?" Violet demanded to know.

"Because every bachelor on *My Dream Man* is allowed to have a relationship adviser, someone close to him to help guide him as he tries to win Jessie's heart. Guys can show up with a buddy, or a sibling, or a coworker, or in my case, my dear old aunt Beatrice, who raised me and knows me better than anyone," Matt said.

Iris shook her head. "This is too dangerous. What if someone recognizes her?"

"I just fooled my two best friends in the whole world," Poppy said, setting the wig and glasses down on an end table next to Iris's couch. "I'm sure I can pull the wool over the eyes of a bunch of strangers."

"I need Poppy with me, she's seen the killer, at least

from a distance. If she's around the set she might pick up on a characteristic or feature that stands out to her, that will help us identify him," Matt said.

"I still don't like it," Iris barked.

"We will be extremely careful," Poppy promised. "Now the next thing I have to do is convince the show's executive producer."

"Detective Jordan got him to agree to let me on the show to ferret out this guy, but we haven't told him about Poppy still being alive, so he thinks I'm coming to LA with my actual Aunt Bea."

"If he hasn't met Poppy, then there should be no problem," Violet said.

"There's the wrinkle—we *have* met," Poppy explained.

"When he found out who I was, he offered his condolences for Poppy's untimely death, and mentioned that he and Poppy dated once back in the mid–nineteen eighties," Matt said.

Poppy shrugged. "I have no recollection of meeting him whatsoever, which tells me the date must not have been all that memorable. It was so long ago, we're probably okay with all this old-age makeup on my face."

Fingers crossed.

It was critical they keep up the charade.

Poppy Harmon had to remain dead because their only hope of catching the killer was for him to keep thinking he had gotten away with her murder.

Chapter 29

"Our relationship was quite serious back in the eighties," Andy Keenan said as he led Matt and Poppy, in disguise as Aunt Beatrice, up the walk to the Los Feliz mansion, where *My Dream Man* was filming. "At one point, I considered proposing to Poppy."

Matt raised an eyebrow and shot a quick glance in Poppy's direction. She shook her head, letting him know this had definitely *never* happened. She barely even remembered this man who was around her age, and although it was entirely possible they had actually dated once, maybe twice, during her *Jack Colt* heyday, there was absolutely no chance the relationship had ever progressed to the point where marriage was ever even remotely considered.

Poppy's take on this entire story that Keenan was selling about his past with her was that the veteran reality TV show producer, just like her vexing rival Serena Saunders, was just embellishing since he believed Poppy was no longer around to refute any claims and correct the record. And she had to resist the powerful urge to tear off her wig and old-age makeup and reveal herself in order to call him out.

"Poppy had a lot of suitors lining up trying to impress

her back then, so you can imagine how special I felt that out of all those adoring men, including big stars like Rod Harper, she somehow, inexplicably, chose me, a relative nobody!" Keenan declared brightly, bolstering his own ego and humbly bragging at the same time.

Poppy could see Matt staring at Keenan, a rather short, stout, balding man, not unattractive, but hardly a stunner, trying to picture him almost forty years younger.

For the life of her, Poppy still could not remember ever meeting this man. She racked her brain, but kept drawing a blank.

"I hadn't spoken to her in years, but she will certainly be missed," Keenan said solemnly.

"Yes, she will," Matt said, suppressing a smirk.

Keenan then playfully nudged Matt in the ribs and winked, "And a real wildcat in the boudoir, if you know what I mean."

Poppy crinkled her nose in disgust.

If she was certain of one thing, it was that she had never, *ever* endured any carnal activities with this lying fool.

Keenan turned to Poppy. "You must be tired after such a long drive from Palm Springs, Aunt Bea!" Keenan shouted, assuming the old woman was hard of hearing. "We have a director's chair with your name on it waiting for you inside so you can sit down and rest!"

"I'm not deaf," Poppy growled. "I have a hearing aid, but I hardly ever need it."

Her irritated tone took Keenan by surprise and he lowered his voice. "Of course. My mother is ninety-two and is still spry and sharp as a tack, just like you."

"Isn't that special?" Poppy sneered in a mocking tone. She was still irked that this man had conjured up a fantasy relationship with her out of thin air.

If Keenan sensed her displeasure, he chose to ignore it.

As they entered the Los Feliz mansion, Poppy soaked in the old Hollywood ambience. Although the furniture had been updated, the design and fixtures evoked a past era, as if right out of the 1930s or 1940s, a Spanish Colonial Revival style abode that could have been used as a location in the Billy Wilder film classic *Double Indemnity*. As they veered right into the large living room with an incredibly high ceiling, they found a full working film crew setting up lights and cameras for the scene to be shot where Jessie Walters meets the five bachelors vying for her attention.

Poppy suddenly found Andy Keenan taking her gently by the arm and escorting her over to a director's chair. "Here we go, Aunt Bea."

"I'm not your aunt, I'm *his* aunt," she said, pointing toward Matt. "Just call me Beatrice."

"Very well," Keenan said, chastened. "Can I help you up? These director's chairs are a little high off the ground, kind of tough to climb for someone so . . ." His words trailed off. He knew he had stepped in it.

"I'm fine, thank you," Poppy said curtly, hopping up in the chair and taking in her surroundings, hanging her cane on the arm.

"Okay, I'm going to go check on Jessie. Why don't you two get to know the other bachelors and their advisers?" Keenan suggested before rushing off.

Matt leaned down and whispered in Poppy's ear. "I said in my video interview that Aunt Bea was a soft-spoken, sweet, kind, adorably cute old lady. You're coming across as a little . . . cranky."

"I'm sorry, but he totally made up that story about us dating in the nineteen eighties. Why do people feel the need to misrepresent how close they were to someone after they're dead?"

"Beats me. Maybe it makes them feel more special," Matt said. "Are you sure you never met him?"

"No, I met hundreds of men back then. I just have no recollection of him ever wooing me, or me allowing him to try to woo me, for that matter," Poppy huffed.

Matt chuckled. "I believe you. I've seen your old *Jack Colt* reruns. You were definitely way out of his league."

Poppy scanned the living room set and quickly identified the other four bachelors, who were milling about waiting for the shooting to start. She recognized them from the dossiers put together by the casting department that Andy Keenan had shared with Matt.

All of them were handsome, professional men, impressive picks in their own right.

There was Neal, the astronaut.

The rodeo cowboy, Ty.

The NASCAR driver, Beau.

And finally, Antony, a purported English royal.

Now this being television, Poppy knew that upon closer inspection, all of their titles were tenuous at best. Wyatt had done his own research on the four men and quickly discovered the cover of the book was far more exciting than what was actually inside. Neal claimed to be an astronaut, but in reality, he was just starting a training program. Only a few in the program ever advanced to the next level, and it turned out Neal had already been cut and so would not be jetting into space anytime soon, not in this lifetime anyway. Rodeo star Ty worked on a ranch in Montana as a low-paid ranch hand, and had been in one rodeo, as a clown that popped out of a barrel during a bull-riding competition. NASCAR driver Beau from Texas had never actually been in a race, just a few trial runs. And British royal Antony, although his accent was convincing, was only a distant cousin twice removed. No serious royal watcher had ever even heard of him. But physically they all fit the bill, tall and good looking, perfect Prince Charmings, at least on paper. And all four men made for good television, so the producers didn't want to ask too many questions.

Poppy zeroed in on them chatting with one another,

meticulously examining them one by one, as Matt glided over to introduce himself as "the actor" bachelor.

Neal.

Ty.

Beau.

Antony.

All of them were clean shaven and seemed to have disparate personalities. Try as she might, Poppy simply could not identify any of them as her would-be killer. Without the beard or the cap, none of them looked even remotely familiar. If he was indeed one of these four bachelors, he was, as they had already determined, truly a chameleon.

Poppy diverted her attention over to the group of dating advisers, of which she was one. They were a motley-looking group consisting of two best bros, a sister, and an ex-girlfriend. If the killer was one of the bachelors in this room, then his adviser was a fake, an accomplice, and had to be lying.

But which one?

Suddenly there was a flurry of activity as Jessie Walters, the bachelorette in search of her dream man, swept into the room. She was stunning in a strapless metallic bustier gown, hair coiffured, her neck adorned with an expensive eighteen-karat Glamazon Mini Disc Pendant Necklace with Diamonds. She sported a blinding smile that showed off her perfectly white teeth. A vision of loveliness tailor made for a reality dating show. The whole room seemed to stop as if frozen in time as everyone, both men and women, took in her staggering beauty.

Even Poppy, who had previously met Jessie in a less formal setting, was taken aback by the startling transformation. She was like a Disney princess come to life.

After a nauseatingly long introduction by Andy Keenan, the director hurriedly called action so they could film Jessie's first introductions to her suitors and capture all their flirty exchanges. Poppy watched from the sidelines, as the advisers would not be introduced in this scene. The bachelors fell all over themselves to get face time with Jessie, including Matt, who was, not surprisingly, very adept at grabbing the spotlight and effortlessly steering Jessie's focus toward him.

Poppy could tell that he was in it to win it.

At one point, Jessie's gaze fell upon Poppy, in her Aunt Bea getup. Her eyes lingered momentarily, but then glazed over and moved on without a hint of recognition.

This is good, Poppy thought to herself. Her cover was working. She knew she had to be perfect and make no missteps because the stakes were far too high.

It was imperative they unmask this killer before he had the opportunity to strike again.

Chapter 30

After production wrapped on the first day's cocktail party, where Jessie had the opportunity to meet and have initial conversations with her five handsome suitors, the cast and their advisers headed off to their assigned rooms in the mansion for a few hours' sleep before filming was scheduled to resume the following morning on the first group date.

Jessie met the men in front of the house at seven-thirty sharp, where they were all transported by shuttle bus to a nightclub on nearby Hollywood Boulevard, where the men would compete in an exotic dance revue for Jessie, which was basically an excuse for five hot guys to perform a striptease in front of the camera with a delighted Jessie clapping and cheering them all on. Of course, the entire goal of the date was to excite viewers and show off the ripped bodies of the bachelors, rather than illuminate any of their personalities for Jessie.

Matt had shown up earlier in the morning at Poppy's door. He had been tipped off by Andy Keenan on what he would be doing today, and was nervous about taking off all his clothes in front of a camera. Poppy had given him a pep talk, encouraging him to just go with the flow and use the whole demeaning scene as an opportunity to grill his fellow contestants to see if he could get the killer to somehow slip up and give himself away.

"Think of this as just another acting challenge," Poppy had said encouragingly, although she could see Matt was still stressing. He did not want videos of himself bumping and grinding and swinging around on a pole half naked living forever on the Internet. But Poppy had reminded him that he had a job to do—they were here to ensure no one else got killed. And that had to be worth the sacrifice. That finally seemed to do the trick. Matt was outside in the driveway waiting with the other bachelors when the shuttle bus pulled up to ferry them to the nightclub.

The advisers were not needed on this day, so they were instructed to stay behind at the house until further notice. Poppy received a note under her door that breakfast would be served outside by the pool, so she quickly applied her old-age makeup, pinned her gray wig in place, and dressed in a soft print dress that looked more like a surgical gown. Donning a beige knitted shawl even though it was nearly eighty degrees outside, she grabbed the wooden cane she had brought with her and made her way outside, where she found the other four dating advisers gathered around a patio table, eating eggs and waffles and fruit.

There was a food station set up off to the side, so Poppy grabbed a plate and gingerly scooped some cottage cheese onto it. A server behind the station offered to make her an omelette but Poppy politely declined, settling for a sliced piece of melon, a bit of scrambled eggs, and a plain piece of toast before sitting down with the others. She took a forkful of the cottage cheese and shakily raised it to her mouth as the others watched silently. After dropping a bit down the front of her dress to really sell her cover, one of the advisers, Maggie, a vibrant young blonde with bright red lipstick and too much mascara, leaned over and touched Poppy's arm.

"How are you doing this morning, Aunt Bea?!" Maggie shouted in a thick Southern drawl.

Poppy adjusted her fake hearing aid, straining to hear her. "Huh?"

"I said, how are you this morning?!" Maggie shouted louder.

"Oh, fine, fine, thank you, dear," Poppy answered in a scratchy, almost weak voice.

"That's a lovely dress you're wearing," the other young woman at the table said in a clipped tone. This was Kate, very regal, very British, with long dark hair, pursed lips, and a pert nose.

Poppy did everything she could not to burst out laughing. It was obvious the girl was humoring her with a healthy dose of condescension, so she just nodded while pretending to struggle to keep some scrambled eggs on her fork as she gamely tried to shovel it into her mouth.

A server appeared with a pot of coffee to fill everyone's ceramic mugs with the MY DREAM MAN logo on them.

Maggie was NASCAR Beau's sister and Kate was apparently English royal Antony's ex-girlfriend. From what Poppy could gather from their brief introductions the night before at the cocktail party, Maggie, as overprotective sister, was always suspicious of any girl who entered her cherished brother Beau's orbit, and so she was going to be a very strict adviser, more concerned with Jessie's ulterior motives than her beloved brother Beau's. Kate, on the other hand, was more easygoing and carefree. She had told everyone, with the cameras rolling of course, that she and Antony had dated for almost two years, but had come to the conclusion that they were better friends than lovers. She stuck around, wanting the best for her unlucky-in-love ex, determined to find him a woman who would make him happy. Of the two young women, Maggie was the friendlier one, telling Poppy, or Aunt Bea, that she reminded her of her own beloved aunt who recently passed away, and describing "Bea" as "cute as a bug in a rug" and "sweeter than cherry pie."

As for the two men who were also at the table, they occasionally eyed the two younger women with wolfish grins, but pretty much ignored Poppy altogether, having no use for a lovable little old lady. They were far too busy talking sports and becoming fast buddies. They were both well built, probably from spending a lot of time in the gym, one short and compact with a shaved head and goatee, the other medium height with blond hair and a fading scar on his cheek. The taller one, Monty, best friend of Cowboy Ty, described himself as "a surfer dude" with no interest in horses or rodeos, but he and Ty had bonded in a Texas bar two years ago over a shared love of baseball when LA-based Monty was visiting family there. The scar on his face, he explained, came from a giant wave in Australia that got the best of him, which unfortunately caused his face to collide with his surfboard. The shorter, quieter one, Charlie, who was Astronaut Neal's pal, was stingy on details about his relationship with his bachelor, except for the fact that he had been in the same astronaut training program as Neal.

Poppy did her best to pump each one of them for more information, but the foursome, all of whom seemed to be exchanging flirtatious looks and sexually suggestive banter, soon abandoned Poppy at the table and scattered to undress for a fun dip in the pool. Poppy waited by herself, exchanging pleasantries with the caterers and staff, and soon all four advisers returned, the women in skimpy bikinis, the men in tight Speedos. They splashed around in the giant pool playing water polo, but using the game as more of an excuse to dunk and grab and touch each other.

Poppy retreated to a lounge chair with a Louise Penny mystery novel, but kept a keen eye on the goings-on. Her initial assessment of the advisers seemed to suggest that three of them, Maggie, Kate, and Monty, struck Poppy as legitimate because they all seemed to freely spool out significant, even intimate details about their friends. Only Charlie, who was less forthcoming, appeared, at least on the surface, to be suspicious because he was less willing than the others to discuss his friendship with Astronaut Neal, either by design or because he just didn't really know the guy well, which would suggest he was a fake plant.

When the foursome finally emerged from the pool and disappeared, quite likely to hook up with one another, Poppy suspected, she returned to her room, where she waited for Matt to show up after his day of shooting. She knew a dinner was scheduled for all the bachelors, their advisers, and Jessie for eight o'clock, and so she expected Matt to seek her out before then.

By seven-thirty, she was starting to get worried, but then there was a knock at the door, and she opened it to find Matt, looking completely worn out.

"How did it go?" Poppy inquired.

He grimaced. "There was a lighting issue so they had to reshoot my striptease *three* times. It was humiliating. But Jessie seemed to enjoy it."

"What about the other bachelors?"

Matt shrugged. "It's hard to tell what's going on with any of them. They're all holding their cards pretty close to the vest, but I chalk that up to seeing me as the competition. The cowboy, Ty, and the British guy, Antony, were both affable enough, at least. But the other two didn't want to give me the time of day. Beau was just cold to me. Every time I approached him, he'd just walk away. And Neal, man, when I tried chatting him up, he just looked at me with these dead eyes and said, 'I'm not here to make friends, I'm here to win Jessie.' I took the hint and kept my distance the rest of the day."

Poppy relayed her suspicions about Neal's friend, Charlie, and how his unsociable demeanor had raised a red flag, compared to the others, and how it had prompted her to review the dossier on Neal one more time.

"I spent half the afternoon staring at the photos he submitted to the casting department. . . ."

"And?"

Poppy slowly shook her head. "Nothing. I tried picturing him with a beard and cap. I even drew them on him with a black marker. But I just can't be sure. It could be him. But then again, it might not be him. Then I drew beards and caps on all of the others. It just made me more confused than ever."

Poppy sighed, frustrated.

Matt put a comforting arm around her shoulders. "Don't worry, Poppy, I know in my gut he's here. We will find him."

Poppy prayed he was right.

Chapter 31

The one advantage you have when everyone around you believes you are ninety years old is the constant stream of people wanting to make sure you are comfortable and that you have everything you need. Poppy certainly appreciated all the young production assistants on *My Dream Man* who adopted her as their own mostly because, she assumed, her Aunt Beatrice character reminded them of their own grandmother.

As the production moved ninety-five miles north of Los Angeles to a posh privately owned winery on the outskirts of town, Poppy found herself inundated with helpful kids bringing her hot tea, a pillow to slip behind her back in her director's chair, a cookie from craft services. And although grateful for their attentiveness, she would have much preferred they just simply ignore her because she was determined to keep a low profile and observe the proceedings unnoticed.

The company was filming the second group date, Jessie and her five suitors at a wine tasting, where they could interact and get to know one another some more. After a brief tour of the premises, the crew set up in the main wine-tasting room, where Jessie and her men would enjoy a mixed flight of red and white wines. The dating advisers, Aunt Bea included, were shunted off to the side, where they could watch but stay out of the way.

Tension appeared to be mounting among the five bachelors as they angled to get some private time with Jessie while the three cameramen recording all the action worked hard running around to capture every moment.

Much to Poppy's surprise, Matt exerted an unexpected brazenness by pushing his way past the other fellows first, and landing right in front of Jessie, taking her gently by the arm and requesting they slip away to the corner of the room to enjoy their wine and have a more intimate conversation. Jessie nodded, and they retreated from the others to be alone, except for the two dozen producers and crew members following them around on their heels and hanging on to their every word.

Poppy could tell Matt was revving up the charm, drawing Jesse in with his intoxicating personality, which, as Iris once described it, was "his superpower."

"I can't tell you what a thrill it is to finally have a quiet moment with you. I've been so looking forward to getting to know you better, to find out what makes Jessie tick," Matt said, raising his glass. "Here's to the beginning of something great."

Jessie gamely clinked glasses with him, but Poppy could tell instantly that something was on her mind.

To his credit, so did Matt.

He zeroed in on her slight grimace.

"Did I say something wrong?"

"No," Jessie replied, shaking her head slightly. "You have been perfect since you got here. Almost *too* perfect."

The whole room fell into an uncomfortable silence.

Poppy noticed the other bachelors stop talking with each other, glancing over in anticipation of what was about to come.

Jessie took a dramatic pause before continuing, almost

as if she had been trained to do so. "Matt, you seem like a lovely guy, and on the surface you check all the boxes. . . ."

"But?"

"My worry is you're an actor. Actors can convey different emotions at will. It's what they do. And . . . and so I fear you might be acting, that doing this show is a way to promote your Hollywood career. . . ."

"I can assure you, Jessie, that is absolutely *not* the case."

Poppy knew he was being sincere in the moment.

He wasn't here for his acting career.

He was here to protect her and keep her safe, but perhaps Jessie was picking up on the fact that he was not here to find true love. Poppy also knew Matt would never carelessly toy with a woman's emotions. He had always been so earnest and honest with her own daughter, Heather, during the time they dated. But this was a real conflict, and if Jessie dismissed Matt today, their investigation would be dead in the water.

"The thing is, I dated an actor last year, and he too said all the right things, but in the end he broke my heart," Jessie explained quietly. "It hurt me deeply, to the point where I wasn't sure I would ever be able to trust a man again."

"I'm not that man, Jessie, I promise you," Matt said.

But there was a strain in his voice, almost imperceptible, but Poppy picked up on it because she was so close to him. He was intrinsically such an honorable, decent man he could not completely hide the ulterior motive for his presence.

"I just want to be up front with you about my feelings," Jessie said, eyeing him suspiciously.

"And I appreciate your candor," Matt said, his mind obviously racing on how to stay in the game. "I know you're genuinely here to find love, and I hope you take a chance to get to know me, the *real* me."

Poppy could see the producers practically salivating over this unexpected twist, Jessie's heartbreak at the hands of a callous actor, Matt inadvertently stirring up those past emotions—it would make for great television.

Matt went in for a hug. Jessie allowed it, but her body stiffened and she turned her cheek away in case he instinctively tried to land a kiss on her lips. Everyone could plainly see how cold and remote she was acting.

This did not bode well for Matt's future on *My Dream Man*.

"We should probably go back and join the others," Jessie suggested.

"Of course. I don't want to hog all of your time," Matt said with a defeated tone.

Matt turned to Poppy and gave her a tight smile.

She knew he was unwilling to fake it, to assure Jessie he was developing authentic feelings for her when he actually wasn't, but that inability was going to cost him.

As Jessie returned to the wine-tasting table, her electric smile instantly returned, especially as she gabbed and flirted with Ty and Neal. Jessie appeared to Poppy to be laser focused on the cowboy and the astronaut, less so with NASCAR man and Mr. British royalty. Matt hung back a respectful distance, still demoralized from his frank encounter with Jessie.

As Jessie laughed and cooed with Neal, at one point running a hand through his thick, wavy hair, Antony the royal was growing visibly frustrated that he was being denied his own personal time with Jessie. He quite noticeably began gulping down glass after glass of wine—red, white, rose, it really did not matter. Poppy watched with concern as he began to stumble and sway. When Neal finally stepped away and Ty tried to slide in and get some face time with Jessie, Antony, whose previously perfect complexion was now red and splotchy, forcefully body-checked Ty out of the way to get to her.

"I am here now, darling, so what are your other two wishes?" Antony spit out, then downed the rest of his wine and grinned lasciviously.

Jessie stared at him incredulously. "Is that really the pickup line you're going with, Antony?"

He ignored her, cupping a hand to his mouth and calling out, "The British are coming! The British are coming!" Then he pointed a finger in front of her face. "And it's all your fault, baby. . . ."

Jessie's face darkened. "Are you *drunk*?"

Wobbling from side to side, his eyes at half-mast, Antony gasped with fake indignation. "What?" He looked around at the crew, shouting, "She thinks I'm off me face!"

"Oh, dear," Kate, Antony's ex-girlfriend, whispered, as she suddenly appeared next to Poppy, who was sitting in her director's chair. "I was afraid this might happen. Antony tends to get a bit out of sorts when he's nervous."

"Do I detect a cockney accent?" Poppy asked.

Kate knelt down slightly so she was eye level with Poppy. "Liverpool."

"Not exactly the House of Windsor," Poppy said.

Kate bristled a bit, but did her best to defend Antony's purported lineage. "You may not see him in any photos at Princess Eugenie's wedding, but he is definitely related to the royal family, and anyone who insinuates otherwise is dead wrong."

By now, Antony was so inebriated he was spraying spittle directly into Jessie's face as he desperately, sloppily tried engaging in a conversation with her. She was clearly over him, and was desperate for someone to swoop in and rescue her. Both Matt and Ty picked up on her cues and rushed over, each taking Antony by an arm and escorting him out.

"Where are we going? I haven't tried the Sangiovese or the Petite Syrah!"

That left Neal and Beau to happily move in to check on Jessie's well-being and commiserate with her on how she had to endure the antics of a drunken fool. They reveled in bad-mouthing the competition.

Poppy turned to see Andy Keenan laughing, thrilled with the turn of events.

"It looks like you should rethink your screening process," Poppy said to Andy in an admonishing tone in line with her ninety-year-old grandmother persona.

Andy raised an eyebrow. "Why? Because the Brit got rip-roaring drunk and caused a little drama?"

"He clearly has a drinking problem," Poppy said.

"Duh," Andy replied, rolling his eyes. "That's what I was counting on. Everyone we talked to about him said he was a booze hound. Which is *exactly* why we chose him to be on the show. I was praying he'd drink too much and cause a scene, and that's what we got! It's going to make for a great episode. Why do you think we came up with this whole wine-tasting date in the first place?"

Poppy's mouth dropped open.

Andy excitedly skittered away to talk to his cameramen to make sure they got every last embarrassing moment recorded.

Poppy turned to Kate, who just shrugged it off and walked away to refill her own glass of wine.

Even though they were here for a good reason, Poppy found this whole enterprise utterly distasteful.

Chapter 32

The courtyard by the pool at the Los Feliz mansion had been decorated with Italian lights. Jessie's spot where she would be selecting the four bachelors to remain in contention was set up in front of a lovely, shimmering fountain with a stone statue of a cherub brought in to give the appearance that Cupid himself was watching over the hopeful bachelorette.

The crew worked feverishly to make everything look perfect before nightfall so they could begin shooting this pivotal sequence in which Jessie would call out the names of the four lucky men, and then, of course, say a tearful good-bye to the one who would be eliminated and sent home.

All five bachelors gathered around the fountain, standing shoulder to shoulder as if they were about to be put through a police lineup. They were similarly dressed in slacks, open-collar shirts, and sharp sports jackets with the exception of Antony, who wore a Union Jack necktie.

The advisers, including Poppy as Aunt Bea, stood by just off-camera, ready for their cue. Whoever was attached to the loser of the evening would rush forward to offer comfort before he bid adieu to Jessie and hopefully wished her all the luck in the world in her search for true love. A young production assistant hovered nearby in case Matt was ousted in order to offer a helping hand to the "frail" Aunt Bea, who might need assistance in reaching her beloved nephew. Poppy had to constantly make a show of trying to act slightly feeble in order to sell her cover.

Poppy's phone buzzed and she used her cane to step away from the other advisers, who were all mingling with each other and basically ignoring her anyway, to answer the call.

She glanced at the screen.

It was Violet.

She tapped the green answer button and raised her phone close to her ear, whispering, "What have you got, Violet?"

"Wyatt's been busy researching the British royal, what's his name again . . . ?"

Poppy whispered, almost inaudibly, "Antony."

"Yes, him. Apparently he's telling the truth about his lineage. He is related to the royal family, but just barely, and not by blood. However, he certainly is connected. We also have been tracking his social media presence over the past few years and have talked to enough people in his orbit to verify all the details. He is definitely legit. And so is Kate, his ex-girlfriend. Her Instagram account is an endless stream of photos of herself with Antony. Wyatt seems to think she still has feelings for him since they broke up last year because she is still posting about him practically every day."

Poppy directed her gaze over to Kate. She had broken away from the other advisers and was staring over at Antony, who was nervously adjusting his tie. It was suddenly obvious to Poppy by the way she looked at him that Kate was still very much in love with him, despite what she was telling everybody.

"So he's not the killer. Great, let me tell Matt," Poppy said.

"How's Matt doing? We're all dying to know back here at the boring office!" Violet said.

"I'm nervous. Jessie has made it crystal clear that she has an aversion to actors, and I'm afraid she's going to give him the boot tonight."

"But how could she possibly do that? Matt is perfectly adorable!" Violet protested.

"Just keep him in your prayers, light some candles, do whatever it takes to send good vibes," Poppy said before ending the call. She couldn't very well drag Matt off the set to alert him to the news about Antony, so she texted him. She watched as Matt felt his phone buzz in his back pocket, pull it out, and read the text. He gave Poppy a conspiratorial wink before wandering over to Andy Keenan, who was standing by the pool. The two men huddled together as Matt filled him in while the other four bachelors watched curiously, not sure what was going on.

Poppy then watched Andy pat Matt on the back and head over to Jessie, who had just swept onto the scene looking stunning in a silver sequin side-cut-out halter gown. Andy and Jessie talked in hushed tones.

Matt bounded over to Poppy.

"Can I get you anything, Aunt Bea, before we start?!" Matt shouted loud enough for everyone to hear.

"No, dear, everyone has been so sweet checking on me, but I'm just fine," Poppy replied.

Matt leaned in close. "I told him Antony's not the killer, so he's going to try to convince Jessie to send him packing tonight so we have one less guy to worry about."

"Do you think she'll agree?"

Matt shrugged. "Who knows? She's a tough read. I thought she liked me until the group date at the winery."

Poppy watched Jessie listening intently to what Andy had to say. Then after a brief exchange, Jessie walked away and took her place in front of the fountain.

Andy approached Matt, then pulled him aside, but still close enough for Poppy to overhear their conversation.

"No dice," Andy said in a low voice. "Despite him causing that scene at the winery, she wants to keep him around and give him a second chance. I guess she has a thing for royalty, probably a big fan of *The Crown*."

"So who's she going to send home?"

Andy flashed him a sympathetic look.

"Oh . . . ," Matt groaned.

"Sorry, bud, I tried talking her out of it, but she is pretty set in her decision. Just promise me you will act surprised when it happens."

"Can't you talk to her again? I'm here to keep her safe. We think there's a killer among us and her life could be in real danger—"

"That's why I let you on the show in the first place, but we have security all around protecting us, and as much as I can nudge her and give her my opinion, at the end of the day it's her decision. Otherwise, if word got out we put a lot of pressure on her, then we'd be done. No one would ever watch another season again."

The assistant director scurried over to Andy. "We're about ready to go, Andy."

He clapped the guy on the back. "Thanks." He turned back to Matt. "Remember, you have no idea you are going home tonight."

Andy trotted off.

Matt turned to Poppy. "Looks like we're done."

Shooting soon got under way after Matt rejoined the other bachelors. After a champagne toast to their time together so far and an impassioned speech from Jessie about how her eyes had been opened to the possibility of true love with one, perhaps two of the men standing before her, and how excited she was to explore these budding relationships even further, it was time to announce the names of the men who would continue on this life-changing quest.

After a long, almost interminable dramatic pause, Jessie's eyes settled on the astronaut.

"Neal," Jessie said with a tender smile. "Would you continue on this journey with me?"

Neal dropped his head in relief, then marched forward and took Jessie's hands in his own. "Yes, of course I will."

He gave her a peck on the cheek and then stepped aside, allowing her to return her attention to the four remaining men.

Another endless pause.

"Ty," Jessie said, eyes twinkling. "Would you continue on this journey with me?"

Ty whooped and hollered like a true cowboy before vaulting toward her and enveloping her in a bear hug that nearly ripped her jaw-droppingly expensive dress. "Yes, ma'am!"

She pulled away first, with a hand raised in front of her as if signaling him to calm down. He quickly got the message and joined Neal off to the side.

Beau was next.

He was more subdued in his reaction to his name being called, but Poppy could tell that all the women around watching, Jessie included, found his smoldering remoteness incredibly sexy.

Only two left.

Poppy held her breath.

It was painstakingly nerve wracking despite knowing the outcome. Matt stood resolutely, hands clasped in front of him, waiting for the inevitable. Antony was sweating, not sure if he was still going to be in the game after the spectacle he had caused at the winery.

Jessie flashed her eyes toward Antony, then to Matt, then back to Antony, as if she were debating with herself, even though her mind was already made up. They finally settled on Antony and she opened her mouth to speak.

"Wait!" a man cried.

All eyes turned to Cowboy Ty.

Jessie stared at him, confused.

Ty took a deep breath and then slowly exhaled. "I promised myself I wouldn't do this, but it's been bugging me all day, and I can no longer stay silent about this." He stepped forward, his phone in his hand. "I didn't come here to sabotage the other dudes, or cause any trouble, but I think it's only fair that Jessie know what's really going on."

Poppy noticed Andy's eyes practically popping out of his head. He was in the dark like everyone else.

Ty raised his phone and showed everyone a video. It was Antony, outside the winery, still drunk, on the phone with a friend back in London.

"She's pretty enough, yeah, but not a lot upstairs, if you know what I mean," he slurred. "Spark? Are you kidding? No, but I can tell she's enamored with me so I'm still a serious contender. Just think, if she actually picks me in the end, that's going to raise my profile to the point where those idiot royals who have been ignoring me my whole life will finally be forced to sit up and take notice. I may get an afternoon tea with William and Kate out of this yet."

The video froze and Ty slowly lowered the phone.

There was a stillness, a stunned silence except for the water fountain flowing behind a now teary-eyed Jessie.

"I-I can explain . . . ," Antony stammered.

A production assistant rushed over and handed Jessie a tissue. She slowly, methodically wiped her eyes, making sure not to mess up her mascara, then turned her steely gaze toward Matt.

"Matt . . . ," Jessie said, sniffling. "Would you continue on this journey with me?"

Matt stepped over to her and gently placed his hands on her bare arms. "Yes, and I am so sorry you had to hear that. It's inexcusable."

"Thank you," she said, quivering.

"Are you all right?" he asked, concerned.

She nodded and forced a smile.

Then she turned to Neal, Ty, and Beau. "Thank you, gentlemen. I will see you tomorrow. Good night, everyone."

She scurried off like Cinderella at midnight except she didn't leave a shoe behind.

"Jessie, wait!" Antony cried.

But he didn't chase after her because he knew it was over for him. He glared angrily at Ty, who refused to be intimidated by him, before stalking off.

Kate, who was standing next to Poppy, said, "I'd better go check on him. He doesn't handle being embarrassed and humiliated well. He's going to need my support."

"You seem to always be there for him," Poppy said.

"Yes, I am, for better or worse," Kate said, chuckling to herself.

"You're still in love with him, aren't you?"

Kate turned to Poppy. She pursed her lips as she considered Poppy's observation. "I suppose I am."

"Then it must be a relief to know that he's not going to end up with Jessie."

"Oh, I knew he would never end up with her," Kate said with a knowing smile.

"How?"

"Who do you think took that video and texted it to Ty?"

And then she hurried off after Antony.

Chapter 33

Poppy found the following day's challenge utterly barbaric, in her opinion. The producers had cooked up a wrestling match, going so far as to erect a large rectangular ring in a nearby Los Feliz parking lot. The official reasoning behind the idea was for the four remaining bachelors to demonstrate their physical strength to Jessie, and to show her how fast they could think on their feet. Poppy, however, had no illusions that this was all designed as some sort of faux Olympic competition to highlight each bachelor's athletic prowess, but rather more of an excuse to show off their bare chests and hard muscles to the viewing audience yet again.

Matt had lamented all morning to Poppy about his distaste for physical violence, how he preferred a battle of wits instead. But unfortunately, that was not to be. The other three men were primed and raring to go. Jessie, for her part, cooed and clapped at the whole notion of men fighting over her, as if she were some noblewoman in ancient Rome presiding over her devoted gladiators battling to the death to impress her in the Colosseum as the bloodthirsty packed crowd cheered them on.

There was a much smaller crowd in the parking lot

just behind an Arby's, mostly the crew and the bachelors' advisers. With the cameras rolling, Astronaut Neal and NASCAR Beau, stripped to the waist and wearing rather immodest sports briefs, psyched themselves up for the imminent battle as a couple of production assistants rubbed their bodies down with oil just to make it more interesting and demeaning and of course visually exciting.

Poppy, as Aunt Bea, watched from her perch in her director's chair as Matt, wearing a white robe, approached her, looking nervous and agitated.

"This might be the most degrading thing I have ever been forced to do," Matt whined. "I thought the striptease was going to be the low point!"

Poppy smiled sympathetically. "You're just going to have to buck up and do it if you want to stick around."

A referee, probably an actor, climbed into the ring as a bell clanged, kicking off the match. Neal and Beau flew out of their respective corners, chests colliding, then grappling, trying to get a hold on each other, made all the more difficult by the slippery oil covering their bodies.

"Look at these guys, they're out for blood," Matt muttered uneasily.

Jessie jumped up and down, clapping and yelling. She was loving every minute of this circus.

Within two minutes it was over. Neal got his arms around Beau from behind in a bear hug and drove him down on the mat, then managed to crawl on top of him and hold him steady for ten seconds until the referee blew his whistle again, declaring the match over and Neal the winner.

Neal pumped his fist in the air triumphantly, strutting around the ring, muscles flexing as Jessie appeared to melt on the spot. Beau crawled to his feet, humiliated for losing in record time, and with a hangdog look jumped out of the ring. His sister, Maggie, was waiting to console him. She had told Poppy she was a nurse during a brief conversation earlier, so it was no surprise that she took a moment to inspect the scratches on Beau's back and slight bruising on his arm.

Neal's adviser, Charlie, leapt into the ring and slapped his bro on the back a couple of times as they celebrated his quick victory.

Matt bowed his head. "This is going to be a total exercise in humiliation," Matt sighed.

"Didn't you once tell me you took a stage combat class?" Poppy asked.

"Yes. I was doing Shakespeare's *Richard the Third*, and we had to stage a sword fight, but it was all fake and the swords were not real—they had blunted tips."

A radio crackled on the hip of a nearby PA. "We're ready for Matt and Ty."

Before Poppy could respond, Matt was whisked away to the wrestling ring, where he reluctantly shed his robe as another PA began rubbing oil all over his chest and arms. Ty, on the opposite end of the ring, was also being prepared for battle. He asked a nearby makeup woman to put some concealer on his lower back to cover a mole he was self-conscious about.

Before Poppy even had a chance to get anxious and worried, the bell rang and she saw Ty furiously charge at Matt, who, much to Poppy's surprise, expertly sidestepped him, tripping him up enough so Ty lost his balance and flew into the ropes. This sudden move surprised Ty long enough for Matt to seize the opportunity to attack from behind, just as Neal had done with Beau. Matt twisted Ty's right arm behind his back, wrenching it hard enough that Poppy could see Ty wince in pain. Then Matt shoved him forward as hard as he could, sending Matt hurtling to the mat. However, unlike Neal, Matt did not react quick enough and jump on top of him, which allowed Ty to pop back up on his feet, his face now filled with a mix of embarrassment and rage.

Poppy glanced over at Jessie, who was obviously impressed with Matt's unexpected physical skills.

Maybe he had learned more in that stage combat class than he realized.

Ty angrily charged again, like a toro in a Spanish bullfight ring. Matt ducked to avoid him, and once again Ty tripped over Matt, landing facedown on the mat. This time Matt acted faster, jumping on top of him and managing to get an arm around Ty's throat. Ty thrashed and growled, but Matt held firm, flipping himself onto his back and holding Ty down on top of him. Ty tried kicking and biting, but Matt miraculously held on for dear life, and ten seconds later, the ref blew his whistle.

Matt was the winner.

Poppy found herself springing out of her director's chair, excitedly yelling, before it dawned on her that although her Aunt Bea character was sprightly, she might not be so youthfully energetic, so Poppy quickly reined it in, grabbing her cane that leaned against the chair and using it for effect to dawdle over and congratulate Matt.

Jessie dashed over and hugged Matt, gushing about how magnificent he was in the ring, how sexy she found it watching him take down Ty. He was more than happy to accept her adoring accolades.

However, much to his chagrin, it turned out Matt was not finished.

Andy Keenan gleefully announced that the two victors, Matt and Neal, would face off with each other in the ring for a final battle. The winner would have a private dinner with Jessie.

Charlie, a confident smile on his face, sauntered up to Poppy and said, "Sorry to tell you, Bea, but your boy's toast."

"I wouldn't be so cocky. Matt handled himself quite well against Ty," she said, annoyed that he was trying to provoke her.

"Yeah, but Ty is used to staying in a saddle on top of a bucking horse, not pinning it to the ground. Neal wrestled in college, he was state champion. Matt's gonna get creamed."

Poppy's face fell.

She tried signaling Matt to warn him, but he was already nose to nose with Neal in the ring, ready to rumble.

"Don't worry, Jessie, I know how you feel about actors, so you can count on me to make sure you don't have to have dinner with this guy tonight," Neal sneered.

"Oh, that wouldn't be so bad. I'm starting to see him in a whole new light," Jessie said, smiling seductively at Matt.

Neal's arrogant smile faded as the bell clanged.

Poppy cried out, "Matt, be careful—"

But it was too late.

Her attempt at a warning only distracted him.

Neal, head down, plowed into Matt, knocking the wind out of him. In three seconds, Neal had Matt flat on his back, Neal's hands pinning his wrists, Matt's legs locked down by Neal's lower body. Matt struggled futilely to free himself, but Neal's strength looked almost super human. Then, Neal let go of Matt's wrists and wrapped his own hands around Matt's neck, squeezing as hard as he could, choking him.

Matt used his fists to frantically pound on Neal's back, hoping to inflict enough pain that he would be forced to release his vice-like grip on his throat, but Poppy could see the pure enjoyment in Neal's eyes as he strangled Matt.

The mood in the room suddenly changed as everyone suddenly realized that Neal was not about to let up, that he might continue wringing Matt's neck until he lost consciousness or worse. The ref blew his whistle. But Neal, as if in a trance-like state, did not budge. He kept squeezing, crushing Matt's windpipe, relishing the fear in Matt's eyes as he coughed and sputtered.

Finally, the ref ran up behind Neal, grabbed him from behind, and forcefully yanked him off Matt, who rolled over on his side, still coughing, gasping for air, his hand gingerly touching his neck.

Neal then popped up and took a bow.

But no one was applauding.

They were all still in shock.

Instead of congratulating the winner, Jessie climbed into the ring and rushed over to make sure Matt was okay.

This did not sit well with Neal at all.

He scowled, insulted, as if it were somehow bad form to pay any attention to the loser.

With Jessie's help, Matt managed to get up on his feet, although with a stumble.

"Enjoy your dinner tonight," he said in a scratchy, weak voice before hobbling off to join Poppy.

"That guy's totally unhinged," Matt insisted, wheezing, glancing back at Neal. "He's got to be the killer."

Poppy pulled out her phone and pulled up one of the photos Wyatt had digitally doctored of all the bachelors, adding a red cap and beard. This was the one of Neal. Poppy scrutinized it, trying to recall the few glimpses she had managed to get of her stalker.

At the grocery store.

In the courtroom.

Outside the apartment building.

But even after having been so up close to Neal, she still could not be certain it was the same man.

There was still a lingering shadow of a doubt.

"I just don't know . . . ," she sighed.

Matt started slowly hobbling back to the mansion with Poppy by his side. "I think I need to go lie down. . . ."

Worry lines formed on Poppy's forehead. "Are you okay?"

Matt nodded wearily, rubbing his neck with his hand. "I will be, although it feels like he made mincemeat of my Adam's apple."

Using her cane until they were out of sight of the *My Dream Man* cast and crew, Poppy escorted Matt the rest of the way back to the mansion. She was relieved that tonight most of the attention would be on Jessie's dinner date with Neal, so Matt would be able to get some much-needed rest. When they arrived at Matt's room, they were surprised to find the door slightly ajar, and it appeared as if the lock had been jimmied.

Matt pushed the door open, and Poppy gasped.

The room had been ransacked.

Matt hurried in to inspect the damage. Suitcase busted open, clothes on the floor, drawers yanked out of the dresser. Matt made a beeline to the nightstand.

He slowly turned back around toward Poppy. "My wallet's gone."

"You left it here in your room?"

Matt shrugged. "I knew I was going to be stuck wearing a Speedo for most of the day—where was I going to put it?"

Poppy suddenly feared the worst.

That someone was on to them.

Chapter 34

"I must admit, Neal can be pretty intense," Jessie said, wearing a sleeveless white chiffon dress and with her hair styled in such a way that she could have easily re-created the iconic Marilyn Monroe pose atop the subway grate from *The Seven Year Itch*. She was seated on a burgundy love seat in a small room on the second floor of the Los Feliz mansion with a skeleton camera crew, to film her post-date confessional. "However," she continued, "he was very direct with me at our one-on-one dinner last night. Neal makes no bones about how he feels about me, and that level of passion and candor can be a bit overwhelming. . . . But, on the other hand, it's incredibly romantic, and when I came into this I said forthrightly I want to find a man who puts me first, makes me his priority, and there is no denying that Neal is willing to do that."

Poppy, as Aunt Bea, loitered in the hallway just outside the room, casually eavesdropping. She knew if she got caught she could just play up the confused senior stereotype, wandering the halls lost, if it came to that. But so far, no one had noticed or cared about her presence.

Jessie smiled shyly. "That's why tonight I will not be asking him to continue this journey with me. . . ." She took a dramatic pause. "Because I already have. I want him in the final three. We have a connection and I am looking forward to exploring that with him even further."

She was smitten with the almost astronaut.

There was no doubt about it.

The one bachelor Poppy fervently disliked, especially after what he had done to Matt in the wrestling ring.

Suddenly a chirping sound filled the air.

The crew curiously looked around at one another.

More chirping.

Jessie stood up, annoyed. "Who forgot to turn off their phone?"

Everyone fumbled to check their phones.

"Am I going to have to do this whole thing again from the beginning?" Jessie snapped.

Poppy suddenly realized it was coming from her own pocket. She usually kept her phone on vibrate but had enabled the sound when she took a bath in her room earlier.

She glanced up to see Jessie and the crew all staring at her.

"I am so sorry. I got turned around going back to my room and saw you all here, and just stopped to see what was going on," Poppy said before adding, "Oh, Jessie, you look so lovely."

That did it.

Jessie's anger faded, replaced by a gentle smile. "Thank you, Aunt Bea, that's so sweet of you to say."

No one dared shout at a sweet little old lady wandering the halls of this giant mansion, lost, so they all just nodded and smiled.

Poppy raised her phone. "I'd better take this, it's my doctor checking in. I'm on a new heart medicine."

Poppy shuffled off down the hall as a PA shut the door to the room to prevent any further disruption.

Glancing around to make sure no one else was in the vicinity, Poppy looked at her phone to see who had been calling. There was a voicemail from Violet. She quickly rang her back. "Hi, Violet, what's up?"

"It's not just me, you're on speaker! Iris and Wyatt are here as well!" Violet shouted.

"You do not have to yell, Violet, she is only pretending to be hard of hearing as part of her undercover assignment!" Iris barked.

Violet ignored Iris but did lower her voice just a tad. "The three of us have been working very hard at the office researching the three remaining bachelors and we have some new information, or I should say my brilliant grandson does. He did most of the work. Go on, tell her, Wyatt...."

"Hi, Aunt Poppy! I wanted to bring this information to you in person so I could see Jessie again, but Maw Maw said no because it would blow your cover."

"Your maw maw is correct, dear. What do you have for me?"

"So Beau, the NASCAR driver, apparently was in some dirt bowl town in Texas driving in a qualifying race on the day Adelaide Campbell was forced off the road in your car and killed. He didn't drive out to LA to appear on the show until several days later, arriving *after* your air conditioner blew up."

"Are you sure it was him driving in the race? He could have enlisted someone else to take his place at the last minute," Poppy suggested.

"We thought that at first, too, because in all the photos posted on social media that he was tagged in before and after the race he was wearing a helmet and face goggles, so it was hard to see what he looked like. But we talked to a lot of his friends and family and officials in charge of the race that day who interacted with him, and everyone confirmed it was the real Beau."

"He arrived in LA only a day before *My Dream Man* began production and reported to the producers immediately, so it would have been nearly impossible for the killer to have had the time to somehow sideline him and take his place," Violet added.

"It's not him!" Iris insisted.

"What about the other two?" Poppy asked.

"The astronaut and the cowboy were both already in California weeks before the start of shooting," Wyatt said. "Unlike Beau, Ty's social media posts show a lot more of him! They're all beefcake shots! And they are all on the *My Dream Man* Instagram and Twitter accounts."

"I have never seen so many pictures of a shirtless man riding a horse on the range in my life," Iris snorted.

"I enjoyed them immensely!" Violet cooed.

"Gross, Maw Maw!" Wyatt groaned, before continuing. "Apparently the first thing Ty did when he got to LA was schedule a photo shoot at Sunset Ranch in Hollywood to prove what an authentic cowboy he really is to Jessie and the producers," Wyatt said. "There were a ton of flattering close-ups of him in his cowboy hat and wider shots of him flexing his muscles in the saddle. But in one of the photos we were able to see an identifying mark. Maw Maw saw it first while she was drooling over him."

"He has a noticeable mole on his lower back," Violet said.

Poppy recalled the wrestling match she had witnessed between Ty and Matt. "Yes, I remember him asking a makeup girl to cover a mole he had with concealer."

"So it sounds like the guy with you on set is the real Ty," Wyatt concluded. "Which leaves . . ."

"The astronaut," Poppy said, hardly surprised.

"He has no real social media presence that we could find, which is unusual for anyone who wants to be on a reality dating show," Wyatt said.

"Have you learned much from your fellow dating advisers?" Violet asked.

"No, not really, they're all young and more interested in

engaging with each other than a sweet elderly aunt. But from what little interaction I have had with them, Beau's sister, Maggie, is very protective and suspicious of other people. Ty's friend, Monty, is pretty much a blank slate. I haven't detected much of a personality. The only one who stands out is Charlie, Neal's friend and fellow astronaut wannabe, but only because he is rather loud and obnoxious. But that doesn't necessarily mean he's untrustworthy."

Poppy heard a commotion coming down the hall. The crew was turning off the lights in the confessional and moving to the pool area, where Jessie would announce the next elimination.

"Listen, I have to go. Jessie is about to send another bachelor packing."

"Fingers crossed it's not Matt!" Violet cried.

"I will keep you posted."

Poppy ended the call, and then hurried down the stairs and outside to where Matt, Beau, and Ty had already gathered to await Jessie's arrival. She could hear them speculating with each other as to why Neal was so far a no-show. They finally came to the consensus that the dinner date did not go well, and Jessie had already sent him packing.

The crew arrived shortly, lights were turned on, mics were adjusted, touch ups were done to ensure Jessie and her men were all camera ready, and within a half hour it was showtime.

Jessie took her place in front of the fountain as the three adoring bachelors gazed lovingly in her direction, eager to hear her final verdict.

"Sorry I'm late," Neal announced as he strutted onto the scene, in a sharp navy Brooks Brother sports coat, powder blue dress shirt, and tan slacks, looking sexier than ever.

Instead of taking a spot next to the other bachelors, Neal made a beeline for Jessie, gave her a hug and a cursory peck on the cheek, and then took a step to the side, a knowing grin on his face.

The other bachelors were all visibly confused.

Jessie turned to the three men. "The reason Neal is not joining you is because . . ." She stopped to flash Neal a co-quettish smile. "I already asked him at the end of our date last night to continue on this journey with me."

All three bachelors suddenly looked stricken.

The cameramen zoomed in to capture the surprised re-actions.

"Which means he will not be going home tonight, but one of you, I'm sad to say, will be," Jessie added, stating the obvious.

This was, after all, television.

Jessie bowed her head, pretending she was taking time to consider this momentous decision, though all indica-tions were she had consulted with Andy Keenan and the other producers hours ago and already knew who would be booted out of the mansion next.

Jessie raised her head and flicked her hair back, a res-olute look on her face. "Ty . . ."

A wave of relief washed over the cowboy.

He bounded over to Jessie and took her hands in his own.

"Ty, will you continue on this journey with me?"

"Of course, darlin'," Ty said, euphoric.

They hugged and he joined Neal.

Two men left standing.

Matt averted his gaze momentarily from Jessie over to Poppy. She could see there was a flicker of uncertainty in his eyes. He had made some progress with winning over Jessie, but had it been enough? Or was he simply out of time?

Jessie waited, making sure the cameras got enough shots of the two last bachelors and the insecurity written all over their apprehensive faces.

"Matt . . ."

Poppy audibly exhaled.

She hadn't even realized she had been holding her breath during those preceding tense moments.

Matt, beaming, crossed over to Jessie.

"Matt, will you continue on this journey with me?"

"It would be my honor," Matt said, hugging her.

He then joined Neal and Ty.

All eyes were now on Beau, who was devastated.

Everyone stared at him, waiting for his reaction.

Would he go quietly or cause a scene?

He took a moment to collect himself, and then marched over to Jessie and locked eyes with her. "You are truly a special woman, Jessie. Any man would be lucky to have you. I hope you find what you're looking for."

Jessie sighed with relief. "Thank you, Beau."

"May I hug you good-bye?"

"Yes, of course."

They embraced, and for a moment it appeared as if Beau might not let her go, but when Jessie shifted her stance, signaling to him that she was done with the hug, Beau mercifully released her and, head held high, walked out of the gate to the driveway, where another camera crew was waiting to film his obvious heartbreak and a hopeful message about him not giving up on love yet.

All eyes were glued to Beau as he left.

But not Poppy's.

She was laser focused on Neal, with his cocksure smile and conceited self-confidence. With each passing day, she was becoming more and more convinced that the would-be astronaut was their man.

Chapter 35

Perch, the rooftop restaurant and lounge in Downtown Los Angeles, with its French small plates, hand-crafted cocktails, and sweeping, grand, unobstructed views of the LA skyline, had been Poppy's choice for Matt's one-on-one date with Jessie. Just after the start of production, the producers had requested that each bachelor sit down with his adviser and design the perfect date, which could be prearranged for when or if he was given the opportunity to show off his romantic side.

Although Poppy would not be allowed to go on the date and watch from the sidelines—only the crew and producers would be tagging along—Andy Keenan had invited Poppy to come to the home theatre at the Los Angeles mansion the morning after and watch the raw footage that had been hastily edited together from the previous evening.

Perch had been shut down to the public so Matt and Jessie could have the whole enchanting, glamorous setting to themselves. A waiter and wine steward were standing by to fulfill their every need. And Matt, looking sharp and casual chic in a charcoal blazer, black T-shirt, and black jeans, sat across the table from Jessie, in a blossom chiffon bell-sleeve sheath dress that accentuated every one of her curves. They looked maddeningly adorable together.

As an expensive Bordeaux blend was poured, Jessie picked up on Matt's nervousness when he fumbled to raise his glass and make a toast.

"To finally having the chance to get to know each other better," Matt said.

They clinked glasses and each took a sip of their wine.

Jessie's face lit up. "Oh, this is good."

"I have to give credit to my aunt Bea. She's the wine connoisseur in the family."

"Well, then here's to Aunt Bea," Jessie said brightly.

They toasted again.

The waiter, cued by the assistant producer, suddenly appeared at the table to go over the five-course menu, which included an amuse-bouche, *fromage* and charcuterie plate, baby beet salad, boeuf Bordelaise, and an orange cardamom crème brûlée, all of which Jessie enthusiastically approved of, which was a huge relief to Poppy, who had also been in charge of selecting the menu.

After the waiter scooted away, Jessie flashed Matt a playful smile. "I can see your hands shaking slightly."

Matt self-consciously put them in his lap.

"No, I think it's sweet that I make you nervous. Actors are usually so used to performing and playing a character, but you seem different."

"Maybe I'm just not a very good actor," Matt joked, shyly glancing down at his hands.

"Why do you think I make you nervous?"

Matt shrugged. "I'm not really sure. To be honest, when I got here I wasn't nervous at all. But these last few days, being around you . . ." His voice trailed off.

Jessie leaned forward expectantly.

Matt was tongue-tied.

He shrugged again.

Poppy had never seen Matt like this.

He always came across so confident and self-assured.

She instinctively knew it was not an act.

This woman really did make him nervous.

Was it possible that he was actually falling in love with her during this completely artificial, forced process?

In any event, it seemed to be working.

Jessie loved seeing this vulnerable side of him.

"Tell me more about yourself," Jessie said. "When was your last relationship?"

"About a year ago," Matt answered quietly, eyes still downcast. "We had only been together a little over a year, but it didn't work out."

"What happened?"

"She moved to New York."

"Ah, the long-distance thing is always a challenge," Jessie said. She took a pause before asking, "Did you love her?"

Poppy knew Matt was talking about her daughter, Heather, and was just as riveted to what he was going to say as Jessie was up on the screen.

Andy Keenan, who was sitting in the same row as Poppy in the home theatre but a few seats away on the aisle, suddenly piped in, "This is where he really gets her. Look closely, he's got tears in his eyes! What an actor!"

On screen, Matt nodded. "Yes, but it just wasn't in the cards. She had gone through some things, which I won't get into, and she wanted to make a big change in her life, and that change just didn't include me."

Poppy could plainly see Matt was being utterly sincere.

Jessie was smart enough to see it, too.

Matt fought to hold it together. He reached for his glass and took a sip of his wine and offered her an apologetic smile. "Sorry, I didn't expect to react like this."

"No need to be sorry. I appreciate you opening up to me. So many men pretend to get real with me, but it's so obvious they're not actually doing it, that it's more of a game. The ironic thing is, you're the actor, you're supposed to be acting all the time, but you're the most genuine man I've met here so far."

The conversation went back to safer, more superficial topics, Jessie spending a good portion of the meal prattling on about her own past boyfriends, how they constantly disappointed her, how she yearned to find a man who would finally put her first.

Poppy found none of this surprising.

One look at Matt, however, and Poppy felt an overwhelming sense of dread.

"Oh dear . . . ," she muttered.

Andy Keenan sat up in his seat. "What?"

"I think he really might be starting to fall for her."

"I know, isn't it great?" Andy cried with an excited grin.

He was more wrapped up in making binge-worthy television than the real reason Matt was here.

After dessert, the couple held hands and gazed at the magnificent skyline before taking an elevator down to street level, where a limousine was waiting to whisk them off to their next destination, Capitol Records.

This part of the date had been Matt's idea.

A recording engineer greeted them at the front entrance and escorted them up to a studio. Jessie looked around with anticipation, as if expecting her favorite pop star, like Taylor Swift or Drake, to come out of hiding and perform a private concert for them. But that wasn't the plan. It was Matt who entered the studio, leaving Jessie behind in the booth with the engineer.

"I don't understand what's happening," Jessie said, confused.

The engineer put on a pair of headphones. "Ready, Matt?"

Matt took his place behind a microphone that hung down in front of him. "All set."

The engineer turned up the volume so they could hear the intro to a song.

" 'Just the Way You Are'! Bruno Mars! This was, like, my favorite song in high school!" Jessie cooed.

The engineer cued Matt, who started singing the lyrics.

Poppy had no doubts that Matt would knock Jessie out with his melodic, soothing voice. She had heard him sing before, and when he suggested off the cuff recording a song for Jessie, she strongly encouraged him to do it because, after all, what woman would not enjoy a man singing her all-time favorite love song to her?

And true to form, Jessie practically melted on the spot.

When Matt finished and joined her in the booth so the engineer could play the performance back for both of them, Jessie suddenly could not keep her hands off him. She was hugely touched by his effort and honest in her assessment of the whole evening.

"Best. Date. Ever."

There was no cameraman in the limo on the ride back to the Los Feliz mansion, but Andy eagerly told Poppy that the kiss good night they had shared before adjourning to their respective rooms was *epic*.

When the screening of the footage was over, Andy announced it was time to film an adviser interview with Jessie where she could ask questions about a bachelor.

"Crew's already set up in Jessie's room. Let's go. She's waiting for you," Andy said, gently taking Poppy by the arm.

Poppy had to keep reminding herself to slow down her pace and hunch over a little, to try acting more like a ninety-year-old, although Iris typically golfed with plenty of ninety-year-olds who could run circles around kids in their twenties.

When they reached Jessie's room, they found her sitting on a couch, her face glowing. She jumped to her feet to hug Poppy, not squeezing too hard, out of fear she might break a few of her brittle bones. Poppy took her place in a chair opposite Jessie, set her cane down, and waited for the director to call action so they could pretend to be having this very spontaneous, casual exchange.

"Aunt Bea, I've always considered myself a good judge of character—usually right from the get-go my first impressions hardly ever change—but in this case, with Matt, I have to admit, he's nothing like what I thought he was."

"I am happy that you are finally seeing the Matt whom I see every day, the kind, empathetic, good man he is and always has been, even as a young boy," Poppy said.

All true in her mind except the knowing him as a young boy part, of course. She just threw that in to cement her cover.

Jessie stared intently at Poppy, hanging on her every word.

Poppy shifted in her chair, uncomfortable, fearful that Jessie was seeing through her disguise since they had previously met recently.

Jessie picked up on her wariness instantly. "Are you all right, Aunt Bea?"

Poppy had to think fast. "Yes, just back pains. Can someone get me a pillow?"

A production assistant dashed out and returned seconds later with a plush throw pillow, then slid it down between Poppy and the back of the chair.

"Better?" Jessie asked with genuine concern.

"Much. Now where were we? Oh, yes, Matt."

Jessie fired off a barrage of silly questions, like what was his favorite food, did he play sports in high school, did he always want to be an actor?

Poppy was prepared for all of them.

But not the last one about to come.

"Did you know his previous girlfriend, the one who broke his heart?"

This one caught her off guard.

She couldn't very well tell the truth.

Poppy hesitated before answering. "Yes, I met her. She seemed nice. They just weren't meant to be, I guess."

Not an outright lie.

She had, of course, met her own daughter.

Heather was indeed nice.

And she and Matt were not meant to be.

"I can see the pain in Matt's eyes when he talks about her. Do you think he still has feelings for her?"

This one was going to be tricky.

Poppy was fairly certain that Matt *did* still have feelings for Heather, but if she admitted it, Matt's future on the show would be in jeopardy. If he was still in love with someone else, Jessie would more likely than not give him the boot.

"No, I believe he has moved on, and he is ready emotionally for whatever might come next."

Jessie smiled, satisfied. "Good. I was hoping you would say that."

Poppy breathed a heavy sigh of relief.

Matt was definitely still in the running to be selected as Jessie's "Dream Man."

She reached across and touched Poppy's knee. "Thank you, Aunt Bea. You've been super helpful. But I still have a very difficult choice to make. The last thing I expected was to have feelings for not one, not two, but *three* men. And I have to send one of them home tonight. I have no clue what I'm going to do."

Poppy wasn't sure if Jessie was talking to her or the viewing audience at home. The only thing she was sure of now was that Matt might not be a shoo-in to stay after all.

Chapter 36

"Ty . . . ," Jessie said.

Ty bounded forward, relieved, grabbing Jessie's hands as she stood resolutely in front of the fountain, after announcing to everyone how difficult this evening was for her, how she had gone back and forth so many times on who should go, but in the end felt she was making the right decision for her.

"Ty, will you continue on this journey with me?"

Ty, who wore a brown cowboy hat that matched his sports jacket, plucked it off the top of his head and tossed it in the air. "Yee-haw!"

Jessie giggled. "I take that as a yes!"

He caught the hat as it came down in his right hand and placed it over his heart. "Yes, ma'am. Thank you."

He stepped to the side, allowing Jessie to focus her attention on the two remaining bachelors.

Matt and Neal.

Poppy could tell Matt was anxious and keyed up.

Neal, at least on the surface, appeared calm and confident. Maybe he knew something Poppy and Matt did not.

Jessie took an unusually long dramatic pause, pretending to be torn about what she was about to do.

The longer she took, the more Poppy could see Neal's

outward bravado slowly chipping away, as if he was finally waking up to the fact that he might not get picked.

Jessie averted her gaze to Matt, then Neal, back to Matt, and then Neal again.

Finally, her eyes remained fixed on Neal.

Poppy's heart sank.

Jessie's eyes always in the end settled on the man whose name she was about to call.

It was over for Matt.

Jessie opened her mouth to speak.

But then, as if changing her mind at the last second, her eyes flicked back to Matt.

"Matt . . ."

Matt broke out into a wide smile and he excitedly jogged over to her, taking her hands into his.

"Matt, will you continue on this journey with me?"

"Absolutely," Matt said, leaning in and giving her a light peck on the cheek.

Poppy, in her Aunt Bea disguise, who was standing next to Neal's buddy, Charlie, could see Neal physically tensing up.

Charlie nervously cleared his throat.

Everyone stared at Neal, who stood frozen in place, a stone-cold expression on his face.

There was utter silence after Matt took his place next to Ty, leaving Neal all alone, odd man out.

Jessie bowed her head solemnly.

Finally, Neal looked around, confused. "I'm sorry. . . . What just happened here?"

Jessie raised her head to face him, teary eyed. "You're a wonderful man, Neal, and I do have feelings for you, but in the end, they just weren't as strong as I had hoped they would be."

"You're kidding, right?" Neal spit out.

Jessie slowly shook her head. "No. But I'm sure you are going to make some lucky girl very happy one day."

But Neal was having none of her flat, fake platitudes. "This is crazy!" He looked around at the crew for some support. "Is she really throwing me over for those two losers over there?" He thrust a finger toward Matt and Ty.

"Neal, please . . ." Jessie begged.

"I'm an astronaut, for crying out loud! I'm going into space someday, I'll be a real American hero, like my name-sake Neil Armstrong, and you're going to pass all that up for some Brad Pitt wannabe and a low-rent Butch Cassidy?"

Charlie hustled over to his friend. "Hey, bro, it's okay, take it easy. . . ."

But Neal violently shoved him away. "No, this doesn't make any sense. . . ." He glared at Jessie. "In my head I totally believed that you were not just a beauty but also a woman of substance. Man, was I wrong. You're like all the rest of those superficial, empty-headed bimbos who do these kinds of shows!"

There were a few audible gasps from the crew.

Jessie burst into tears.

Matt took a step toward Neal. "Hey, man, you're out of line. . . ."

Neal gestured with his hands for Matt to come closer. "You want a piece of me, I'll show you who the real man is around here. . . ."

But before Matt could respond, several muscle-bound security guys in tight black T-shirts descended onto the set and physically escorted Neal out of the mansion. Charlie chased after him like a loyal golden retriever.

Poppy grabbed her cane and followed them as Matt and Ty surrounded a visibly upset Jessie to offer comfort.

Outside the mansion, one of the security men gave Neal a forceful shove, indicating his disgust over how Neal had just spoken to Jessie. Neal stumbled but did not lose his balance and fall to the pavement. With his chest puffed out, he scowled defiantly as they headed back inside.

Charlie joined his friend. "Come on, I know of a bar close by where we can get a drink and decompress."

"She's making a big mistake if she thinks she can treat me that way," Neal growled.

Charlie patted Neal gently on the back. "It's over, buddy, let it go."

"Screw that. This isn't over by a long shot."

Poppy hovered in the shadows outside, witnessing the would-be astronaut becoming completely unhinged, as if he had never been rejected before in his life. As Charlie tried steering Neal into his car to get him away from the mansion as quickly as possible, Poppy overheard him mention a nearby dive bar, Hyperion Tavern. Poppy decided on the spot to tail them and try to find out more information. She knew she had to ditch her Aunt Bea getup because a nonagenarian would most certainly stick out at an East LA indie glam hangout. Going as herself was also out of the question because Poppy Harmon was still supposedly dead. So another disguise was going to be required.

Poppy hurried back to her room, washed off her old-lady makeup, dispensed with the gray wig and frumpy clothes, and totally reinvented herself with a red wig, thick black glasses, and all black attire from her suitcase. She was obviously decades older than your typical Los Feliz hipster, but she just might manage to blend in. She knew Matt would be tied up for hours with interviews about what went down this evening and so she was on her own.

Google Maps got her to the Hyperion Tavern in less than ten minutes, and after parking her car in a very expensive lot, Poppy slipped inside the crowded bar. She ordered a beer and weaved her way toward the back, where she spotted Neal and Charlie huddled in conversation. Luckily the live band performing was just taking a break, so she managed to slide in the booth directly behind them completely unnoticed and casually listen to what they were talking about.

Neal guzzled down the last of his beer and slammed the bottle down on the table, then picked up another and gulped that one down, too. "She lied to me, she said I was special, that I wasn't like the other guys. I won't let her get away with it."

"Dude, you gotta move on, it isn't worth all the aggravation this is causing you," Charlie pleaded, warily keeping an eye on how much Neal was drinking.

Neal got up and pushed his way to the bar, waved down the bartender, and ordered three more bottles. Poppy kept her back to them, her head turned away, pretending to look at a painting on the wall, as he returned and set two of the bottles down for himself and held out the third for Charlie.

Charlie raised his beer, which was still over half full. "I'm still working on this one."

Neal shrugged and grabbed a full bottle and began knocking it back. He stopped drinking long enough to mutter, "Jessie and I belong together. She just doesn't see it yet. I have to somehow get back on the show. Maybe tonight I can sneak back, talk to her, make her see how much she means to me. . . ."

Charlie put a hand firmly on Neal's shoulder. "Dude, that would be a huge blunder. You know how these things go. It would not end well for you."

"I don't care. I will blow up the whole show if I have to!"

Poppy stiffened. Although her back was to him, she could almost picture the manic look in his eyes. He was fast devolving into a dangerous frame of mind.

"Dude, I'm begging you, don't do this," Charlie said. "Forget about Jessie and the stupid show. Why don't you go back to your girlfriend in Palm Springs? You were really into her for a while."

Poppy sprang to attention.

Palm Springs?

Could he be referring to Tanya Cook?

Poppy felt as if she was on the precipice of finally identifying the killer.

And in all likelihood it was Neal.

"We broke up," Neal muttered.

"Why?"

"She was getting way too clingy. I felt suffocated. This opportunity gave me the excuse to finally get away from her."

"Was she at least hot?"

Neal laughed derisively. "Sort of."

"Sort of? Dude, you dated her for something like six months."

"Yeah, because she paid my rent and bought me my Camaro. But she was old enough to be my mother, which was okay, I mean she was still hot, but when she started *acting* like my mother, that's when I told her I'm out."

"I didn't know you were into older women," Charlie said.

"Sure, why not? Especially if they're insecure about being with a younger guy and insist on paying for everything. But seriously, bro, she was a total hottie back in the day. I wish I had known her when she was in her thirties. She was this really well-known actress and was in, like, tons of movies and TV shows."

"Awesome. Have I heard of her?"

"Maybe. Serena Saunders?"

Chapter 37

By the time Poppy got back to her room in the mansion, her mind was still reeling from the revelation that Neal had been romantically involved with Serena Saunders, of all people. She was certainly not surprised by the age difference. Serena had proudly announced her predilection for boy toys when Poppy had first run into her at John Henry's Cafe, but that it was Neal, the aspiring astronaut, a bachelor on *My Dream Man*, that was what was so shocking.

After discarding her wig and glasses, she shed her outfit and slipped into a plush white robe, then texted her news to Iris and Violet, suggesting they find Serena and pump her for any useful information she might have about the mercurial and increasingly dangerous Neal.

Violet was the first to respond, assuring Poppy they would take care of it, and after plugging in her phone to charge it, Poppy crawled into bed and shut off the light, looking forward to a good night's sleep. She was slowly drifting off when there was suddenly a loud knock at the door.

Poppy, startled, bolted up in bed. "Who is it?"

"Jessie."

Poppy felt a twinge of panic. "Jessie? What time is it?"

"I know it's late, but I was hoping we could have a talk, just the two of us."

Poppy snapped on the lamp sitting on her bedside table. She jumped out of bed and was halfway to the door when she suddenly realized she had wiped her face clean of her old-age makeup and did not have time now to put it back on.

"Just a second, dear," Poppy cried, scurrying into the bathroom and staring at her reflection in the wall mirror.

What on earth was she going to do?

If Jessie saw her like this, the jig would be up, their whole ruse foiled. Her eyes scanned the vanity. She spotted her jar of white night cream, hurriedly unscrewed the top, dipped two fingers in, and began slapping heavy globs all over her face in a last-ditch effort to disguise herself.

Jessie knocked again. "Aunt Bea, are you all right?"

Poppy studied her handiwork. Only her eyes and lips could be made out with so much cream covering her face. Satisfied, she then raced out of the bathroom, grabbed her cane by the bed, donned her gray wig, and opened the door to find Jessie in a baby blue satin nightie and matching furry slippers, surrounded by a full camera crew who would be documenting their "private conversation."

Jessie reared back, flabbergasted, at the sight of Poppy's cream-covered face, but quickly recovered. "I apologize for barging in on you like this, Aunt Bea, but it's critical we speak before tomorrow."

Poppy ushered her inside, the crew trudging in behind her. "Don't be silly, dear, we are all here to make sure you have a fairy tale ending, so I want to help in any way I can."

"Thank you, Aunt Bea, you're such a peach," Jessie said.

The crew quickly set up some lights and the perfect shot of Jessie and Aunt Bea sitting side by side on the bed as if the two women were having some kind of impromptu slumber party.

When the assistant director announced they were good to go, Jessie gave Poppy a puzzled look.

"Would you like to wash all that cream off your face before we start so the viewers can see you, Aunt Bea?"

"Heavens, no," Poppy gasped. "I need to keep this on all night. Otherwise, tomorrow I will look like the Crypt Keeper."

"The what?" Jessie asked, crinkling her nose, confused.

"Forget it, dear. You're way too young to remember."

Jessie cranked her head around to address the director. "Can you live with her looking like this, Stan?"

The director checked his watch and nodded. "She's fine. All eyes are going to be on you the whole time anyway," he said, gesturing toward her revealing nightie.

Jessie liked that answer. She adjusted her cleavage to show off a little more, and then cleared her throat as the director called, "Action."

Jessie, grave and earnest, turned toward Aunt Bea. "I am so grateful you agreed to sit down with me."

Poppy smiled.

The director yelled for them to cut the scene and then he added, "Let's start again. This time, Aunt Bea, say what you said before the cameras started rolling, the stuff about how we're here for Jessie's fairy tale ending and all that crap."

Poppy nodded tentatively. "Okay . . ."

The director called, "Action," again.

Jessie leaned in and hugged Poppy, repeated her line about being grateful for the sit-down, and on cue, Poppy responded with her line about everyone being here to facilitate Jessie's fairy tale ending and how she just wanted to help.

"The thing is, Aunt Bea . . . I'm . . . I'm . . ." Jessie took another one of her signature long dramatic pauses before continuing. "I'm falling for Matt. Hard."

"That's wonderful news!" Poppy said, this time initiating another hug herself.

When Jessie withdrew, Poppy instantly noticed the hesitancy in Jessie's eyes.

"What's bothering you, dear?"

"It's just that I have very strong feelings for Ty as well. You seem like such a sweet and caring person, Aunt Bea, and well, I guess I was hoping you might offer me some motherly advice, since my own mother is all the way back home in Louisiana."

The intense heat from the lights was starting to make Poppy sweat to the point where she could feel the cream starting to slide down her face. This was a disaster. If enough of the cream melted away, everyone would be able to see Poppy out of makeup, and they would know Aunt Bea was a big fake.

She had to think fast.

"Follow your heart!" she declared.

Jessie waited for more but Poppy had already turned to the director. "Was that good? Are we done?"

The director signaled with his hands that he wanted her to stretch it out, keep going, tell her more.

Poppy, now panic stricken as gobs of white cream began dropping into her lap, spoke at double speed. "The heart always knows what it wants. Take some time and try picturing your future with each of them, what that looks like, and how that makes you feel inside. They're both good men. Of course, I would be lying if I said I had no bias given how much I love my nephew, Matt, and want him to come out of this with his own dream woman, but that's not for me to decide. This is about your journey, Jessie, and your happy ending."

Poppy glanced over at the director, who seemed delighted with her off-the-cuff advice.

So did Jessie, who popped back up to her feet. "Thank you, Aunt Bea, you have given me all the clarity I need. I can see why Matt chose you as his personal dating adviser. You seem to have all the answers."

"It's a miracle I'm even coherent right now given how it's so far past my bedtime," Poppy said pointedly as more cream dissolved, showing more and more of her real face.

The director gave Jessie a thumbs-up and yelled for them to cut the scene. He had what he needed.

"You're a real trouper for doing this. The producers say, judging from the footage, you're going to be *the* breakout star of the season," Jessie said. "Everyone's going to want their own Aunt Bea."

"Maybe they'll make me into a doll, like Mrs. Beasley in that old show *Family Affair*," Poppy cracked.

Jessie crinkled her nose, lost again. "Who? Family what?"

"Never mind," Poppy said, sighing. "Good night, everyone." She pretended to hobble with her cane as quickly as possible into the bathroom and slammed the door behind her. She could hear the crew on the other side of the door breaking down the lights and hauling the equipment out of Poppy's room. She snatched up a washcloth and removed the last remnants of night cream, waiting until the last crew member was gone and the door shut before finally emerging and crawling back into bed.

As she turned off the light, she worried about Jessie's own intentions. Poppy was already convinced that Matt was sincere in his rapidly developing feelings for Jessie. It was undoubtedly a complication in their investigation. None of them had expected Matt to become so emotionally invested while posing as one of Jessie's bachelors, but as she had just told Jessie, the heart wants what it wants. And Matt had always worn his on his sleeve ever since the day she had first met him.

But Jessie was more of an enigma. Was this late-night visit to Aunt Bea just for show, a way to play up her dilemma on camera, or was she genuinely torn between the last two men standing?

Poppy had witnessed firsthand just how heartbroken Matt had been after Heather broke it off with him not so long ago. He had been so obviously hurt and devastated despite his best efforts to put on a brave face. And she just couldn't bear to see that happen to him all over again.

Chapter 38

"Poppy most certainly did not have an easy life, I can tell you that. Her career all but collapsed after *Jack Colt* was cancelled, and then I heard that her last husband, the one with the awful gambling problem, left her penniless," Serena Saunders said with a forced frown, although it was clear she was endlessly pleased about this downbeat assessment of the life of Poppy Harmon.

Iris, who was sitting on a white leather couch across from Serena, a glass-top coffee table between them, visibly bristled. "Chester had his problems, but he was a good man and he loved Poppy very much."

Serena halfheartedly nodded. "Yes, I suppose he might have loved her at the onset, but how can you both still love someone and betray her on such a grand scale at the same time? It begs the question, was he unhappy? Did all that gambling provide some sort of solace and release outside the marriage?"

Iris appeared to shift from minor annoyance to burning rage in five seconds flat. "Are you now blaming Chester's gambling on Poppy?"

Violet could be heard saying, "Iris, calm down."

Serena, sensing she had set Iris off, quickly retreated.

"Poppy and I regrettably lost touch over the years, so I am just speculating."

"So you really do not know what you are talking about!" Iris bellowed.

Serena's face twitched. "Please stop yelling."

"I'm not yelling!" Iris yelled.

"Yes, Iris, you are yelling," Violet squeaked.

Poppy could not see Violet on the video that she played on her phone because Violet was the one secretly recording the visit to Serena Saunders's midcentury home in the fashionable Movie Colony area of Palm Springs. Wyatt had rigged a tiny video camera and disguised it as a clasp on Violet's purse, which she perched on her lap for the entire conversation so Serena would not suspect she would be on camera. Iris could be seen in the corner of the screen opposite Violet, red faced and fuming.

Poppy was not surprised that Serena was seizing yet another opportunity to trash-talk her. But the cold reality was that Serena was not wrong. Poppy's acting career did wane after *Jack Colt* and her late husband did indeed leave her broke due to a gambling addiction she knew nothing about. She just hated the fact that Serena was enjoying her past misfortune so much.

The video image shook as Violet shifted and the purse moved slightly.

"But we're not here to talk about Chester, are we, Iris?" Violet said.

Poppy could visualize Violet's pursed lips and stern gaze.

Iris finally got the message. "No, we're not. We are here to discuss *your* relationship."

Serena, clueless, leaned forward in her chair. "Which one?"

Iris sighed. "The boy toy, the young one."

Serena's eyes twinkled and she chuckled. "I'm afraid you're going to have to be more specific."

"Neal," Violet offered.

"Neal . . . ," Serena said, the name dripping off her tongue like sweet honey, her mind appearing to wander to more unbridled, lustful thoughts. "Strong, commanding, passionate. One of the best lovers I ever had."

Iris reflexively rolled her eyes and sighed again, this time louder. "We do not need to hear about that!"

"Then why *are* you here? I know you two are Poppy's friends, I saw you at her memorial service. Frankly I thought you had come by for a donation to cover the cost of her funeral arrangements given the paucity of her estate."

Poppy's jaw tightened as she clenched her teeth.

"We work with her as private investigators," Violet said.

"*Worked*," Iris piped in, correcting her.

"Yes, before . . . ," Violet whispered as she probably tried to work up a few tears. Poppy and Matt were not the only actors in the Desert Flowers Detective Agency. Violet was a natural when she needed to be.

Serena's eyes widened in surprise. "Really? You two were Poppy's partners?"

Serena gazed at them for a moment in stunned silence, and then burst out laughing.

"What's so funny?" Iris snorted.

"I'm sorry, I'm just picturing the opening to the old *Charlie's Angels* show, you know, 'Once upon a time, there were three little girls who went to the police academy,' except instead of those pretty young girls running and jumping and driving fast cars, I'm seeing you two and Poppy. . . ."

Iris had heard enough. "When you are done, we would like to get back to Neal."

Serena finally managed to get control of herself and her smile slowly faded. "Neal and I are no longer together. I don't know where he is now. I heard a rumor he went back to LA and is on some reality show, but we're not in touch anymore. Why are you interested in him?"

"We have reason to believe that he might have been stalking Poppy," Violet said.

Serena sat back languidly, a skeptical look on her face. "Why in heaven's name would he do that?"

Violet proceeded cautiously. "We suspect he wanted revenge for Poppy testifying against another woman he was seeing. . . ."

"A *much younger* woman!" Iris noted.

Serena's eyes narrowed. "That's impossible. When Neal was with me, he was completely faithful. He had no interest in any other women."

Now it was Iris's turn to display an overabundance of skepticism, which was not lost on Serena, who grimaced.

Serena suddenly sat up. "Wait, are you suggesting that Neal might have been responsible for Poppy's death? I thought the cause was faulty electrical wiring in her house or something like that?"

"It was murder, and not only Poppy. There was another woman who had the bad luck of driving Poppy's car when he . . . someone forced her off the road and over a cliff to her death," Violet quietly explained.

Serena shot to her feet, eyes now blazing. "It *wasn't* Neal."

Iris folded her arms. "How can you be so sure?"

"Because he was with me the entire week before Poppy died in that explosion. After I ran into her at John Henry's Cafe, Neal and I left for Las Vegas. We checked into the Bellagio, played blackjack, dined at a few trendy restaurants, took in a whole slew of shows. But most of the time we stayed in our room. It was my attempt to rekindle our relationship, but both of us realized that sadly it had run its course, and it was now time to move on. We were both still in Vegas together when I heard about Poppy. So Neal could not have done it."

Iris pulled out her own phone, pulled up a photo, and handed it to Serena. "Is that him? Is that Neal?"

Poppy knew what photo Iris was showing Serena. It was from the wrestling match. The one Poppy had surreptitiously taken of Neal battling Matt. It was a clear, full-body shirtless shot. Matt's head was turned away, so Serena could not recognize him from Poppy's funeral.

Serena didn't have to study it. All it took was a quick glance. "Yes, that's him."

"Are you sure?" Violet could be heard asking.

"Of course I'm sure! It's Neal. And I recognize the scar on his lower abdomen from a recent surgery he had to remove his gallbladder. It's not something I can forget since he didn't have health insurance and I had to pay for the whole damn operation."

There was a trace of sadness on Serena's face.

She was probably recounting the breakup again in her mind.

Neal coldly walking away from Serena once he squeezed her dry and was done with her.

Although Serena was no friend, Poppy could not help but sympathize. Nobody deserved to be used like that. However, Serena was not about to show any vulnerability. Instead, she fought to maintain an unfazed demeanor. "So is that it? Are we finished with this little interrogation? I have a coffee date with a charming young man I met online, a doctor, if you must know." She couldn't resist showing Iris and Violet a photo on her phone. He was certainly handsome, dark features, perhaps of Asian or Middle Eastern descent, and in his midtwenties.

"I know him. He's no doctor. He works at the pharmacy where I pick up my prescriptions," Iris cackled. "He's not even the pharmacist. He just rings up the pills on the cash register!"

Before Poppy could see Serena's horrified reaction, she was distracted by shouting down the hall from her room in the Los Feliz mansion. She quickly stopped the video and sprang to her feet, then rushed out the door to investigate the loud commotion. She found Neal struggling in Matt's grip. Matt had one arm slung around Neal's neck while he held Neal's right arm, twisted behind his back. Jessie stood a few feet away, crying, her face buried in her hands as a small camera crew was on the scene to record the ensuing drama.

Poppy as Aunt Bea, realizing she had bolted from her room without her cane, which was such a key part of her disguise, quickly grabbed the wall as if she needed its support to move forward. Neal's buddy and fellow astronaut Charlie suddenly was at her side, gently taking her by the arm to assist her.

Poppy turned and gave him an appreciative smile. "Thank you, Charlie. What is going on?"

"Neal insisted on coming back to the mansion to make one Hail Mary pass to get back in the game. He was convinced Jessie had made a terrible mistake sending him away and wanted another chance. I tried talking him out of it but he can be so pigheaded and he wouldn't listen to me. Jessie freaked out, Matt showed up and had to stick his nose in it, and everything just got way out of hand."

Several producers were now on the scene desperately trying to bring down the temperature on the situation, although Poppy strongly suspected they had been the ones to encourage the whole ploy in order to ratchet up the drama before Jessie's final big choice between Matt and Ty, for the good of the show. But what they hadn't counted on was Neal's fiery temper and unpredictability.

With producers and security all around now, Matt released Neal. But instead of leaving quietly, Neal made a beeline for Jessie. "Please, listen to me, Jessie, I didn't come back to upset you, I just feel I haven't explained my feelings for you properly. We're meant to be together, and I need you to see that!"

Jessie refused to make eye contact. "Go away! I'm never going to choose you! I don't want you near me! You're acting like a *stalker*!" She raced into Matt's arms for comfort. He held her tight, tenderly patting her back with his hand as she buried her face in his chest, sobbing. "Please, make him go away."

Two beefy stone-faced security guards flanked Neal from both sides, making it clear his time on the show had officially come to a close.

For once, he didn't put up a fight.

He knew he was outnumbered.

There would be no touching good-byes, or wishes that Jessie would find what she was looking for, but Poppy judged from the gleeful expressions on the faces of the show producers that this episode cut together would be a ratings bonanza.

Neal stalked off, Charlie shuffling after him again.

Matt, who still hugged Jessie, glanced over at Poppy, a bit shaken from the run-in, but relieved the ill-tempered, easily stoked Neal was finally gone and hopefully never to return.

Leaving just two bachelors vying for Jessie's affections.

And most likely one murderer.

Chapter 39

"Oh, dear, I overslept this morning and I'm not quite ready yet," Poppy as Aunt Bea said to the maid who stood at her door, her cleaning cart parked right behind her. "Could you start with the room across the hall, and then come back to me?"

The maid, seeing no reason to object, nodded with a polite smile, and then crossed the hall and used her master key to open the door and step inside. Poppy wasted no time bounding after her with a piece of duct tape and a coin. She quickly pressed the quarter over the door's latch and secured it with the tape so when the maid left and closed the door it would not lock. Poppy had heard Ty leave twenty minutes earlier for breakfast, and she knew he would be shooting a scene directly after and would unlikely be returning for some time. She scooted back to her own room, listening at the door until the maid finished changing sheets, emptying the garbage pail, and cleaning the bathroom. Finally, just as the maid emerged, Poppy grabbed her cane and opened her door, startling the maid.

"Perfect timing!" Poppy declared, hunching her back as she gestured toward the room with her cane. "I'm off, it's all yours."

Again, the maid gave her a polite, perfunctory smile and

hustled past her into Poppy's room. Making sure the maid's back was to her, Poppy dashed across the hall, removed the coin and tape from the door, and slipped inside Ty's room, quietly closing the door behind her.

She then began opening the drawers of a dresser but found nothing but socks and underwear before moving to the closet, where she rummaged through his rack of suits and modish shirts. She dropped down to her hands and knees, scanning the floor that was lined up with half a dozen trendy pairs of shoes and shiny cowboy boots. Ty had come prepared to impress. She was about to climb back up to her feet when she noticed a brown paper bag in the corner of the closet. Reaching out, she grabbed the folded top and dragged it toward her. She opened it up and peered inside. At first she thought it was some kind of dead animal, but then she lightly touched it.

No, it was a wig.

But when she pulled it out, she suddenly realized it was not a wig, but a fake beard. Glancing back in the bag, she saw that underneath the beard was a red baseball cap and a pair of dark sunglasses.

Fake beard.

Red cap.

Dark sunglasses.

It was him.

Ty was her stalker and would-be killer.

And she finally had the evidence to prove it.

But wait, she thought, *how can this be?*

How could Ty be in two places at once? Unless all of those clear, recognizable photos of him online taken at the time he was supposedly stalking Poppy were of his identical twin.

She quickly put the fake beard back in the bag, rolled the top closed, and stood up to leave with her newly discovered evidence when she suddenly heard a key being inserted into the lock. Poppy froze in place as the door swung open and Ty entered, stopping in his tracks, his mouth agape at finding Matt's doddering old aunt Bea in his room.

"What . . . what are you doing here?"

Poppy opened her mouth to speak, but realized she had no idea what she was going to say.

Ty's mind raced and then his face darkened. "Did Matt send you here to try to dig up dirt on me? Is that it?" He snatched his phone from the back pocket of his jeans. "I'm calling the producers. I'm sure they are going to want to hear about Matt using his poor old aunt to sabotage me so Jessie picks him!"

"That's not why I'm here," Poppy said, dispensing with her well-rehearsed "granny" voice.

The change in her tone surprised Ty, who slowly lowered his phone as Poppy removed her gray wig and glasses, setting them down on the bed.

Ty's eyes popped wide open. "What the . . . ?"

Then she dipped her hand into her purse for a wad of tissue to wipe off her makeup, at least enough to reveal her true identity.

"Who are you?"

"My name is Poppy Harmon. You don't recognize me?"

He studied her. "Wait, aren't you that faded actress who died recently?"

"You could have avoided using the insulting word *faded*, but yes, that's me."

"But how can you still be alive? Reports of your death were all over the news."

"It was a calculated strategy, a strategy that brought me straight here, to this room. To you."

Ty appeared thoroughly confused.

Poppy considered the possibility that it was all an act, that he was just pretending not to know what was going on so he would not implicate himself further.

"Lady, I have no clue what you're talking about."

Poppy emptied the contents of the paper bag onto the

bed next to her wig and glasses. "Would you mind explaining these?"

He stared at the fake beard, cap, and glasses, dumbfounded. "I've never seen them before."

"I found them in the corner of your closet."

Ty stared at the items, baffled.

"*Someone* put them there," Poppy said accusingly. "And you're the only one staying in this room."

"I swear, they're not mine."

"Then to whom do they belong?"

Ty shrugged. "How the hell should I know? Monty's room connects with mine, we've been going back and forth through that door day and night, hanging out, drinking beers, maybe they belong to him. Why does it matter?"

"I will tell you why it matters. Someone wore this beard, this cap, and these glasses to disguise himself so he could freely stalk me and try to kill me in Palm Springs. He succeeded in murdering a friend of mine, and came close to succeeding with me as well, and I want to find him and make him pay."

"And you think it's one of the bachelors on this show? That's why you conjured up this whole sweet Aunt Bea act?"

Poppy nodded.

Although she had never considered the possibility that the killer might not be one of the bachelors. If he had been rejected and could not somehow con his way onto the show posing as one of the bachelors who *had* been chosen, then another option would be tagging along as one of the bachelor's "dating advisers."

Which meant, Monty could very well be guilty.

"How well do you know Monty?"

Before Ty could answer, the door swung open again.

It was Jessie.

At first her eyes were focused on Ty, ignoring Poppy. "Ty, we need to talk. . . ."

Poppy was confounded by the fact that Jessie was not

being trailed by a camera crew. The point was for every move she made to be recorded. But she had come here with the express intent of having a private conversation with Ty out of view of a worldwide audience, which Poppy found curious.

Jessie suddenly noticed Poppy standing in the room. She stared at her, mystified, then at the wig and glasses on the bed next to the other items. She raised her eyes back up to Poppy's face and then was thunderstruck by recognition.

"You're her. . . . You're Poppy. . . ."

Chapter 40

Jessie continued staring at Poppy, slack jawed. "I thought you were . . ."

"As you can see, I'm very much alive," Poppy said.

"I don't understand what's happening here. Are you . . . ?"

"Yes, I'm Aunt Bea."

"Why would you lead people to believe you were dead? And why would you dress up as some doddering old aunt to crash the set of *My Dream Man*?"

"Because I am here to protect you. Please, come in and close the door so we can talk privately. I don't want anyone else to see me."

Jessie hesitated.

Ty shot across the room to Jessie's side, snatching up her hands and holding them tightly. "We should get the producers up here immediately. This woman is obviously here under false pretenses. This is disqualifying. Matt should be kicked off the show right now." He stopped short from adding, *So I can be the last man standing.*

Jessie's eyes flicked to Ty, then back to Poppy.

She sighed and finally stepped into the room, wriggled one hand free from Ty, and closed the door.

Ty deflated. "Jessie, no, the woman is clearly deranged. You shouldn't give any oxygen to her ridiculous claims."

Jessie ignored him, her attention focused squarely on Poppy. "Does this have to do with our previous meeting, your worries about some crackpot stalker?"

"I only wish you had taken me seriously at the time—we might have avoided this entire charade," Poppy said sternly. "Jessie, I cannot stress enough, your life could be in real jeopardy. This man is still on the loose, and extremely dangerous. We just want to catch him before he causes any more harm. To you, to anyone."

"*We*? So Matt's in on this, too?" Ty insisted on pointing out.

This time Poppy ignored him. "This man has already killed once, an innocent woman who just happened to be in the wrong place at the wrong time. I have no doubt, if given the opportunity, he will have no compunction about doing it again. He already believes he's done away with me as well."

Rattled, Jessie moved to the bed to sit down.

This was all too much for her.

She folded her arms in front of her, rocking her body slowly back and forth.

Ty wasted no time in bounding over to join her, slinging his muscled arm protectively around her shoulders, but she winced, and he quickly got the message that she did not want to be touched at the moment. He slowly withdrew, allowing her some space, but looking like he was dying inside.

Jessie looked up at Poppy, frightened. "Who is he?"

"We don't know yet, but we have a few ideas."

"One of the bachelors?" Jessie squeaked.

"Possibly, although the only two left are Matt and Ty. We have ruled out the others you let go."

"It's not *me*!" Ty roared, puffing out his chest.

"Have you noticed anyone acting suspicious, perhaps one of the crew?" Poppy asked.

Jessie shook her head. "No, everyone on the crew has

been with the company for years, they're like a tight-knit family. I simply cannot imagine it could be one of them."

Ty couldn't resist touching Jessie again, placing a hand on her bare shoulder as she absentmindedly straightened her tight black dress, distracted and disturbed. She angrily shoved him away. "Ty, please, back off, you're suffocating me!"

Ty, wounded, instantly moved away to the opposite end of the bed, where he sulked in silence.

Poppy took a step toward him. "Just before Jessie came into the room, I asked about your friend Monty."

"Yeah, what about him?" Ty spit out, scowling.

"How long have the two of you known each other?"

"Around two years. We lost touch for a while. Nothing happened, we didn't have a fight or anything, we just had different interests, me riding bulls in Texas, him riding the waves in SoCal. But recently we reconnected and I remembered how much I liked having him in my life. We've been close bros ever since."

"So it's possible he reunited with you knowing you were going to be on *My Dream Man* in order to get close to Jessie," Poppy said.

Jessie glanced up, suddenly interested.

"What are you saying, that this guy on the loose is Monty? You're insane, lady!" Ty snapped.

Poppy refused to back down. "Was he with you while you were back in Texas competing in that rodeo the week before production started on the show?"

"No, he was here, in LA. This is where he lives. We met up when I got to town," Ty said, noticing Poppy's arched eyebrow. "Just because he was in Southern California doesn't mean he's guilty of murder! Show me your proof!"

"Where is he now?" Poppy pressed.

"The producers didn't need him. He has the whole day off, so he planned a date."

"A date? With whom?"

"Some girl, I don't know!"

Poppy folded her arms. "If he's your 'close bro,' wouldn't he give you a few more details?"

Ty noticed Jessie's demeanor quietly changing.

She was becoming less enamored with him the more agitated he became, signaling he had to change his tack pronto. He took a deep breath and calmed himself down. "He didn't tell me her name, but I know where he took her. They went to Venice Beach. The waves are mellow there. He was going to teach her how to surf."

Poppy scooted over and picked up her wig and glasses. "I would appreciate it if you both granted me your discretion. It's imperative you not reveal my true identity to anyone, not until we find this man," she implored before adding pointedly in Ty's direction, "For the sake of Jessie's safety."

Jessie nodded, hugging herself, fretting.

"What about Matt? He's a fake. Jessie, please don't tell me you're going to keep him around."

Before Jessie could speak, Poppy interjected, "For what it's worth, I can assure you, Matt's feelings for you are genuine. I've known him for quite some time now, and he's absolutely not faking anything."

"He lied about why he's here, he didn't come for you, his intentions are clearly not honorable, Jessie!" Ty bellowed.

He could see her wavering.

Ty threw his hands in the air. "He's a plant!"

"Matt stays," Jessie said to Poppy. "For now." She then turned to her discombobulated suitor. "And if you blow his cover, Ty, you *will* regret it. . . ."

Ty opened his mouth to object.

"I mean it," Jessie hissed.

Ty nodded obediently but was obviously fuming inside.

Chapter 41

Poppy found Matt by the pool surrounded by the crew, where he was taping a confessional about the final elimination scheduled for later in the day. Poppy waited for him to finish talking about his state of mind, his excitement and anticipation, his deep genuine feelings for Jessie, which caused a nervous twinge in Poppy's stomach as she heard the words gushing out of his mouth.

Matt finally stood up and, with a hopeful smile, entwined the index and middle finger on his right hand, and raised it up in front of the camera. "Fingers crossed."

The producers thanked him and told him to stick around in case any reshoots were required. The crew remained on standby waiting for Ty to appear for his own confessional.

Matt bounded over to Poppy, who hastily recounted what had just transpired in Ty's room, the evidence she uncovered in his closet, the possibility of those items belonging to Ty's buddy Monty, and how Poppy was now planning to drive out to Venice Beach to find him.

"You shouldn't go alone, I'll come with you," Matt said, concerned.

"No, you need to stay here, keep an eye on Jessie, in

case we're wrong about Monty, and the killer is still around here somewhere."

Matt nodded, agreeing. "Just be careful."

"Always," Poppy said assuredly. She paused, then added, "You sounded quite convincing just now." She gestured toward the camera set up where he had recorded his thoughts about Jessie.

Matt's face lit up, his whole face glowing. "I don't know what to say, Poppy. I'm head over heels for this girl. I know I came into this with the intention of just acting the part of an adoring suitor, but as I've gotten to know her better through this intense, strange, totally surreal process, I've begun to see her for who she really is, and now I can no longer suppress my true feelings." He took a deep breath. "And I am pretty certain she feels the same." He instantly registered the hesitancy in Poppy's demeanor. "What, you don't?"

"No, it's not that, I just don't know enough about her yet, that's all," Poppy said, choosing her words very carefully. "I've grown rather fond of you, in case you haven't noticed, Matt, and I would hate to see you get hurt."

He cupped a hand behind her neck and kissed her sweetly on the forehead. "I appreciate your concern, and the feeling is mutual. . . ." He stepped back, full of faith and certainty. "But I've got this."

Poppy tried projecting confidence, but knew she was failing miserably. All he could see in her expression was hesitation and worry, enough for him to feel the urge to repeat himself.

"Seriously, Poppy, I've got this."

"Okay," Poppy said with a thin smile.

There was nothing left for her to say.

She was a motherly figure to Matt, and sometimes no matter what advice a mother doles out, to take things slow, not make any rash decisions like proposing marriage on a reality TV show, sons could be stubborn, especially when their heart was involved. Poppy worried that Jessie might be playing him, pretending to be in love with him, all to fulfill the producers' specific agenda to keep the drama at a high-pitched level for the big reveal finale. . . . Will Jessie pick Matt or Ty?

Still, on the other hand, she could in the end be 100 percent wrong. As just Matt's adviser, she had not witnessed all the private time they had shared together. Perhaps a real, solid relationship was developing. Poppy had no way of knowing anything for sure.

All she knew right now was that she had to find Monty.

The 10 Freeway west to Santa Monica was predictably clogged with midday traffic, most likely due to an accident or stall out, so the journey to Venice Beach from Los Feliz took Poppy nearly an hour in her car. She used the Waze app to find the exact spot Ty had told her Monty liked to surf by typing in the address of a frozen lemonade stand on the boardwalk just up from the beach. According to Ty, Monty always liked to stop there for a drink before trudging across the sand with his surfboard down to the water.

After parking her car in another ludicrously expensive all day lot, Poppy marched down the buzzing boardwalk with its funky shops, skateboarders, and street performers, not to mention endless walls of vibrant murals. Poppy had remembered in her twenties roller-skating down the boardwalk in the early eighties, in a pink halter top and tight cutoff jeans, epitomizing the youthful bohemian spirit that still resonated to this day.

After purchasing her own frozen lemonade from Monty's favorite stand, Poppy slipped out of her Burberry latticed leather espadrilles, then carried them in her hand as she made her way down the beach barefoot. It didn't take her long to zero in on a beautiful blue resin tint Solana Twin Fin Fish surfboard, the exact one Ty had described in detail for Poppy, lodged in the sand nose first. She knew if that was Monty's board, he had to be around somewhere.

It did not take her long to locate him.

She spotted him splashing around in the surf, bare chested in brightly colored Pacific Wear board shorts, chasing after a shapely young woman in a white bikini, who was giggling and screaming. He tackled her and the two stumbled and fell, disappearing beneath the water's surface as a wave crashed over them. They reemerged moments later, lying in the wet sand, Monty on top of the young woman, their lips smacking, in a moment reminiscent of the classic scene with Burt Lancaster and Deborah Kerr in *From Here to Eternity*. Both of them were also blissfully ignorant of several middle school children at the water's edge gaping at them.

Finally, they came up for air as Monty jumped up and extended a helping hand to the woman, who took it and then playfully slapped him in a mock show of displeasure, although her electric smile revealed unbridled joy.

When Poppy finally got a clear view of the girl in her immodest beachwear, a slight gasp emanated from her lips.

She had seen her before.

The woman Monty was frolicking with in the ocean was none other than NASCAR Beau's dating adviser, his sister, Maggie.

Chapter 42

"Here for a little fun in the sun?"

Poppy turned to her right to take in the sight of a balding man in his mid- to late sixties, stretched out on a beach lounger underneath an umbrella, sporting big round sunglasses, a visible dollop of sunscreen on the tip of his nose, and a protruding bare beer gut. A tuft of white hair in the middle of his chest blew in the light breeze.

"I'm sorry . . . ?"

The man grunted as he leaned forward and stuck out his hand. "Horace Sunday, and you are?"

"Poppy."

She decided not to provide a last name.

"May I say, you are one fine-looking woman, Poppy, mighty fine. Care to join me?"

"No, thank you," she said curtly, keeping an eye on Monty and Maggie, who were now walking hand in hand back up the beach toward her.

"Awww, come on, I promise I won't bite," he said before adding with a leering grin, "Unless you ask me to."

Poppy quickly realized Monty and Maggie's own blanket, tote bags, and umbrella were set up in the sand just to the left of Horace. She reflexively dropped down behind Horace's umbrella to hide, although she was plainly aware in all likelihood they would not recognize her out of her Aunt Bea disguise.

Horace beamed, rolling over on his side. "Well, I'm glad you changed your mind, beautiful."

Poppy ignored him and raised her head just enough above the top of the umbrella to see Monty and Maggie grabbing towels from their bags and drying themselves off while staring lustfully at each other. Monty then dropped his towel, reached out, and pulled Maggie toward him until her whole body was smashed up against his chest and he was able to cover her mouth with his own. Maggie enthusiastically threw her arms around his neck and seemed to melt in his embrace as their tongues ravenously explored each other.

"Oh, to be young and energetic again. These days, just putting on my socks can tucker me out," Horace said, erupting in laughter, his giant belly jiggling.

Poppy threw him a sideways glance before returning her attention to Monty and Maggie, who were now lying prone on a turquoise beach blanket, hugging each other, Monty's fingers slowly caressing Maggie's lower back.

Poppy managed to hear Maggie say, "Who would have thought I would meet my own dream man on the set of *My Dream Man*?"

Monty laughed heartily.

Poppy wondered why Monty could be so passionate about a woman he had just met if he was indeed the stalker who had up to this point been so singularly fixated on Jessie. It struck her as an implausible sharp turn. Unless Monty was not the man they were looking for.

Horace, who had lost sight of the young attractive couple once they had lain down on the blanket, struggled to get up from his lounger. The wheezing and grunting and herculean effort garnered Poppy's attention.

"What are they doing now?" Horace gasped, finally managing to lift himself up.

Poppy raised a hand to stop him. "Please, don't draw attention. . . ."

Suddenly Horace was pointing a pudgy finger at Maggie. "Hey, I know you. . . ."

Monty and Maggie separated, perturbed by the interruption.

"You're the girl from that mattress commercial I see on TV all the time. . . . The Sweet Dreams girl. I know I'm right! That's you, isn't it?"

Resigned, Maggie reluctantly nodded. "Yes, it's me."

She pretended to be annoyed, but Poppy could see there was a tiny part of her that was thrilled to be recognized.

"She doesn't just do commercials, she's been in some big shows, too, like that Netflix show where you played a courtesan. . . ."

"*Bridgerton.* I didn't have any lines but the director did move me to the front so everyone could see me in the shot. I think he had a little crush on me," Maggie said, humbly bragging.

An actress?

This made no sense.

Poppy stood up, revealing herself.

Monty and Maggie stared at her blankly, neither of them with even a hint of recognition.

"You said you were a nurse," Poppy said firmly.

Maggie appeared visibly shaken. "Who are you?"

"My name is Poppy Harmon."

She flicked her eyes toward Monty, who appeared painfully confused. He did not look as if he was seeing a ghost, which indicated to Poppy that he was not the man who had tried to kill her. Twice.

"Why did you lie to everyone?" Poppy pressed.

"I don't need to explain myself to a complete stranger," Maggie snapped.

"No, you don't. But you will have to explain yourself to

the police, your true relationship to Beau, otherwise they could charge you with murder *and* attempted murder."

Maggie turned to Monty. "What is she talking about?"

"She's a raving lunatic," Monty said, jumping to his feet and then helping Maggie up. "Let's get out of here."

"I am a private investigator, and I've been on the set of *My Dream Man* in disguise as Matt's dating adviser to find a killer on the loose, and right now, the clues are pointing to your supposed brother Beau, and you as an accessory," Poppy explained.

Maggie's mouth dropped open in shock. "You're Aunt Bea?"

Monty hurriedly stuffed the towels back in their tote bags, tossed the blanket over his shoulder, and snatched Maggie's hand to drag her away from the uncomfortable scene. "Come on, Maggie."

Horace just watched the whole intense drama unfolding, slack jawed.

Maggie wrenched her hand free. "No, wait. . . ."

"You don't have to say anything to her," Monty advised.

Maggie locked eyes with Poppy. "I am an actress. But I had nothing to do with what you're talking about. I was between acting jobs and I was perusing a casting Web site and I saw a posting from a guy looking for an actress to play his sister. It was a paying gig, and I needed rent money, so I applied and he hired me. It was as simple as that. Once Jessie dumped Beau, my job was done."

"What's your real name?"

"Evie Hart. You can find me on IMDB. And I'm repped by Lance Hunter at United Creative Management. He'll vouch for me. Look, I had no idea Beau was some kind of dangerous criminal!"

"Did Beau tell you why he needed someone to pretend to be his sister?" Poppy asked.

"He said he was in a bind. His real sister couldn't make it out to LA at the last minute because of some family emergency, and he was worried they might boot him off the show if he didn't have a dating adviser, so he decided to get creative. He didn't want this once-in-a-lifetime opportunity to slip through his fingers."

It was a lie.

There was no family emergency.

Because the man on the show was no NASCAR driver.

He wasn't the real Beau.

He was Patrice, aka Pete, aka Bobby.

The Talented Mr. Ripley.

Poppy reached for her phone in her bag.

Maggie took a step forward. "Who are you calling?"

"The police."

"Please, you have to tell them I had nothing to do with anything illegal," Maggie pleaded, her green eyes pooling with tears as Monty slid a protective arm around her trembling shoulders.

Horace put his chubby hands on his hips and marveled at Poppy. "Man, I thought you were a wonder when I believed you were just a fellow retiree looking to get a suntan. Now that I know you're a private eye, I'm all the more excited."

Poppy dashed away, kicking up sand as she ran for her car in the lot adjacent to the beach.

"Wait!" Horace yelled after her. "Can I at least get your number?!"

Poppy was already behind the wheel and roaring back down the Pacific Coast Highway on her way to the Los Feliz mansion, when the operator finally put her call through to Detective Jordan.

"This is Jordan," he said through the car speakers.

"It's Beau, the NASCAR driver! He's the one!"

"I know," Detective Jordan said in a tense voice.

Poppy gripped the steering wheel and kept her eyes fixed on the road. "How?"

"We just got word from the authorities in Arizona that a body was found just outside Flagstaff that matches the description of the real Beau. He was last seen on security footage at a truck stop the day before production on the show began."

"So the killer must have tracked him down somewhere between Texas and California, murdered him, and then took his car and identity and showed up on the set pretending to be the real Beau," Poppy said, fretting. "He's already been eliminated from the show, which means he could be anywhere at this point."

And able to strike at any moment.

Chapter 43

Andy Keenan's ashen face betrayed such a profound sense of shock, Poppy initially believed he might pass out on the spot. Eyes bulging out, bottom lip quivering, his exaggerated reaction looked almost comical, as if he were embodying a Looney Tunes cartoon character like Wile E. Coyote after the Road Runner led him off the cliff and in that split second realized there was no ground underneath him and the only way to go was down.

Andy closed his eyes for a moment and then opened them again, almost expecting the perceived apparition before him would be gone in a puff of smoke.

But Poppy was still there.

"Yes, Andy, it's me. I'm alive," Poppy barked, annoyed.

"B-but I don't understand. . . . Wh-what is happening?" he stammered, moving his arm forward, about to reach out and touch her to confirm that what he was seeing was real, that his eyes were not playing tricks on him. He thought better of it at the last second.

Poppy had rushed back to the Los Feliz mansion, ditching all pretense at continuing her Aunt Bea deception. The clock was ticking. And she had to know how her would-be killer had conned his way onto the set of a national reality TV show. She grasped Andy by the arm and led him from the downstairs foyer, where she had run into him moments after her arrival, and pushed him into a half bath, slammed the door behind them, and turned the lock from the inside so they would have complete privacy.

Andy placed a trembling hand over his chest. "Poppy, my heart is beating so fast. . . . How . . . ? Why . . . ?"

"I have no time to explain, Andy. I need to know how a dangerous killer got past your screening process posing as Beau so easily!"

"Beau . . . ? That's not the real Beau? Then who—?"

Poppy cut him off sharply. "We don't know his real name because he has more fake identities than the police or FBI can keep track of. But how could you not know? You must have done a preliminary interview before you allowed him on the show!"

"Yes, of course," Andy insisted before Poppy noticed a slight hint of dread on his face.

"What? What are you not telling me?"

"No, it's not possible. . . ."

"What, Andy? Tell me! I need to know everything!"

"We did a thorough background check, just like we do with all the potential bachelors. Beau sailed through the entire vetting process, but for the in-person final interview that we always do the day before the start of production in order to sign off on their actual participation, with Beau there was a slight change. He had one more race in Texas he wanted to compete in before driving to LA, and asked if we would be open to conducting the interview over Zoom. . . ."

"So your people never actually met him in person!"

Andy nodded shamefully. "We'd already had so much contact with him we felt like we knew him well enough already. . . . We knew it was a risk, but the producers felt comfortable with him, there were no red flags in his background check."

"What about a psychological evaluation? Someone must have done one of those!"

"Yes, yes, he had one done in Texas with a very reputable doctor, who assured us there was nothing to be concerned about."

"Because the doctor in Texas evaluated the real Beau, not the homicidal imposter who murdered him in cold blood on his way to LA and took his place!"

Andy Keenan could do nothing but shake his head in utter dismay. "Oh God. This is a nightmare. . . ."

Poppy's mind raced.

If the killer was posing as Beau, why did he leave the mansion so gracefully after Jessie eliminated him? Wouldn't her outright rejection have set him off, especially if in his demented mind the two of them belonged together? Why not show his true colors right then and there?

Unless he had some kind of backup plan.

"Where is Jessie now?"

Andy, unnerved and shell shocked, stared off into space.

Poppy snatched him by the arms and rattled him hard. "Tell me where to find Jessie!"

Andy finally snapped out of it. "There is no need to worry. She's safe in the garden, surrounded by dozens of crew members. They're setting up for the Last Man Standing ceremony. Trust me, there is no chance she's in any danger."

"You will forgive me if I don't trust you," she said acidly.

Poppy spun around, flipped open the lock, and bolted from the tiny bathroom, leaving a disconcerted, wobbly Andy Keenan behind.

Chapter 44

Poppy darted past the pool toward the garden that stretched all the way around the house. The Last Man Standing ceremony had been set up in another location on the property, not near the fountain but in a private rose sanctuary, to give this weighty moment the truly unique and romantic setting it called for. Poppy stopped just past the swimming pool, trying to decide which direction she should go, not entirely certain where the sanctuary was located. Off in the distance, she could hear faint voices. The crew assembling for this critical reveal, Jessie's final choice.

Poppy was about to continue on, to follow the sounds to where she hoped she would find everyone and warn them to be on the lookout for Beau, when the jarring sound of ominous whistling suddenly filled the air.

Someone nearby was whistling a frighteningly familiar tune.

A deep chill ran down her spine.

Poppy's eyes darted back and forth nervously as she tried not to panic.

There was no mistaking what she was hearing.

Twinkle, twinkle, little star.

Sensing a presence behind her, Poppy spun around, her

teeth clenching at the terrifying sight of Beau, brandishing a Glock pistol, with a sick, twisted smile on his face.

"It's a miracle! You're alive!" he spouted with a knowing wink. "I have to give you credit, Poppy, I totally bought you perishing in that unfortunate explosion at your home, which by now you no doubt realize was not *exactly* an accident. But bravo, nicely done, you had me thoroughly convinced."

Poppy kept her eyes laser focused on the gun he was pointing at her chest. "What's your real name?"

"Why Tom, of course. Tom Ripley."

"That's a fictional character."

"It's real to me. I have modeled my entire life after him."

"Can you actually even remember your real name at this point, after using so many aliases over the years?"

"I'm sure I could dig up a birth certificate if I put my mind to it, but why bother? That guy was a total loser and I knew a long time ago I had to kill him off and reinvent myself if I was ever going to get what I want in this world."

"You mean *take* what you want," Poppy spit out disgustedly.

He shrugged. "Sure, why quibble?"

"You were the real brains behind Tanya Cook's burglary and fraud operation. She and her BFFs did all the work and you just sat back and reaped the benefits."

"What can I say? She loved me with all her heart. I would have been stupid not to have taken advantage of her side business bilking all those useless geezers and sad dust bags."

Poppy cringed. "But then when I, along with my colleagues, put an abrupt stop to the whole operation, we effectively cut off your financial lifeline and that set you off."

"Yeah, I guess by now you've figured out that it's not a good idea to get on my bad side."

"Yes, you have made that crystal clear," Poppy said evenly, glancing around to see if there was someone, anyone in the vicinity, but it was apparent that she and this demented madman were all alone.

Poppy redirected her attention back to Tom Ripley. She could see the whites of his knuckles from gripping the gun so tightly. "You tried intimidating me first, following me to the grocery store, on the hiking trail, whistling that nursery rhyme, all in an effort to scare me off from testifying so Tanya had a better chance of beating the rap and you could continue to enjoy the lifestyle to which you had grown accustomed."

"But brave, heroic Poppy Harmon stubbornly, stupidly refused to back down, and she resolutely marched into that courtroom and sank poor Tanya's whole case. I couldn't let you get away with that," he said, sneering.

"So you took it upon yourself to get revenge by ramming my car from behind and forcing it off a cliff, knowing my chances of surviving a crash like that would be next to impossible."

"How was I to know it wasn't you driving? I have to admit, that one threw me. I almost felt bad for that poor old broad who borrowed your car."

"But you couldn't let it go. You decided to get creative and strike closer to home the next time. You staked out my neighborhood. You knew I had a new air-conditioning unit installed in my backyard, and that became your new plan."

"It was surprisingly easy to hack into your smart home system. Frankly, there is quite a big brain behind this impossibly handsome face."

"Don't flatter yourself."

"Believe me, I have a shockingly high IQ."

"I was talking about your face. You're not that handsome."

He grimaced but quickly recovered, not wanting to give her the satisfaction of knowing she had effectively insulted him. "I was able to remotely shut down your whole heating and air system, making you think there was a problem with the unit, which forced you to call the company and request they send out a technician. After that, it was pretty much a cake walk. I called the company and cancelled the appointment on your behalf. I told them the unit was working again. I was the one who showed up to fix it, allowing me plenty of time to plant that pipe bomb. I even hot-wired a company truck so I wouldn't arouse any suspicion, and had it back to them before anyone even noticed it was ever missing."

"And when you read online that I had perished in the explosion, you thought your job was done. Tanya was going to waste away in prison for the foreseeable future, so you decided to set your sights on your next project, claiming Jessie as your next prize."

He gazed wistfully past Poppy. "She's perfect, isn't she? Everything I want and deserve in a woman."

He absentmindedly lowered his gun.

Poppy made a move to the right, as if she might try to make a run for it, but in a flash, he brought the gun back up, aiming it squarely at her chest again.

"Given your remarkable talent at assuming other people's identities, you decided that your best shot for getting some real face time with your object of affection was to replace one of her suitors. You studied all the profiles of the four competitors the show's producers had publicly named on their Web site, and zeroed in on the NASCAR driver, Beau."

"He was the easiest option given our physical similarities and his pathetic lack of an online presence. Hell, in most of the professional photos of him online he's wearing a helmet and face shield. In the few shots of him out of his racing uniform, we look enough alike that anyone who didn't know him well would never be able to tell the difference. And all of his friends and family back in Texas wouldn't have a clue I wasn't the real Beau until the show aired on TV months from now. I only had to fool the cast, the crew, and, most importantly, Jessie."

"How did you track down Beau on his way to LA?"

He chuckled. "That was the easy part. I just called his family in Texas, posing as one of the show's producers, and said I needed to know when Beau would be arriving in Los Angeles. They were super helpful—they even offered the name of the motel where he reserved a room for a night in Flagstaff—so I drove all night to intercept him, followed him until I had a chance to take care of him at a truck stop. He never saw it coming." He smiled ruefully. "My only mistake was not hiding the body where it would never be found. That obviously was a complication, but I was stuck for time. I had to get out here fast."

"The Tom Ripley in the books would never have made such a rookie mistake," Poppy said sourly.

He glared at her, not appreciating her unsolicited assessment.

"Then there was the issue of Beau's sister, Maggie, whom he had tapped to be his dating adviser," Poppy said.

"That one took a little finesse. I called the real Maggie and luckily caught her just as she was leaving for the airport to fly out here. Again, I said I was a producer and informed her that we had made a creative decision to drop the dating advisers so she was no longer required to come out to California and be on the show with her brother. I could tell she was disappointed because she really wanted to be on TV, but that's life. I also mentioned she probably wouldn't be hearing from Beau until the show wrapped, part of the rules for the show, so I wouldn't have to worry about any nosy family members popping up unexpectedly."

"That's when you hired Evie Hart to play Maggie."

"She was a good sport. As an aspiring actress, she was more interested in how to play the role than asking too many questions about why she was playing it."

"With all the pieces now in place, your mission then became knocking off the competition so you would be the last man standing. I assume you broke into Matt's room to find something incriminating to use against him?"

"He was the wild card, a suspicious last-minute addition. I don't like surprises, so I was determined to find out more about him. Imagine my dismay when I stole his wallet and discovered his connection to the Desert Flowers Detective Agency in Palm Springs, the same outfit that put away my ex-girlfriend Tanya."

The answers for Poppy were flooding in fast now. "You knew something was hinky, and so you planted your Palm Springs disguise, the hat, the fake beard, the sunglasses, in Ty's room in order to throw us off your scent, in case we were getting too close to the truth."

"But then I got eliminated," he lamented.

"That must have been bruising for your inflated ego," Poppy snapped. "I was astonished you took it in stride and acted like such a gentleman."

He shrugged. "To be fair, Jessie was technically rejecting Beau, not me. She still hasn't gotten to know the *real* me."

"Is there a real you?"

He shot her a stern look.

"I'm guessing you took a cue from Neal and conned your way back into the mansion by telling the producers and security you had come back to make one last plea to Jessie to reconsider her decision, thereby adding yet another last-minute jolt of drama into the big finale."

"It worked beautifully. All anyone around here cares about is what makes good television."

"The only problem is, they're setting up for the Last Man Standing ceremony, Jessie is about to choose between Matt and Ty, you're odd man out, and now it's too late."

"Let them go through with their bogus ceremony. Jessie can select whichever one of those weak, pathetic, gutless wonders she wants. I can isolate her at any time of my choosing, pick off her dream man with one shot, and show her why she *will* always belong to me."

"You're insane," Poppy hissed.

He stared at Poppy a long time, his gun still pointed at her. "Maybe to some; others might call me a genius. Just like some might call you admirably tenacious in your pursuit of me, while others might just call you . . . dead."

He suddenly wrapped his finger around the trigger of his gun and began to slowly pull it back to fire off a shot. "Let's hope the third time's the charm."

Chapter 45

"Poppy!"

Momentarily distracted, Tom Ripley swiveled his head around to pinpoint where the voice was coming from.

Poppy seized the opportunity to lunge forward and make a grab for the gun in his hand. She knew he was younger and much stronger and would undoubtedly simply swat her away, but she had to do something.

Ripley roared in anger, furious with himself for allowing her to make even a feeble attempt to get the upper hand. Poppy had her hands locked around his wrist, pushing the barrel of the gun down away from her. With his free hand, Tom grabbed Poppy by the hair, yanking so hard she thought he might tear a fistful out by its roots. She howled in pain, but was not about to give up. Poppy bent her head down low enough where she could manage to bite down on his hand, her teeth burrowing into his skin. His grip on the gun loosened but he did not let go.

As they struggled they heard the same voice call out again. "Poppy!"

This time it was much closer and she knew it was Matt. She bit down harder and Ripley yelped in pain, finally dropping the gun to the ground.

Before Poppy could answer Matt, who was obviously frantically searching for her, Tom Ripley, enraged by her insolence to his obvious superiority, shook his hand free from her clenched jaw and lashed out even harder, shoving her violently away from him. She stumbled back and fell down hard on the concrete surface next to the pool. Lying on the ground, the beating midday sun blinding her, she raised her hand slowly to block out the harsh rays and saw a seething Ripley, taking heaving breaths, bend over and scoop up the gun off the ground. He angrily directed his aim at Poppy. Her heart sank as she feared she was a goner.

But then, Matt came flying out of nowhere at a dizzying speed and tackled a stunned Tom Ripley, whose feet lifted off the ground as the two men vaulted into the swimming pool. The impact sent the heavily chlorinated water splashing everywhere, drenching Poppy, who was still lying on her back on the hard cement. She struggled to her feet, coughing from having swallowed a mouthful of the nasty water, and watched as the two men punched and jabbed each other in the pool. Tom Ripley's eyes were ablaze as he fought viciously, acutely aware that if Matt defeated him, his life as he knew it would be over. His carefree life of crime done, the rest of it would be spent wasting away inside the walls of a maximum security prison. He could not let that happen. He managed to get Matt in a chokehold and dunk his head underneath the water. Matt struggled mightily but was now in a vulnerable, potentially fatal position.

Poppy knew she had to save him.

The gun.

Where was the gun?

Had it gone in the pool with them?

She frantically searched the blue tiled floor of the swimming pool but didn't see it. Then, after she spun around, her eyes searched the entire area before zeroing in on a glint from the sun reflecting off an object in the grass near the loungers. She raced over and retrieved the gun. She hated guns. Even the prop guns she had been required to use in a few episodes of *Jack Colt*.

But Matt's life was on the line.

She pointed the gun at Tom Ripley, who seemed to be enjoying having a firm control over Matt, who was slowly weakening, his last breaths about to escape from his body.

"Let him go!" Poppy cried.

Ripley flashed her a vainglorious grin.

He was proud of himself for vanquishing Matt so easily, and did not appear to be taking Poppy's warning at all seriously.

He had made the wrong bet.

Poppy pulled the trigger.

The bullet nicked his ear.

He shrieked, his eyes popping open in astonishment, as he cupped his ear with one hand. "You nearly shot my ear off!"

She had been aiming for his arm, but she was just grateful she didn't hit any of his vital organs.

Poppy had always been a terrible shot. She knew that from when she visited a firing range in the mideighties for research in preparation for a *Jack Colt* episode where she played a dual role as a Daphne look-alike who was one half of a modern-day Bonnie and Clyde on a crime spree.

"Trust me, I have no problem putting another bullet through your forehead if you don't let go of him right now. You've caused enough damage."

Finally, convinced she was not bluffing, he relented and released Matt, who wrestled free and came up for air, sputtering and choking and coughing violently.

The sound of the gun had drawn the attention of the cast and crew, many of whom came charging around the side of the house to check out what was happening, stopping at the sight of a whining Tom Ripley, whom they recognized as Beau the NASCAR driver, begging for medical help as he clutched his bloody earlobe.

Poppy handed the gun to one of the grips and gestured toward Tom in the pool. "Keep an eye on him. He's extremely dangerous."

Taking the gun, the grip gave her a puzzled look but did as he was instructed, aiming it at Tom, who was now knee deep in the shallow end of the pool and shivering, his hands in the air.

Poppy scurried over to the shallow edge of the pool where Matt had dragged himself, spitting out water and gasping for air. She helped him up the concrete steps, leading him to one of the loungers, where he could sit down and collect himself.

She gently patted his back. "Are you all right, Matt?"

He nodded, shaken but otherwise fine.

"How did you know I was in trouble?" Poppy asked.

"I didn't," he finally answered in a hoarse voice. He took a few more moments to catch his breath. "I was looking for you because we were about to shoot the big finale, and I wanted my aunt Bea there for moral support." He cracked a smile. "But I ended up finding you instead."

The grip, who had the gun squarely trained on Tom Ripley, glanced over at Poppy and Matt, thoroughly confused. "So where is Aunt Bea?"

"She left," Poppy said, relieved. "And I don't think she will be coming back."

Chapter 46

There was a flurry of activity as the hair and makeup people descended upon Matt like a race car pit crew at Le Mans, armed with hair dryers, desperately trying to blow out his wet, matted hair and dry his expensive Hugo Boss dark blue suit. Several of the bulkier crew members had been called to the scene to physically restrain Tom Ripley until the police could arrive, which they did by laying him down on the cement near the pool, one pinning his legs, another his arms, and a third with his knee firmly pressed against his back. By the time a dozen officers were swarming into the backyard, Jessie had finally emerged from the house in a silver sequin high-neck sheath gown, bejeweled, her hair curled and coiffured. She had obviously been alerted to the commotion outside by the pool, but did not appear to be overtly disturbed or distressed by it. Her eyes fell upon Matt, who was still drenched and in a state of disarray.

"How long do you think it's going to take to make him look presentable?! I really want to get on with this!" she shouted to no one in particular.

"Hopefully we'll be ready to go in a few minutes! Just hang tight!" the director called back in a feeble attempt to calm any frayed nerves.

Jessie frowned but did not cause any further fuss.

The cops hauled Tom Ripley to his feet, cuffed his hands behind his back, and frog-marched him away. He cranked his head around, yelling desperately, "Jessie! Jessie!"

She didn't answer him.

In fact, she didn't acknowledge him at all, and it was only a few seconds before the cops had spirited him away that the situation appeared to be back to normal.

Poppy walked up to Jessie and placed a comforting hand on her arm and offered her a reassuring smile. "You're safe now, Jessie. He's no longer a threat to you."

She stared at Poppy blankly. Then, as if a tiny voice inside her suggested it might be a good idea to recognize the severity of the situation, her close call with a deranged and deadly stalker, she nodded slightly. "Yes, what a relief," she said robotically, her mind clearly elsewhere.

There was no *thank you* for ferreting him out and possibly saving her life. No, Jessie's main concern at this moment was that she had a show to do, it was her big moment, and she did not want to disappoint her legions of fans. She was too self-absorbed to worry about being abducted, or worse.

The makeup and hair people were just about done repairing the damage done by Matt's wrestling match in the pool, and after pressing out a few last wrinkles from his jacket with a travel iron, he was whisked back to the sanctuary so they could finally begin taping the finale.

Andy Keenan quietly suggested Poppy might want to don her Aunt Bea disguise in the interest of continuity so viewers wouldn't wonder why Aunt Bea was AWOL for the big finale, but Poppy firmly dismissed the idea. She was done dressing up now that the case was officially closed.

Keenan wisely did not argue with her.

It took another forty-five minutes for the company to be ready to shoot, making the set even more tense since

Jessie's mood continued to sour and everyone was sub-jected to her bellyaching, but finally, the cameras rolled in the intimate, perfectly romantic setting.

Matt and his rival, Ty, dashing in a gray Giorgio Ar-mani suit and a white cowboy hat, congratulated each other on making it this far, then quickly focused their at-tention on the stunning Jessie, who slowly entered the sanctuary, eyes fluttering, hands trembling, as if she was still unsure which bachelor she was going to choose to spend the rest of her life with. Poppy, who stood off to the side with Ty's buddy, Monty, eyed Jessie skeptically, not buying her act for one second. She strongly believed Jessie had made up her mind which man she was going to pick a while ago, and that she was just going through the mo-tions of uncertainty for the cameras.

Matt and Ty stood erect, hands by their sides, like loyal soldiers about to be knighted by their queen.

Jessie took her place in front of a latticed wall of color-ful roses, pausing as she smiled and nodded at the two stoic men who awaited her final decision. "I came here hoping and praying to find love, and then, to my utter sur-prise, I actually found it. I never thought it was possible to fall in love with not one, but two men, at the same time, but this journey I've taken has been eye opening in a lot of ways, and things I thought were impossible have been proven otherwise. But I can only choose one, and to do that, I can only follow my heart. Ty . . ."

He snapped to attention, eyes widening in anticipation.

"You have taught me how to be more adventurous, to take chances, not to be afraid of the unknown. I had never been in a saddle on top of a horse before meeting you, and I've got the sore butt to prove it!"

Titters from the onlookers and crew.

"And Matt . . ."

Matt gazed at her adoringly.

Poppy's stomach twinged. He was so genuinely taken

with this woman, and that made her very nervous because Poppy's instinct told her Matt was not going to be the last man standing.

"Matt, you make me laugh so hard. When I'm with you, I let myself go in a way I never have before. You've shown me how to get the most out of life, not sweat the small stuff, which I know is a book, but you could have written it. . . . I can be silly and just be myself when I'm around you. . . ."

She paused dramatically, of course.

"Coming into this, I thought at this point it would be easy, I would obviously know what to do, but right up until this moment I have been confused and unsure of myself. However, standing here now, in front of both of you, I can see clearly for the first time where my heart truly lies. . . ."

Another painstakingly long pause.

Poppy could picture in her mind the final edited version of the show: close-up of Jessie, cutaway to Ty, then Matt, then back to Jessie, then back to Ty and Matt, drawing out the suspense for as long as humanly possible.

"Ty . . ."

Ty couldn't help but break out into a wide grin. He whipped his cowboy hat off his head and held it up against his heart.

Jessie dropped her eyes all the way down to her Christian Louboutin sparkling stilettos then back up again. "When I was a little girl, I played this dating board game and I would always choose the cowboy because he was so strong and manly but also sweet and caring. He was the embodiment of my dream man, and after all these years, here you are. . . ."

Matt lowered his head, devastated.

"And I'm sure I'm not the only woman out there who has fantasized about meeting a man like you, and I know one day you will meet that woman and she will make you very happy. . . ."

Ty's wide grin slowly began to fade.

"You are truly a special person and I feel privileged having had the opportunity to meet you. . . . But . . ."

Matt popped his head back up, eyes fixed on Jessie.

"But when Matt showed up, my heart sang like it never has before. I tried to turn down the volume because he was an actor, and I never had much luck with actors, but the more I tried to ignore the signs the louder they got . . . until I could no longer deny how I truly felt. . . . Matt, will you be my Dream Man?"

Matt bounded forward, threw his arms around Jessie, kissed her passionately as she melted in his embrace in classic TV fashion.

Ty stood bravely by, trying to hide his sorrow.

And Poppy's stomach continued to twinge, causing her an uncomfortable amount of distress.

She wanted to be happy for Matt.

She really did.

But she just couldn't.

Because something just didn't feel right.

Chapter 47

"Be sure to call me when you get back so I know you made it safely," Matt said as he lifted Poppy's suitcase and shoved it into the trunk of the car.

Poppy tried adopting a light tone so as not to overtly show him her deep concern. "Are you sure you don't want to come back with me to Palm Springs, at least until you and Jessie have time to figure out how this is going to work?"

Matt smiled knowingly. "No, I need to be here with Jessie."

"All of this is just so sudden. You two have never even had any alone time when there haven't been cameras around. It might be prudent to take things a bit slower."

"I love how protective of me you are, Poppy. In some ways you're more of a mother to me than my own mother, who is somewhere in Europe bouncing around with her latest boyfriend, but you have nothing to worry about. I know this whole . . . process has been a whirlwind, but in the end, against all odds, it actually worked. . . . I found the one."

Poppy had to fight the urge to address her suspicions about Jessie. Matt was a big boy, he could handle himself, so she decided to keep her mouth shut and simply offer him her unconditional support.

She hugged Matt. "I'm so happy for you."

She circled around toward the driver's-side door and was about to get in when she heard someone yell, "Poppy!"

Andy Keenan hustled down the stone steps of the Los Feliz mansion, his face flushed and sweaty, brown hair dye streaming down both sides of his cheeks. "I was hoping to catch you before you left!"

He had to stop and catch his breath for a few moments, breathing in and out, before continuing. "I want to thank you both for keeping Jessie safe and finding that nut job before he did any serious harm."

"We are just grateful it all worked out," Poppy said coolly, not eager to engage with this man who had so blatantly lied about having some kind of sordid past with her.

"And, Poppy, I can't tell you how ecstatic I was to find out that you are definitely alive and well. You look fantastic, by the way! And that got me thinking. We should talk about setting up a reality show about this whole experience. A former actress, a sex symbol from the nineteen eighties, fakes her death, fools the entire world, and then, boom, jump-starts a whole new career when she reveals that she's not really dead! We could call it *The Resurrection of Poppy Harmon*. What do you think?"

Poppy stared at him, incredulous. She chose her words carefully. "I must say, it's an unusual idea."

Andy's face lit up. "Then you'll consider it?"

"I said unusual. I did not say it was a good idea, or one that I would ever consider. So my answer is a firm no, Andy."

Like any tenacious, tireless producer, he didn't appear at all disappointed or rejected. He was already moving on to his next thought. "Okay then, what about staying in LA a bit longer? I know this intimate little restaurant hidden away up in Topanga Canyon with an impressive wine list—"

"Again, no," Poppy said. She reached into her purse and fetched some tissues, then handed them to him. "Here."

"What are these for?"

"You're melting."

Matt tried suppressing a snicker.

Andy used them to wipe his face and then finally saw the hair dye stains on the tissues. "Oh, thanks." Desperate to change the subject, he turned to Matt. "I also want to congratulate you, Matt, on your stellar performance."

Matt gave him a puzzled look. "What do you mean?"

"Coming onto the show, pretending to fall in love with Jessie like that, it was a real tour de force."

"I wasn't acting. I really did fall in love with Jessie," Matt said steadfastly.

There was a pregnant pause.

Andy noticeably blanched.

"What's wrong?" Poppy asked.

"Oh . . . wow . . . I didn't expect this. . . . I thought, wow, I thought you were just here undercover, that your participation in the show was just an act."

Matt tensed. "Well, it wasn't. It got real pretty quickly."

"The thing is, Matt . . ."

Poppy braced for the worst.

"The thing is, when you're in the middle of taping a reality show, the number one goal is to keep the audience invested, keep the drama and suspense going all the way up until the end. We knew right from the start that you would be a breakout, that the audience would fall in love with you, and want you to be the last man standing, but . . ."

Poppy could see Matt physically deflating.

"But what?" Matt asked.

"But she was already romantically involved with another bachelor even before the show began production. The plan was for them to wind up together in the end, but when you arrived on the scene, and you were so charming, we knew we had to create a whole new storyline . . . and so I persuaded Jessie to choose you for the sake of the ratings. Honestly, I didn't think you would mind because you were here for other reasons. Never in my wildest imagination did I ever believe you would *actually* . . ."

They all suddenly heard Jessie's signature giggle and turned to see Jessie and Ty, the cowboy, coming out the front door of the mansion like a pair of newlyweds, smooching and hanging off each other as they bounded down the steps to a red sports car. As Ty opened the passenger-side door for her and she slinked in, she noticed Poppy, Matt, and Andy nearby, watching. She smiled brightly, offering a tiny wave, and then Ty was behind the wheel and they roared off into the sunset to begin their new life together post–reality show.

"I-I-I'm so sorry, Matt," Andy stammered.

It all made sense now to Poppy.

That's why Jessie had just shown up in Ty's room when Poppy was there. It had not been just a coincidence. It was a pre-planned rendezvous, undoubtedly one of many.

Andy found this entire exchange painfully awkward and just wanted to get away. "Well, I have work to do, a ton of postproduction to get through. Poppy, if you ever change your mind about dinner sometime—"

"Oh, believe me, Andy, I won't."

He nodded, the finality of her rejection finally sinking in. "Okay then, safe travels back to Palm Springs."

And he was off like a shot.

Poppy reached out for Matt's hand. "Matt . . ."

She could see him trying to put on a brave face. "I had a feeling it was all a game. What are you always telling me, listen to your gut?"

Poppy squeezed his hand. She knew he was deeply hurt. "You will find the right girl, Matt, I promise you."

He nodded, embarrassed. Then tried laughing it off.

"You know what, on second thought maybe I will hitch a ride with you back to the desert. Let me just go grab my bag. You wait right here." He whipped around and dashed up the stone steps and back inside the house.

Poppy would wait for him.

And she would always be there for him.

So would Iris and Violet.

Because, for better or worse, they were a family.

And whether Matt yet knew it or not, he was going to need his family.

Chapter 48

It was unseasonably chilly up in the mountains of Big Bear, California, disconcerting for the fact that down below in the Coachella Valley the temperatures were creeping over a hundred degrees. Sam's cabin, nestled in the woods above the banks of Big Bear Lake, was especially warm and inviting with a fire crackling in the hearth of his sparsely decorated living room. The few pieces of furniture were all made of wood, some of which Sam had built himself. After arriving back in Palm Springs from New York, Sam had talked Poppy into accompanying him in his SUV back up the mountain to his cozy hideaway, and after all she had been through, Poppy certainly did not feel the need to deliberate too much. She was grateful for the chance to get away and be with the man she loved. Poppy always felt safe when she was with Sam, and right now, she craved that safe feeling more than anything.

Upon their arrival, Sam had insisted on making them a romantic dinner. He asked a few questions about the unpleasant Tom Ripley ordeal during their meal, but picked up on Poppy's reluctance to dwell too much on the whole sordid story. So he popped open a second bottle of wine, then steered Poppy to the couch facing the fireplace, where they sat down and cuddled together, Sam pulling Poppy close to his chest with a protective arm.

They gazed at the dancing flames in front of them for the longest time until Sam turned his head and gently kissed Poppy on the cheek. Oh, how she had missed him while he was gone. She peppered him with questions about his trip, which he answered politely with one- or two-word answers. He was less interested in reliving his past few weeks on the East Coast working on a TV show and more focused on being present in this moment with Poppy. Finally, Poppy rested her head on his chest, her ear pressed against his wool sweater, taking in the firm, rhythmic beats of his heart, which had now mostly recovered from a serious attack last year.

She sat up and clinked his wineglass with her own, but didn't say anything.

Sam arched his right eyebrow. "What are we toasting?"

"To how grateful I am."

"Okay, I'll go with that."

They each took a sip.

"What are you grateful for?"

"When I saw how crushed and disappointed Matt was when he discovered Jessie had only been using him and didn't really love him, I felt so helpless because I knew I couldn't make that hurt go away. But at the same time . . ."

Sam studied her curiously.

"At the same time . . . I felt lucky and grateful because I knew I had already found *my* dream man. . . ."

Poppy could see Sam suddenly start to get emotional, the rims of his eyes beginning to moisten. He was close to full-on crying, and a tough guy like him couldn't do that, so he glanced away, cleared his throat, and took another manly swig of his wine.

Poppy chuckled. "You asked."

He grinned at her, then cupped his thick calloused hand around the back of her neck and slowly drew her in for another kiss, this time square on the lips. Then, he took her by the hand. "It's late. You ready for bed?"

"Sam, it's not even eight o'clock. I'm hardly tired."

"Who said anything about sleeping?"

She playfully swatted his shoulder. "No, I can't just yet. The world thinks I'm dead. I need to compose some kind of public statement letting people know that, despite previously published reports, Poppy Harmon, former co-star of the nineteen eighties detective series *Jack Colt, PI*, is actually still very much alive."

"Can't it wait until morning? You know once you hit SEND, it's going to be a relentless storm of attention. You'll probably trend on Twitter. You'll become one of those ma'ams for memes. Who needs all that crap?"

She patted his knee and stood up. "That reminds me . . ."

"Where are you going?"

"I need to make a very important call."

She walked over to her bag, which was sitting on a chair at Sam's wooden dining room table, which was cluttered with all their dirty dishes from dinner. She rummaged through her bag for her phone, scrolled down until she came to the name she wanted, tapped the screen, and then held the phone up to her ear.

Sam stood up from the couch. "Who are you calling?"

She smiled and put a finger to her lips, and then when someone answered, she said in a stern, commanding voice, "Hello, Serena, it's Poppy, *Poppy Harmon.*"